JUSTICE
LOST

OTHER TITLES BY SCOTT PRATT

JUSTICE LOST

SCOTT PRATT

Text copyright © 2018 by Arthur Scott Pratt

No part of this book may be reproduced, or stored in a retrieval system, or transmitted in any form or by any means, electronic, mechanical, photocopying, recording, or otherwise, without express written permission of the publisher.

Published by Thomas & Mercer, Seattle

www.apub.com

Amazon, the Amazon logo, and Thomas & Mercer are trademarks of Amazon.com, Inc., or its affiliates.

ISBN-13: 9781542049689
ISBN-10: 1542049687

Cover design by David Drummond

Printed in the United States of America

This book, along with every book I've written and every book I'll write, is dedicated to my darling Kristy, to her unconquerable spirit, and to her inspirational courage. I loved her before I was born, and I'll love her after I'm long gone.

At his best, man is the noblest of all animals; separated from law and justice he is the worst.

—*Aristotle*

PART I

CHAPTER 1

I looked around at the circle of empty chairs. There were two empty seats to my right and two to my left. I was back at Farragut High School outside Knoxville, Tennessee, in the classroom assigned for in-school detention. I'd been there several times in my youth for fighting, but this seemed more serious. The doors were made of iron bars, the walls were concrete block and painted Old Glory Blue, the same color as that on the American flag.

Hovering over me at the front of the class was Mrs. Judge, a woman I'd dealt with before. Her appearance had changed dramatically, though, since I'd last seen her. Her face was as gray as bone ash, and she was staring at me through tinted glasses that were as thick as the bottoms of old beer bottles and looked almost like goggles. She was wearing a red silk robe with a white lace collar. In her right hand, she held a set of pan mechanical balance scales, and in her left she carried a double-edged sword that looked, from where I was sitting, to be razor sharp. When she'd come into the room a few seconds earlier, she hadn't walked like a normal human. She'd floated across the floor like a ghost.

I was trembling. There wasn't much in the world that I feared, but this version of Mrs. Judge terrified me. She seemed to radiate power and danger, and I couldn't escape the feeling that she could incinerate me with one blazing look from her eyes. And if she was quick with the sword—which I was certain she was—my head could be rolling across the floor at any second.

"Where are your friends, Mr. Street?" Mrs. Judge said in a slow, gravelly Southern accent.

"I don't know what you're talking about," I said.

She raised her hands, the sword and scales gleaming, and fire began to swirl around my head.

"Don't lie to me, Mr. Street. You know exactly what I'm talking about. Where are your four friends who are supposed to be sitting in these four seats?"

"They're not my friends," I said. I looked up at her hideous face and then back down at the floor.

"Do you dare trifle with me? I have no qualms about turning you to dust and blowing you to the far edges of the universe. You will speak the truth in this room."

"I had to do something," I said.

"You mean you had to take justice into your own hands. You had to become a vigilante."

"Call it whatever you want. I'd do it again."

"I want to hear you say it," she said. "I want you to look at me and tell me exactly what you did."

I forced myself to look at the face. It was the face of a person—no, an entity—that had been twisted and betrayed and misunderstood and beaten and defeated, yet stood defiantly and continued to fight.

"There is no such thing as justice, you know," I said. "There are only random acts followed by revenge."

"Tell me what you did!" Her voice was so forceful it nearly shattered my eardrums. "Confess! Right now! What did you do to the four men who should be sitting in these chairs?"

"I killed them," I said. "All four of them. Are you happy? I shot Donnie Frazier and Tommy Beane in a bar in West Virginia. I blew them to hell. They didn't have a chance. I helped hang the former federal prosecutor, Ben Clancy, in a barn up by Gatlinburg, and then I fed his sorry ass to a pen full of hungry pigs. And Big Pappy Donovan? He wanted to kill me. He actually wanted to have an old-fashioned duel in the mountains near Petros. He was crazy. He'd gone completely off the rails. So I met him and we had our duel. He lost, and then he wound up in the same pigpen as Ben Clancy."

"And you got away with all four of the killings," she said. "You faced no consequences from the laws of man."

"I got away with the killings."

"Do you feel no remorse for the taking of human lives?"

"None. Frazier and Beane murdered my mother. Clancy falsely convicted me of murder and sent me off to prison for two years. Big Pappy was a sociopath, if not a psychopath, who wanted to kill me. It was him or me."

"What makes you think you get to make these choices?" she said. "What makes you think you have the power to decide who lives and who dies?"

Mrs. Judge was judging me, and I wasn't having it. I didn't know whether or not I was dreaming, but what I was feeling was very real to me. My fear was suddenly replaced by anger, and I gave no thought to what might happen to me for confronting this powerful force.

"What makes *you* think you have that same power?" I said. "You're nothing but the product of the wealthy protecting themselves from the poor. You're a hypocrite and a false idol, and as far as I'm concerned, you can take your hypocrisy and go straight to hell."

I felt the air go out of the room and heard the metallic whoosh of her sword being raised into the air.

"Get on your knees," Mrs. Judge said.

I looked up at her and stood.

"I don't hit my knees for you or anybody else," I said. "If you're going to take my head, you're going to do it while I'm standing."

Her smile revealed pointed, yellowed teeth.

"Have it your way," she said, and the sword dove toward me at the speed of . . .

* * *

I felt the hand on my shoulder, and my eyes immediately popped open. I looked around the den, heard the television, and couldn't believe I'd dozed off.

"Is it time?" I said.

"Are you all right, Darren? You sounded like you were having a nightmare."

"I'm fine. I was dreaming about this teacher I had in high school named Mrs. Judge. It was strange. What about you? How are the contractions?"

"I think we should go," Grace said. "They're about sixty seconds, and they're coming every three or four minutes."

"Do they hurt?"

"Ever had somebody push on your lower abdomen with an anvil?" she said.

"Can't say that I have."

"That's what they feel like. The longer they get, the heavier the anvil."

Grace's contractions had begun the day before, but they'd been intermittent. Over the past several hours, however, they'd become more intense and had come at much shorter intervals. I looked at the clock next to the couch. It was 7:45 p.m. on Friday night. We were both dressed and had everything packed in my car. Grace called her mother and father—both of whom lived in San Diego, California—and told them we were heading to the hospital.

The thought struck me that it was rather pitiful that I didn't have anyone to call. My son, Sean, who was nine years old, had just returned to Hawaii after having spent the summer with Grace and me. He knew

Grace was going to have a baby and seemed excited by the fact that he was going to have a sister. But I knew if I tried to call him, his mother, Katie, would ignore the call, so I just let it go.

Grace took my arm, and we walked out of the building into the mid-August heat and humidity. Twenty minutes later, we arrived at the birthing center just south of Knoxville, Tennessee. Everything was pre-arranged. Grace had been the perfect mother-to-be. She'd taken good care of herself, gotten plenty of exercise and rest, and eaten well with the exception of an unusually large intake of french fries that she chalked up to cravings. She'd worked her job at the federal defender's office until the previous week and was planning to take a month off after our baby girl—her name was to be Jasmine Cathleen Alexander—was born. Grace had chosen the name, and I liked it. Since she and I weren't married and had no immediate plans in that vein, we'd agreed the child would take Grace's last name. If we decided to take the vows at some point, we'd talk about names then. What we called the child didn't really mean that much to me. All I wanted was a healthy, happy baby girl, and I planned to love her with everything I could muster.

A nurse told me to take a seat in a small waiting room and she'd come to get me when Grace was settled into her birthing suite. I sat down and began to reflect.

Grace and I were getting along well. She'd kicked me out of her apartment when she suspected I'd been involved in killing the two men who'd murdered my mother, but her stance had eventually softened. I'd finally opened up and been honest with her about what had happened to Ben Clancy and Big Pappy, and she had allowed me back into her life with the stipulation that I see a psychiatrist on a weekly basis, both to overcome Post Traumatic Stress Disorder from my time in prison and to try to make sense of the violence that had been visited upon me and my reactions to that violence. Eventually, Grace became akin to a wife whose husband had volunteered for a combat tour overseas and had taken lives and seen terrible things in the line of duty. She didn't really understand the things I'd done, but on some level she accepted that in my way of thinking, I'd really had no choice. I had to avenge my mother by killing the men who had killed her. I had to force justice upon Ben Clancy because the system that was in place wasn't going to do a thing to him, and I had to protect myself from Big Pappy Donovan because he was a dangerous killer.

I'd been a criminal defense lawyer for more than a decade and knew the judicial system inside and out. It had failed me again and again, so I'd taken matters into my own hands and used my knowledge of the laws of evidence and the individual protections afforded by the Constitution not only to dole out my own brand of justice but also to do so in such a manner that the police and the lawyers and the judges never got a chance to hold me accountable. Grace still looked at me strangely sometimes, but I believed she had forgiven me.

I'd visited a shrink for months—never mentioning any of the murders I'd committed—before Grace allowed me to stop. It was good she let me stop when she did, because the doctor was beginning to annoy me so much that I'd begun to fantasize about strangling her and hauling her up to Granny Tipton's pigpen.

Grace hadn't renewed the lease on her apartment when it came time two months earlier and had moved in with me. I had an extra bedroom, and she slept in there. There was no sex, but we'd become closer than ever during those two months. I found myself doting on her, which she enjoyed. I was a perfect gentleman, holding doors and holding hands and saying please and thank you. I felt the baby moving in Grace's womb, listened to her heartbeat. I also listened intently to everything Grace said, and if she asked me a question, I gave her a thoughtful and honest answer.

I hadn't said "I love you" to her since before she kicked me out of her apartment, but it was the first thing I planned to say as soon as the baby was born. I thought it would be a good start to our lives together as parents. I didn't know how she'd react, but I was going to say it, anyway. Like I said, I still sensed just a bit of distrust from her. I knew she wanted me in Jasmine's life, but I wasn't sure at this point whether she'd totally committed to our relationship as husband and wife. Grace cared for me and she let me know it, but I sensed that she also regarded me warily sometimes, the way a trainer of dangerous lions regards the animals. I wondered occasionally whether she stayed with me out of an old-fashioned sense of duty. She'd made the choice to sleep with me, she'd become pregnant, and now it was her duty to stay with me and to attempt to successfully hold the family together. Maybe she didn't want to disappoint her parents. I barely knew them, but from what Grace had told me, they were conservative and old-school. Her father was a career marine corps officer, and her mother was a journalism professor. Maybe Grace didn't want them to have the stigma of a bastard grandchild, so she stuck with me in the hope that I would be able to resist some of my behavioral and emotional urges and we'd eventually marry.

A nursing assistant opened the door of the birthing suite and motioned me to come in. I settled in on the couch while a nurse attached leads to Grace so they could monitor her and the baby's vital signs. The nurse attaching the leads was pretty, maybe thirty-five, with black hair and dark-brown eyes. She'd written "Jenny Diaz" on a board that hung on the wall near the bed.

"Who's on call?" Grace said to Jenny.

"Dr. Fraturra."

Grace crinkled her nose.

"Is that a problem?" I said.

"It's fine. I've seen him twice at the office. He just seemed a little distracted."

I expected a comforting phrase from the nurse, something like, "Oh, Dr. Fraturra is excellent. You're in good hands." But none was forthcoming. She just continued to adjust the monitors.

"What do you think of Dr. Fraturra, Jenny?" I said.

"I've been a labor-and-delivery nurse for ten years, but my husband and I just moved to Knoxville," she said. "I've only been here six weeks, so I'm not very familiar with the doctors yet. I've already paged him, though. He should be here soon."

"He isn't in the building?" I said. "We called before we left the apartment and were told he'd be here."

"He must just be running a little late. Nothing to worry about. We still have a little while. She's dilated six centimeters."

The door opened, and a thin, dark-haired, midthirties man with a receding hairline walked in.

"Ah, here's the magic man," Jenny said.

"I'm Dr. Sams," the man said, nodding to both Grace and me. "I'm the anesthesiologist, and I'm here to administer your epidural."

"Thank God," Grace said.

They asked me to leave the room again, and ten minutes later, Dr. Sams walked through the door.

"You can go back," he said. "I'll check on her regularly."

I found a different woman when I returned, one whose face was no longer pale and drawn. She looked relaxed, almost angelic.

"Anesthesia is the bomb," Grace said. "It was like he walked in here and sprinkled fairy dust all over me."

CHAPTER 2

In a trendy bar near Turkey Creek on Knoxville's West Side, Dr. Nicolas Fraturra raised a glass of fifteen-year-old bourbon in a toast to the blonde sitting on the bar stool next to him. His pager vibrated against his side again, but he ignored it.

"To your good health, your beautiful face, your gorgeous body, and my prospects of getting you out of that very sexy dress in the near future," he said beneath the din of young professionals who crowded the bar every Friday night.

The blonde, a financial analyst from Nashville named Danielle Davis, who was at least ten years younger than Fraturra, raised her eyebrows.

"Don't believe in wasting time, do you, Doctor?"

"That's something I learned early on as a doctor," Fraturra said. "Life is short, and it is precious. There is absolutely no sense in wasting time."

"There is such a thing as decorum, though, don't you think?" Davis said as she clinked her glass of Chardonnay against his bourbon.

"You said you were here to close a deal with one of your firm's biggest clients," Fraturra said, ignoring the question. "Where's your client?"

"We're close to getting it done," she said, "but it's his thirtieth wedding anniversary. I'll have to wait until Monday."

"How lucky for me," Fraturra said. "Forgive my lack of decorum, but my experience has been that some women find straight talk sexy. The way I see it, one of two things is going to happen: either the two of us are going to spend the weekend together in luxurious and amorous bliss, or we aren't. I would prefer that we do. You can stay at my house if you'd like—I'm single—or you can stay at your hotel and we can maintain a little space if you're more comfortable doing so. Everything will be on me—food, drink, mood-altering substances, if you're into that sort of thing. I have a five-thousand-square-foot home overlooking the Tennessee River, an incredible pool, absolute privacy, and an insatiable sexual appetite. All you have to do is say yes, and we're out of this place."

The beeper vibrated again, and Fraturra became irritated. He pulled it from his belt and looked down.

"What kind of medicine do you practice?" Davis said.

"OB-GYN."

"Why doesn't that surprise me? The look on your face says something is wrong. Is there an emergency? Someone having a baby?"

"No, no. Nothing wrong. No emergency. I'm not even on call this weekend. I just need to take care of something. Will you excuse me for a few minutes?"

"Of course."

"Don't go anywhere. I'll be right back."

Fraturra made his way out of the crowded bar and into the men's room. He would have gone outside, but a severe thunderstorm had suddenly blown into Knoxville, and rain was falling in sheets. He dialed a number on his cell.

"Bernie? Yeah, yeah, I need a favor. I'm on call tonight. A patient has come in, and I can't make it. Can you cover for me?"

Fraturra listened to the answer, something about a daughter's volleyball game. He stepped into a stall and lowered his voice.

"C'mon, Bernie, I've done you plenty of favors in the past," he said.

"Really?" was the response from Bernie Weinstein, a member of Fraturra's medical group. "Name one."

Fraturra cringed. "Give me a break, Bernie. This is important."

"Where are you?" Weinstein asked. "Your speech is slurred. You're drinking again, aren't you, Nick?"

"No, I'm past all that. I just need you to cover for me."

"You're lying. You're drunk. Which bar are you in, and I'll call Bill Taylor, have him come and pick you up. Taylor won't say anything to anyone."

"I'm not in a fucking bar! My mother fell and broke her hip. I'm driving to Murfreesboro."

"And this fall happened when?"

"I don't know. A couple of hours ago, I think. I just found out."

"Why didn't you call Jenkins? He's the boss."

"Jenkins is a dick. You know he doesn't like me."

"He's your ex-father-in-law, and you're the father of his grandson. He's also kept you employed far longer than anyone else in his position would have. He feels loyal to your father. That's the only reason you weren't out on the street a long time ago."

"He also financed his daughter's divorce from me."

"Who can blame him? You were screwing everything you could get your hands on. Listen, Nick, I'd like to help you, but we've been down this road. I just don't believe you. I think you're in a bar some-where, probably trying to get laid, and you're trying to dump your call responsibility on somebody else. I'm not going to risk getting sued, I'm not going to risk my job at the medical group, I'm not going to risk my medical license, and I'm not going to cover for you. So either you call Jenkins right now or I will. Is there a patient who needs care in labor right now?"

"I don't know. I've gotten a few pages and two calls from Southside Birthing Center."

"And you're on call there tonight?"

"Yeah."

"What did they say?"

"I didn't answer."

"Did they leave you a voice mail?"

"I haven't listened to it. Jesus, Bernie, babies practically deliver themselves. How do you think the human race got this far in the first place? The nurses can handle it."

"Are you listening to yourself, Nick? What the hell's the matter with you? Whatever you're doing, stop it right now. Call Jenkins—no, I'm calling Jenkins—but you get your ass over there and see about your patient. I just hope everything is all right."

"Fine, asshole," Fraturra said. "I'll find somebody else to cover."

"I'm calling Jenkins," he heard Weinstein say as he disconnected the call.

Fraturra started going through his contact list of the other doctors in his group as he walked out of the bathroom. He was thinking about cocaine, Viagra, and what he was going to do to that voluptuous blonde named Danielle Davis. When he walked back into the bar, he didn't see her. He stepped to his stool and motioned the bartender over.

"Where's the blonde who was here?" he said.

"She paid and bolted as soon as you went into the bathroom," the bartender said.

"Shit," Fraturra muttered under his breath. "Bring me my tab."

CHAPTER 3

About half an hour after we arrived at the birthing center, I began to get the distinct impression that something was wrong. Fraturra still hadn't shown up, and the nurse's demeanor had changed. Her face was tight. She was moving quickly. She kept checking the monitors, and she kept feeling Grace's baby bump and talking quietly to Grace. She left the room several times.

"Have you heard from the doctor?" I said to her when she walked back in after leaving for the third time.

"I'm sure he'll be here soon."

"Everything okay with Grace?"

"Of course." She turned and gave me a strained smile. "Everything is fine."

She ran her hands over Grace's belly again, looked at all the monitors again, and turned to me.

"Excuse me, I'll be back as soon as I can," she said.

"You just got here," I said as she hurried out the door.

When she came back about five minutes later, she had an older woman with her, also wearing a nurse's uniform.

"Hi," the woman said to me. "I'm Allison Broyles, a registered nurse. I'm just going to take a look at a couple of things."

"What's going on?" I said. "And don't say nothing. Don't tell me everything is fine, because I can tell from the look on your face that everything isn't fine."

"Your baby's heart rate has dropped some," Nurse Broyles said. "That concerns me a little."

"Where's the doctor?"

"We called the head of his group. He's on his way."

"But where is the doctor who was supposed to be here when we got here?"

Nurse Broyles turned, looked at me, straightened her back, and said, "I don't know, sir. We've been trying to reach him, and he isn't responding."

I got up and walked over to the bedside. I took Grace's hand.

"Do you feel okay?" I said.

"I feel a little strange," Grace said, "but I think I'm okay."

"No pain?"

"No. I feel a little woozy, but no pain."

"We're going to need to move you to another room," Nurse Broyles said. "Just to be on the safe side."

"What room?" I said.

"We're going to move her to an operating room. When the other doctor gets here, if the baby needs to be taken out quickly, we want to have her ready."

"This doesn't sound good," I said.

"It's just a precaution. Everything will be fine."

A couple of orderlies showed up just then, and I reached down and kissed Grace on the forehead.

"I love you, Grace," I said. "You're going to be fine. I'll be waiting for you. See you soon."

A tear slipped from Grace's eye, and she smiled up at me.

"I've been waiting for months to hear those words," she said. "I love you, too, Darren."

She blew me a kiss, and they pushed her out of the room.

"Nurse Diaz is going to accompany you to a special waiting room while we take Miss Grace to the operating room," Nurse Broyles said.

Just then, a large man walked through the door. He was wearing a brown sport coat, a white, button-down shirt, and brown slacks and shoes. He was around forty and had curly, dark hair and wore wire-framed glasses. I immediately noticed bloodshot eyes behind the lenses.

"Dr. Fraturra," Nurse Broyles said. "Nice of you to join us. Jenny, would you take Mr. Street to the waiting room?"

As we started to walk out of the room past Dr. Fraturra, I stopped dead in my tracks. Jenny was in front of me, and Nurse Broyles was behind me. "You're Dr. Fraturra?" I said. "Where the hell have you been? Have you been drinking?" I moved up close to him and pointed my finger at his nose. "You smell like a distillery."

"Go on to wherever you were going," Fraturra said. "I don't have time to fool with you right now."

"How would you know that?" I said. "You just got here. You don't have any idea what's going on."

"Are you a doctor?" Fraturra said.

"I'm a lawyer, and you're late, your speech is slurred, and you stink of booze. I'm your worst nightmare right now, you drunk piece of shit."

I turned around and looked at Nurse Broyles. "Is the other doctor here yet? There's no way this drunk is touching Grace."

I felt a hand on my arm. It was Nurse Jenny. I don't know whether she was trying to soothe me or restrain me, but neither was working. Nurse Broyles walked past us and out the door.

"The other doctor is probably here by now," Nurse Jenny said softly. "Let's go on to the other waiting room."

"I asked you a minute ago where you've been," I said to Fraturra. "I want an answer. "You've been in a bar, right? Which one? Or do you just sit at home and drink when you're on call?"

17

"You're crazy," Fraturra said. "Get the hell out of here. Get out of my face."

"Come on, Mr. Street," Jenny said. "Please, there's nothing you can do here."

I pulled my arm away from Jenny and stepped to within a foot of Fraturra.

"You're right about me being crazy," I said, lowering my voice. "And if any harm comes to Grace or our baby, getting sued is going to be the least of your worries."

"Is that right?" Fraturra said, puffing up like a toad and leaning in toward me. I desperately wanted to break his jaw. I saw Jenny out of the corner of my eye as she moved to the doorway. I figured she was ready to push a panic button or call security. Fraturra inched closer. "Are you threatening me?" he said.

I lowered my voice even more, hoping Jenny couldn't make out what I was saying, and locked my eyes on Fraturra's.

"I promise you this. If anything happens to Grace or the baby, I'll cut your head off with a dull knife and bury you in the mountains."

Fraturra took two steps back. I had his attention now. I turned back to Jenny and walked toward her.

"Where's that waiting room?" I said, and we walked out the door.

CHAPTER 4

The waiting room where I was taken was small and isolated. I kept thinking it was the kind of place where bad news would be delivered. I walked out several times and made my way to the nursing station. Jenny wasn't there, and neither was Nurse Broyles. The only person at the station was a thirtysomething brown-haired paper pusher whose dress looked like a denim tent and who wore the tired face of someone who just wanted to get the hell out of there and go sit in front of a television set and eat cookies.

"What's going on with Grace?" I said to her each time I walked in.

"I'm sorry, I don't have any news other than they're working on her."

"What does that mean?" I asked the third time she repeated the phrase. "Working on her? Do you mean they're operating on her? Are they delivering the baby?"

"I really don't know, sir," she said. "I'm just a record keeper."

"I've been in that waiting room for a half hour," I said, my voice rising along with my anger. "I want some answers. I want to know if Grace and our baby are all right. I want you to go, right now, and find someone who can tell me something, or I'm going to go find Grace myself."

"Don't get belligerent with me, sir," she said. "I'll call security and get the police here."

"Good, good, let's just have a reunion. Call security. Call the police. They know me. Tell them it's Darren Street. I've been in prison before, and I'm suspected of committing several murders, although they've never been able to prove a thing. Tell them to come on down. Your choice."

I couldn't believe how cavalier she was acting. I was going crazy with worry over Grace and the baby. I was being cooped up in a small waiting room with only my imagination to tell me what was going on, and what my imagination was telling me wasn't good. And then every time I walked out to try to get some information, I was faced with this cud-chewing cow, who obviously couldn't have cared less about me or Grace or the baby or anything else except when she would eat next.

"Either you can call security and the police and there'll be a hell of a scene, or you can just get off your lazy ass and go find somebody who can tell me what's going on with Grace and our daughter," I said. "What's your name, anyway? I might want to catch up with you later."

"What did you say? Did you just threaten me?"

"Did you hear me say a minute ago I'm suspected in four murders? I wasn't kidding. Go find out what's on."

"Will you go back to the waiting room?" she said meekly.

"For ten minutes, tops."

She got up and waddled off down the hall in the opposite direction of the waiting room. I did what I told her I'd do. I went back to the waiting room and paced. I looked at my phone the second I walked in and marked the time. The countdown began. At the seven-minute mark, a man wearing gray surgical scrubs and looking tired and defeated walked in. He was my height, about five nine, and had short, curly, salt-and-pepper hair, a strong build, and a thick stubble of sideburn and beard on his face. His eyes were hazel surrounded by pink. He appeared to be on the verge of tears.

He offered his hand and I shook it.

"I'm Dr. Frank Jenkins," he said. "I'm the managing partner of the obstetrics and gynecology group that was responsible for Miss Alexander's care."

"Was?" I said, and I felt my legs begin to go limp. I backed up and managed to fall into a chair before I hit the floor. I thought I noticed someone else walk in, but I couldn't really see. The world had gone gray; shapes had become indistinguishable.

"I'm so sorry. I'm going to try to explain this as simply as possible," the doctor said.

He sounded as though he were in a barrel, a canyon, an echo chamber. It was a sound I'd heard only once before, the night a police officer named Bob Ridge told me my mother had been murdered. The echoes began to thicken, like he was underwater. I was able to process only bits of information.

"Uterine rupture . . . extremely rare . . . separated . . . torn . . . baby slipped out . . . abdominal cavity . . . hemorrhage . . . baby suffocated . . . mother bled . . . everything I could possibly do . . . tried to save them . . . there just wasn't enough time . . . again, so sorry . . ."

The noise that began to emanate from me came from a primal place, a place so far removed from present day that I could very well have been sitting in a cave sharpening a spear when I received the news. I cannot describe it because I did not hear it. I felt it, though later I barely remembered the feeling. It was a wail of desperation so deep and painful that the only thing I could possibly have hoped to achieve was to bring Grace and the baby back before they got too far away.

Please, wait for me, Grace. I can't take any more of this pain. I'll be along soon.

CHAPTER 5

Grace and Jasmine were flown to San Diego, where they were buried in a beautiful cemetery on a hill overlooking the Pacific. I didn't call her parents—I wasn't able at the time—but Jenny Diaz, the nurse who worked so hard to save their lives, turned out to be one of the kindest people I'd ever met. She took it upon herself to contact Grace's parents, and they made all the funeral and burial arrangements. I called Grace's mother once, two days after Grace died, and was told that I was not welcome at the funeral or the burial. I didn't know why she was projecting so much anger onto me, although I suppose I had caused Grace more than her share of heartache. But I wasn't responsible for her death, so I ignored what her mother said about the funeral and the burial, and I flew to San Diego. I sat in the back at the funeral, kept my mouth shut, and kept my distance at the burial. I was on a flight back to Knoxville less than twenty-four hours after I left.

Another change had come over me, one of which I was aware but powerless to do anything about. I was back in the same tunnel-visioned, laser-focused, emotionless state that I had entered when my mother was killed and the police told me they had a suspect. I already had my suspect. His name was Dr. Nicolas Fraturra. I had to make certain of two things, though: First of all, I had to gather as much information as I could about exactly what happened in that birthing center. I remembered something about uterine rupture, so I began to research the subject. I learned it was extremely rare and could be deadly to both mother and baby. But I also learned that given prompt attention, both mother and baby had an excellent chance of survival without any long-term effects. The key was to quickly and accurately diagnose what was going on, and once the diagnosis was made, to immediately get the mother into an operating room so the baby could be removed and the doctors could stop the mother's bleeding. Typically, from everything I read, the doctors had between ten and thirty minutes to operate once the uterus ruptured.

I stared at the computer screen in my apartment and thought about that night. It had only been a week. I first knew something was wrong when Jenny Diaz, the nurse, brought the second, older nurse in to look at Grace. That was when they told me they were moving Grace to another room. If Jenny Diaz had noticed something and gone to get the second nurse, the countdown started when Jenny walked out of the room. That moment, I believed, was when Jenny Diaz began to believe Grace's uterus may have ruptured.

Up to that point, the doctor was nowhere to be found. We'd been told he had been paged and that he would be arriving soon, but he didn't arrive until Grace was obviously in trouble, and when he did arrive, he looked and smelled drunk. I needed some answers, so I decided to turn to the nurse, Jenny Diaz. I called the birthing center and asked for her, but they told me she wasn't working until the next day. I asked what time her shift started, and surprisingly, the young woman I was talking to offered the information right up. Jenny would be in at 7:00 a.m. the next day.

"Twelve-hour shift?" I said.

"Right. She gets off at seven."

The next morning, I was in the employee parking lot at the birthing center at 6:30 a.m. At 6:45 a.m., I saw Jenny Diaz get out of a silver Chevy Malibu. I watched her walk into the hospital. I left, but I was back twelve hours later. I got out of my car when I saw her walk out of the building. It was hot, nearly ninety degrees and muggy. I stopped about ten feet from her car.

"Excuse me, Mrs. Diaz?"

She looked over at me, surprised, and then stopped dead in her tracks.

"I apologize if I frightened you. I'm Darren Street. I was here last week with Grace, the woman who—"

"I remember you," she said.

"I wanted to thank you for your kindness."

"You're welcome," she said. "I'm sorry about what happened. I really am."

"Can we talk for a minute?"

"I really shouldn't talk to you, Mr. Street. I'm sure there will be a lawsuit."

"I'm not filing a lawsuit. Grace and I weren't married, and I don't want money for the baby. It wouldn't bring her back. Wouldn't do any good."

"Her parents will probably sue," Jenny said.

"Maybe. Probably. But that has nothing to do with why I want to talk to you."

She looked around the parking lot. "There are cameras out here."

"I know."

It was a part of me now, looking for cameras everywhere I went. I was constantly vigilant about watching for people following me. I did a lot of doubling back in traffic, circling blocks multiple times, pulling in and out of parking lots. The things I'd done in the past had caused me to become paranoid.

"There's a dog park just down the street," she said. "We could talk there for a few minutes."

"Perfect. I promise I won't take much of your time. I'll follow you."

I was relieved to hear that she'd talk to me, and as I followed her out of the parking lot, I wondered why a nurse who would undoubtedly become involved in litigation, who would be deposed, and who could possibly lose her job if anyone found out she had spoken to me would make herself so accessible. Perhaps she felt guilty. Maybe she knew instinctively that when Fraturra didn't answer his pages early on that he wasn't coming and that she should have called the head of his medical group immediately. Perhaps she was simply a genuinely kind person and thought she could be of assistance to someone who was grieving. Or maybe she had some kind of personal grudge against Fraturra. Had she known my real reason for wanting to talk to her, she probably would have fled with her arms flailing, screaming at the top of her lungs for help. But instead, five minutes later, we were sitting next to each other on a park bench in the shade of an elm tree while people and their dogs passed by.

"Long day?" I said.

She looked tired, but she was a pretty woman with high cheekbones, dark, smooth skin, and shiny black hair.

"How did you know when I would be getting off?" she said.

"I called the nurses' station last night. They told me."

"No questions asked?"

"Nope."

"I guess it's a good thing you're not some kind of murderer or stalker."

If you only knew, I thought. "Yeah," I said. "You might want to speak to them about giving out information over the phone."

"I assumed the woman who died was your girlfriend, but I wasn't sure until you said so back in the parking lot. How long had you known her?"

"Several years. We were engaged once, but we went through a rough time and broke up for a little while."

"She was a sweet lady."

"Yes, yes, she was."

"Where is she now? I mean, I know she isn't, you know . . . Was her funeral here in Knoxville?"

25

"She was originally from San Diego. She and the baby are there now. It's a nice spot."

She folded her hands and looked down at the ground. "What did she do? For a living, I mean."

"She was a lawyer. She worked in the federal system, defending criminals."

"Really? That beautiful lady was a criminal lawyer?"

I smiled and nodded my head. "Don't let the pretty face fool you. She was as tough as a pine knot. Smart, too. The world lost a fine lawyer and an even better person."

"I'm so sorry," she said, and her eyes began to fill with tears.

"Please, I know this wasn't your fault. I've done a lot of research, and I know you did everything you could do. There are some things that I have to know, though. I'm not going to do anything rash, but if my suspicions are true, I'm going to do everything in my power to see to it that this doesn't happen to anyone else."

"You're talking about Dr. Fraturra."

I nodded. "I know you said you haven't been here long, but what can you tell me about him?"

"He has problems," Jenny said.

"What kind of problems?"

"Substance abuse. Drugs and alcohol. And from everything I've heard, he's an insufferable womanizer."

"Has anything like this happened before that you know of?"

"Like what? A mother and baby dying because he was out drinking? No, I don't think anything like that has happened before. But he's been late before, he's had other doctors in his group cover for him, he's come in smelling of alcohol."

"You've witnessed all these things firsthand?"

"Just a couple of times. He came in smelling like booze three weeks ago and then last week with your girlfriend. But the other nurses talk about him a lot. They hate him."

"The day we were there, you said you paged him. How many times?"

"Three. I paged him when I was first made aware that you were on your way to the hospital. I paged him again about fifteen minutes later because I hadn't heard anything back from him. I paged him again after I got Grace into the room and the monitors hooked up. And then I called him."

"You called him? Did you talk to him?"

"No. It went to voice mail."

"Did you leave him a message?"

"I did. I told him he had a patient who was within a half hour or so of giving birth. Then I called him again when the baby's heart rate first started to drop."

"Why does he still have a medical license?" I said. "Why is he still working if he does these kinds of things? Dr. Jenkins seems like a good man. Why would he put up with it?"

"My understanding is that Dr. Jenkins keeps him on because Dr. Fraturra's father was Dr. Jenkins's best friend. They started the medical group together. A few years back, Dr. Fraturra's father died of pancreatic cancer, but before he died, he asked Dr. Jenkins to take care of his son. He knew his son was having problems. Dr. Fraturra was also married to Dr. Jenkins's daughter, but she divorced him a couple of years ago. They have a five-year-old boy who is severely autistic. It's complicated, to say the least. I think Dr. Jenkins is just trying to do the right thing by everyone, but Dr. Fraturra keeps getting worse and worse. From what everyone is saying, there could be some real problems over what happened to your girlfriend and your daughter."

"Do you by any chance know what bars he hangs out in? Does he have a favorite that you know of?"

"I've heard a couple of nurses say you can find him at the Portal two or three times a week. I've also heard them mention Spanky's."

I'd heard of both bars. Spanky's was a meat market in the Old City, frequented mostly by upperclassmen and graduate students at the University of Tennessee. The Portal was a high-end bar and restaurant in Turkey Creek.

I looked at Jenny and reached out my hand. She took it, and I squeezed and shook her hand gently.

"Thank you for talking with me," I said.

"What are you going to do, if you don't mind my asking? I probably shouldn't tell you this, but when you and Dr. Fraturra were talking in Grace's room, when it got really tense, I thought I heard you threaten him."

"I don't really remember what I said to him," I lied, "but I don't think I threatened him. If I did, it was an empty threat. I'm not a violent person. I am a lawyer, though, and I think Grace and Jasmine—that was the baby's name—deserve some justice. I'm going to talk to the district attorney general and try to have Dr. Fraturra arrested."

"Arrested? For what?"

"Reckless homicide. Maybe criminally negligent homicide."

"What's the difference?"

"Reckless is a little worse. I think drinking while you're on call, ignoring pages and telephone calls and messages from the hospital, and finally showing up drunk is reckless behavior, especially when a woman and a baby die because of it. I think he deserves to be punished."

"So he could go to jail?"

"I hope so," I said. "That seems like a more just outcome to me than an insurance company having to pay out a bunch of money."

Just outcome, I thought. Here I was, the killer of four men, talking about "just outcomes." But justice, to me, had become nothing more than a hypocrite's word. Justice was a prettied-up term for revenge.

"Speaking of money, Jenny, do you happen to know what kind of car he drives? Guy like that probably drives something flashy and expensive."

"Why would you want to know what kind of car he drives?"

"I don't know. Just curious, I guess."

"It's one of the flashiest cars I've ever seen," she said. "Brand-new Porsche 911 Cabriolet. I've heard him brag about it to other doctors. It's some kind of turbo something or other. He said it cost him more than two hundred thousand dollars."

"Wow," I said. "Have you seen it?"

"Yeah, of course. You can't miss it in the parking lot. It's silver."

I thanked Jenny again for talking with me, and she stood and said goodbye. As I watched her walk away, black hair waving in the breeze, I thought again about the chances of getting the district attorney to agree to prosecute a doctor under these circumstances. It was doable. The facts fit the law for a prosecution for reckless homicide.

I knew Grace wouldn't want me to kill Dr. Fraturra. Her preference, I believed, would have been for me to sue him on Jasmine's behalf and let her parents sue on her behalf, but I thought she also would have gone along with the idea of filing a reckless homicide charge in criminal court. At least that's what I told myself, because I wasn't going to sue anyone.

Filing a lawsuit would take years, involve dozens of depositions and court hearings. Lawyers who defended medical malpractice cases worked for medical malpractice insurance companies, and they were cutthroat litigators and strategists. Their goal was always to drag a case out, especially a big-money case like Grace and Jasmine's, until the other side became so frustrated that they finally gave up and settled. They would come into court and file motions, trying to convince a judge that a cloudless sky was green if it suited their purpose. They would prolong depositions for days, harassing and intimidating witnesses, going through minutiae that had absolutely no relevance to anything, until the plaintiff's lawyer or lawyers finally threw up their hands in frustration and disgust.

So I was going to try another route. I had a plan. First, I would go to the Portal and ask around about the night Fraturra was there. I'd talk to the bartenders, the waitresses, the bouncers—anyone who would talk to me, and I'd find out what Fraturra had done there that night when he was supposed to be taking care of Grace. Then I would go to the district attorney, a man I knew and had helped get elected. I would give the criminal justice system another chance. I would lay out a case for him that was a lock. I would hand him Dr. Nicolas Fraturra's head on a platter and let him make an example out of a man who deserved far worse than a few years in jail. I would give the district attorney an opportunity to garner some excellent publicity for himself and his staff. It would be win/win.

But if that system failed me, as it had in the past, I would have to take matters into my own hands.

And, once again, I didn't give a damn about the consequences.

CHAPTER 6

I was a little surprised Stephen Morris agreed to see me, although we'd been close at one time. Morris was the district attorney I'd helped get elected more than six years earlier after I successfully freed my Uncle Tommy from prison. Morris beat Ben Clancy, my nemesis, largely because of the work I put in on Morris's campaign. It didn't really hurt Clancy, though. He immediately moved on to the US attorney's office where one of his old political cronies gave him a job as an assistant US attorney. He later used that position to frame me for a murder and send me off to prison. I got out, with Grace's help, after two years. Not long after that, Clancy disappeared.

I knew Morris, along with every other local and federal law enforcement officer within fifty miles, suspected that I had killed Clancy. They also thought I had killed a couple of rednecks in West Virginia who were suspected of dynamiting my mother's house. They were right, but they couldn't prove anything, and I wasn't about to offer any admissions.

I tried to get Morris to meet me at a coffee shop or diner somewhere, but he insisted that I come to his office in the City County Building a couple of blocks from Neyland Stadium, where the Tennessee Volunteers had played mediocre football in front of huge crowds on Saturdays for the past ten years. He let me stew in the lobby for half an hour before he finally had his secretary lead me through the maze of hallways to his office. It was one of those ornate, ego offices.

It overlooked the Tennessee River, had plush leather furniture, US and Tennessee flags, a vintage set of the *Tennessee Code Annotated* on a shelf to my left, and framed certificates and photos of Morris with politicians and judges and sheriffs everywhere. He'd even somehow managed to work a chandelier into the office decorating budget.

"Nice," I said as I looked around. Morris was medium height, a stocky, powerful man whose dark-brown hair was perfectly cut and parted on the side. I could easily imagine him as one of those guys in the gym at six in the morning, wearing a spaghetti-strap tank top and spandex shorts. When I walked into his office, though, he was wearing a sharp navy-blue suit with a red tie and a white shirt.

"Had to fight tooth and nail for every scrap of it," Morris said. "Some of the county commissioners would just as soon have the top law enforcement officer in the county work out of a bathroom in the basement. Bunch of damned cheapskates."

He reached his hand across the desk, and I took it.

"Nice to see you again, Darren," he said. "A lot of water under the bridge since the last time I laid eyes on you."

I nodded. "An ocean. Nice suit, Stephen. I'm not an aficionado, but that doesn't look like it came off the rack at Sears."

He smiled. "It's an Armani, actually. Treat from the wife for our anniversary last year."

"Well, you wear it well."

"I was so sorry to hear about your mother when that terrible thing happened," Morris said. "I should have reached out, but I just didn't know what to say. We got the TBI and the ATF involved right away, but—"

"Don't apologize," I said, holding up my hand. "I barely remember anything during that time."

"And then our two main suspects got themselves shot to hell in West Virginia."

"Yeah, I know. Did you ever look at anybody else? I mean, besides me?"

"I hope you're not taking that personally, Darren. The cops just let the investigation lead them. You know how they do it."

"They made up their minds it was me, and when they couldn't prove it, they shelved the whole thing."

"Is that why you're here? Do you want us to reopen the investigation into your mother's death?"

I shook my head. "I don't think it would do any good at this point. I'm here about something else. Did you hear about Grace Alexander and my daughter?"

He nodded and put his elbows on the desk. "I did, and again, I'm so sorry. I met her once, you know."

"Grace? Yeah, she told me. She said it didn't go very well between the two of you."

"She told me I didn't have any balls."

I smiled. Grace had never told me she'd used those exact words, but I didn't doubt it. "She was one of the kindest people I ever met, but if she got riled, she wasn't afraid to speak her mind. It wasn't always what people wanted to hear."

"The worst part about it was she was right," Morris said. "She came to me and told me Clancy had framed you, and she wanted me to help, but I refused. I was afraid of the big fed machine. And then you got out and cleared yourself. That was an amazing feat."

"Like they say, the truth shall set you free."

"What do you think happened to him?" Morris said.

"Who? Clancy?"

"Yeah. You think somebody killed him? I mean, none of his credit cards were ever used, and his money is still in the bank, from what I know. He isn't sitting on a beach, sipping rum punch, but he hasn't been declared legally dead yet."

"Guys like Clancy never die," I said. "They just fester."

33

"So you think he's still around somewhere?"

"He had a lot of enemies. He did a lot of bad things. I think somebody probably got even with him."

"Well, I don't suppose you came here to talk about Ben Clancy," Morris said.

"I didn't. I came here to talk to you about Grace and our baby and what happened to them. Do you know anything about it?"

"Just what I read in the obituary. That Grace and the baby both died during childbirth."

"There's a lot more to it," I said. "Have you ever heard of a doctor named Nicolas Fraturra?"

Morris twitched, almost imperceptibly, when I said the name. His chin came up just a touch, and his head leaned to the right. It was something a normal person might not even pick up on, but I was anything but a normal person at this point. I saw the twitch. He knew him.

"What was the last name?"

"Fraturra. About your age, early forties. Works for an OB-GYN group here in town."

Morris shook his head slowly and averted his gaze. "Fraturra? Can't say that I do."

He was lying. I would have bet my life on it.

"I'd like for you to get to know him," I said. "And then I'd like you to charge him with two counts of reckless homicide and send his sorry ass to the penitentiary where he belongs."

"Darren, do you have any idea how hard medical cases are to prove? That's why they all wind up as wrongful death cases in civil court."

"This one shouldn't be that tough," I said, and over the next several minutes, I laid out everything I knew. I told him what happened the night Grace and Jasmine died, what I'd learned at the bar, how Fraturra had come in late and drunk, and how Dr. Jenkins had tried to save Grace and Jasmine. The only thing I left out was the threat I made to cut off Fraturra's head and bury him in the mountains.

"I can see some problems with this right on the front end," Morris said.

By his tone, I knew he'd already made up his mind. There would be no criminal prosecution. "Really? What problems?"

"The first thing that jumps out at me is that we'll have to prove he was intoxicated if we want to prove he was reckless."

"You do the same thing I did. You send investigators to the bar he was in. It's called the Portal. Like I said, I've already been there and talked to the bartender who served him that night. The bartender's name is Bud. You subpoena the tab. Take a look at his credit card records. Get your investigators to talk to Bud. Get them to talk to the blonde he was bird-dogging. Her name is Danielle Davis. Subpoena his phone records for the pages and the calls and the voice mails that came from the birthing center. Canvass for witnesses. I'll testify that he was drunk when he came into Grace's room, and I'm sure a couple of nurses and maybe a doctor will, too. Do a timeline. It should be open-and-shut."

"Okay, let's say we do all those things. We find out he had too much to drink. We find out he ignored the pages and the phone calls you told me about. The fact remains that he didn't lay a hand on Grace, if I'm understanding you correctly. He didn't do the surgery, right?"

"That's right, but—"

"Then how do we prove he caused the deaths recklessly or other-wise, if he didn't touch Grace or the baby?"

"The whole point is that he acted recklessly by drinking and not responding to the pages when he was the doctor on call that night. When a uterine rupture occurs, the medical literature says they have between ten and thirty minutes to get the baby out and attend to the mother. If he hadn't been drunk, he would have been there and would have been able to take care of her. Instead, he got there late and he was drunk. They had to wait for another doc to show up, and by that time, it was too late."

"And he hires a defense expert who comes into court, a highly paid medical whore, to testify it was something entirely different that killed Grace and the baby. They'll say the birthing center or the OB-GYN group should have a backup doctor on call and immediately available. We get into a war of experts, the jury goes to sleep, and we're dead in the water. Who made the call that Fraturra couldn't do the surgery?"

"What? You mean when he finally showed up?"

"Right. Which doctor or medical administrator gave the order that Dr. Fraturra was too intoxicated to operate on Grace and the baby?"

"I . . . I don't know. I know I told him right there in Grace's room that there was no way he was touching Grace. He was shit-faced, Stephen. He smelled like a distillery, his eyes were red and bloodshot, his speech was slurred. The guy was too drunk to be driving a car, let alone cutting open a human being and performing surgery in a life-and-death situation."

"Was he stumbling? How long did you talk to him? Did you know it was a life-and-death situation at the time?"

"I've been around enough drunks in my life to know the difference between somebody who's had a couple of beers and somebody who's half in the bag. And, no, I didn't know it was life or death at the time, but that wouldn't have mattered. No way was that drunk touching Grace."

"So maybe *you* killed her," he said.

He was stone-faced when he said it. I couldn't believe what I was hearing. He must have sensed something from the look on my face, because he held up his hands.

"Take it easy," he said. "I'm just playing devil's advocate. That's what the defense is going to say, Darren, and you know it. They'll say he was fine and you interfered. They'll blame it on you. Think about it, Darren. What do you really want here?"

"I read the preliminary autopsy report, Stephen. My daughter suffocated. Grace bled to death from hemorrhage. All of it was preventable if only he hadn't abdicated his responsibilities as a doctor that night and decided to go get drunk. You can prove this case. And as far as what I want . . . I want the scales evened."

"You want justice."

"Call it what you like."

His intercom buzzed, and he picked up the phone on his desk, muttered a few words, and put it back down.

"Used up my allotted time?" I said. "Important meeting to go to?"

"I'm sorry, Darren. I can't bring a criminal prosecution under these circumstances."

"And you won't even authorize an investigation?"

He shook his head and stood.

"It'd be a waste of time. It was good to see you again. My deepest sympathies for your loss."

I stayed in the chair and smiled at him.

"Turns out Grace was right," I said through clenched teeth. I wanted to tear his precious chandelier down and strangle him with the shiny strands of fake crystal beads.

"Leave, Darren."

"Fuck you. I'm not going anywhere until you tell me you're going to do the right thing and go after the man who killed my Grace and my baby."

"I mean it, Darren. I know you're upset, but if you don't get up and walk out the door right now, I'll have you arrested."

"For what? Exercising my constitutional right to free speech? The right that allows me to tell the elected district attorney general he's a gutless piece of shit?"

I stood slowly as he reached for his phone.

"Fraturra could have prevented two deaths just by doing his job," I said.

"Sue him, Darren. Get a good medical malpractice lawyer and sue him."

I looked at him and said very slowly, "You could prevent one by doing yours." There was no mistaking what I meant.

I turned to walk out of the office when he said, "What was that? Was that some kind of cryptic threat to kill Dr. Fraturra, Darren?"

I stopped and turned back to face him. The statement was so obvious, the question so idiotic. My psyche was in slow-burn mode, and I knew where it would lead. Fraturra wouldn't last long, and the way I was feeling, Morris might just join him.

"You have no balls. Grace had you pegged."

CHAPTER 7

The Portal was one of those risky ventures for entrepreneurs. You hire a high-dollar chef, build out a first-class bar and restaurant in an expensive space surrounded by even more expensive spaces, you call your bartenders "mixologists" and stock the bar with expensive wine and spirits, you charge extravagant prices, you cater to young professionals—many with expense accounts—and hope people come. If they do, you clean up. If they don't, well, it's off to bankruptcy court.

I'd never set foot in the Portal before the night I went to see whether Dr. Nicolas Fraturra might be there. I was operating on a very strong suspicion that he would, based on my conversation with Jenny Diaz, but I wasn't certain. I hadn't really started my serious recon of Fraturra, the kind of recon that ultimately leads to a killing. I knew where he lived, but I'd only driven by once. I knew a little about his family situation from Jenny, and I knew, of course, what he did for a living and where he worked. But I hadn't really decided to kill him until earlier that day when I met with Stephen Morris, the district attorney, and realized that Morris wasn't going to give me any satisfaction. But since Morris had turned me down flat, I had to figure out how I was going to kill him and get away with it. If I screwed up and the cops were going to be able to come after me, I knew I'd have no trouble putting a bullet in my own head. My attitude about going back to jail hadn't changed since my release from prison. I would rather die than go back.

The restaurant was noisy when I walked in at 7:00 p.m. There were a couple dozen people sitting in the lobby, waiting, and the bar was packed. I'd dressed for the occasion—a navy-blue suit, white shirt, and navy-blue tie—the lawyer's uniform. The bar was to the left, and I walked past the hostess's station and looked around the large, ornately decorated room. There was an avant-garde sort of vibe in the room. The bar was a big square, constructed of river rock with a granite cap. Hanging from the ceiling above the bar was a model of a dirigible. It was lighted purple on the inside, and it cast a soft hue over the entire room. The walls were exposed brick covered with old gears and fans and copper piping and mechanical drawings.

I spotted Fraturra within twenty seconds. He was sitting on the other side of the room at a counter, facing away from the bar. I expected a woman to be sitting next to him, but instead, he was deep in conversation with a man in a suit that was very much like the one I was wearing. I recognized the man immediately. It was Stephen Morris, the district attorney who had looked me in the eye earlier that very day and told me he didn't know Fraturra.

That twitch back at the office. I knew Morris was lying then, and now, here was proof in the flesh. I felt my heartbeat rise and told myself to try to keep it together. I didn't need to go to jail, but how I longed to walk over there and smash Morris in the face. A day or two in jail might have been worth the satisfaction of breaking his jaw.

I squeezed between a couple of people at the bar and finally managed to catch the eye of a bartender. I ordered a beer and stepped back, trying to decide exactly what to do. It didn't take long. I decided to do what I usually did when I was angry—confront the situation head-on without thinking it through—and I worked my way around the bar toward the two men.

When I got to them, I stood directly behind Morris, facing toward the bar so he wouldn't recognize me, and then I turned.

"Well, I'll be damned," I said, and both of their heads shot around. I looked at Morris. "This is a hell of a coincidence, isn't it, Stevie? A few hours ago you told me you didn't know this guy, and here you are, having a drink with him. You must have just met, right? How are you two hitting it off?"

"Get out of here, Darren, before I call the police."

"People say that to me all the time these days," I said. "Go ahead—call 'em up. While you're doing that, I'll call the *News Sentinel* and see if we can get a reporter down here. Get both sides of the story in the paper."

I looked at Fraturra. "On call again tonight, Doc? Ignoring your phone?"

Fraturra looked at me like he wanted to spit in my face, but he didn't say anything.

"I asked old Stephen here to charge you with reckless homicide for killing my girl and my baby," I said. "He made up a bunch of bullshit excuses why he couldn't do it, so you're safe. Doesn't look like you'll be going to jail. He's a good friend. I just thought you should know that. You have a good friend there."

I looked back at Morris. "Where did you guys meet, anyway, Stephen? High school? Frat buddies in college? Hook up in the bathroom of some bar? Was that it? Love at first sight?"

"Darren," Morris said, "I swear to God if you don't walk away right now I'm going to bring a shit storm down on you that you'll never forget."

"Really? What are you going to do? Frame me and put me in prison? Blow my mother to bits? Kill my girlfriend and baby? Because those are all things that have happened to me, Stephen. Really. They happened. I've been through those experiences. What would you possibly think could be worse?"

"I . . . I . . ." He had no answer. "What do you want, Darren? What are you doing here?"

"I just wanted to check this place out. I've heard such good things about it, you know? I've heard the people who come here regularly are stuffy and a little sleazy and think they're better than other people. I was hoping I'd fit right in. And you know what? I feel like I am fitting in. I think I'll come here every night, just to feel superior and sleazy and say hello to my good friend Dr. Fraturra."

Fraturra rose from his seat and hurried away toward the entrance.

"Are you leaving?" I called after him. "Please, don't leave! I was hoping we could bond!"

He walked around the corner of the bar in his gray suit, and I turned back to Morris.

"You lied to me, you son of a bitch," I said. "You said you didn't know him."

"I've known him since high school," Morris said. "We were on the debate team together. We actually got laid for the first time on the same night in the same house by the Williams twins. We're old friends, Darren, but it doesn't matter."

Morris was trying to look tough. He took a long sip from the glass in his hand and said, "You wouldn't have a criminal case whether I knew him or whether he was a complete stranger. Give it up, Darren. Take my advice and go find a malpractice lawyer. He pays a bunch for malpractice insurance. Run it up his ass."

"What were the two of you talking about? Why did you meet him here today? Was I the subject of the conversation?"

"Your name came up."

"In what context?"

"In the context of he needs to hire some protection, some security. I think you're capable of some pretty terrible things."

"And he isn't? He's responsible for two killings, and those are just the ones I know about."

"He didn't *kill* anyone."

Just then I felt a hand on my shoulder. I turned to face two very large men in tight black pants and jackets, wearing white button-down shirts.

"Is this gentleman bothering you?" one of them said to Morris. The man's head was shaved, and he had green eyes. The other one had a buzz cut and brown eyes. The bald guy had tattoos on both of his hands. Fraturra was hanging back about ten feet behind them. I noticed the people close to us go quiet.

"Yes," Morris said. "As a matter of fact, he is."

"We're going to have to ask you to leave," the bald guy said.

I'd been in dozens of fights in prison. I'd fought inmates, cellmates, and guards. I'd fought big guys and small, quick guys. I'd fought grapplers and strikers. I'd taken punches and kicks and been choked out and even stabbed. There was probably nothing at that point I hadn't seen as far as hand-to-hand combat. I figured I could kick the bald guy in the groin and punch the other dude in the throat before they knew what happened, but then I'd just wind up in jail for a day or two and have to go through the system after the cops found me and charged me with assault.

"Why?" I said to Mount Baldy. "What have I done?"

"Dr. Fraturra is one of our best customers, and he says you've been harassing him. The gentleman right there, as I'm sure you know, is the district attorney. If they say you have to go, then you have to go."

I took a swig of my beer and set it on the bar.

"Fine," I said. "I'll walk out, but if you so much as lay a finger on me, both of you muscle heads will be eating through a tube for a while."

"Ah," Buzz Cut said. "Are we a badass?"

"Touch me and you'll find out real quick."

"Great to see you again, Stephen," I said to Morris, and I started walking toward the entrance. Baldy and Buzz Cut parted like a gate and let me walk past, but they followed close behind. As I passed Fraturra, I winked at him.

"Be seeing you soon, Doc," I said, and I walked out of the bar.

I got into my car, looked toward the mist-covered Smoky Mountains in the distance, and headed for Gatlinburg.

CHAPTER 8

"You never call," Luanne "Granny" Tipton said when she opened the door and saw me standing on her front porch.

Granny and two of her grandsons lived atop a mountain on two hundred acres about thirty minutes outside of Gatlinburg. I'd driven along the steadily climbing mountain road among lengthening shadows, negotiating sharp turns and switchbacks, until the asphalt ended and turned to gravel. A chat driveway eventually led to the Tipton compound. I'd climbed out of my car and walked up onto her front porch and knocked on the door.

Granny was in her early seventies, lean and still ramrod straight. Her hair was fine and white, and her eyes a deep brown. She smiled warmly at me. I don't know what it was about Granny, but we connected at a deep level. She was always glad to see me, and the feeling was mutual.

"I apologize," I said. "Do you have some time for an old friend?"

"Always," she said. "I was about to go for my evening stroll. Care to join me?"

"That would be nice."

"Let me get a shawl," she said. "I know it's warm, but these old bones start to chill."

It was a little after eight o'clock, and the sun was dropping steadily toward the rounded humps to the west. I stood on the porch while she retrieved a white shawl and came back out. We walked down the steps, crossed the driveway, and began to follow a path that skirted a creek and a tree line. It led back toward the road, away from her house and the two large, beautiful log cabins on either side. The cabins belonged to her grandsons, Eugene and Ronnie.

"Haven't heard from you in a while, Darren," she said as we walked slowly along the path. "How have you been?"

"I have another favor to ask," I said quietly. My hands were folded behind my back, and I was looking at the ground.

"So you haven't been doing well," she said. "What kind of favor?"

"Very similar to two I've asked in the past."

I had a long history with the Tipton family. One of them, a grandson named James, became entangled in the murder trial in which Ben Clancy framed me. James was a witness against me and later recanted and helped get me out of prison, but the psychological and emotional damage inflicted upon him by Ben Clancy eventually drove him to shoot himself in the head. I was there, trying to talk him out of it, when he pulled the trigger.

Eugene, Ronnie, Granny, and Big Pappy Donovan later helped me hang Ben Clancy in their barn after Big Pappy and I kidnapped him. When I killed Donovan during our duel, I also disposed of him at the Tiptons'.

"So something has gone wrong," Granny said.

"You haven't heard what happened to Grace?"

Granny looked at me, puzzled, and said, "No, Darren. What happened to her?"

I told her about the night Grace and the baby died. I told her I'd tried to take it to the district attorney, but that he and the doctor were connected somehow and he wasn't going to help.

"So you're going to kill the doctor," she said.

"Yes, I'm afraid I am. I don't feel like I have a choice. If I don't kill him, it's almost like Grace's death, the baby's death, didn't happen.

There is no consequence to the doctor's actions. It all just seems so unfinished. Do you understand?"

"I understand, Darren. The question is: when does it stop for you?"

"I don't know. I suppose it stops when people stop killing those I love, and since there really isn't anyone I love left except my son, Sean, maybe it stops after this one."

"When do you want to do it?" Granny said.

"Soon. I think the district attorney warned him I might be coming after him and told him to hire some security. It'll probably be off-duty cops or retired cops. If the doctor really thinks he needs protection, I think it'll take him at least a week to get his act together. He's a drunk, isn't exactly on top of things."

"How do you plan to kill him?" she said.

"I was thinking about that on the drive up here," I said. "From everything I read about what happened in the operating room, my daughter suffocated, so I thought about strangling him. But Grace bled to death from a hemorrhage, so I think I'd like to look into his eyes while he bleeds out."

"Which means you're going to gut-shoot him or cut his throat," Granny said.

"I was thinking more toward the throat."

"You've become a cold-blooded killer, Darren. Do you know that? Is that something you're ready to concede?"

A coyote howled in the distance as the sun continued to sink. I looked in the direction of the coyote and thought about what Granny had just said. It was a big statement. Me, Darren Street, son of a violent, alcoholic father whom I eventually threw out of the house when I was thirteen, leaving me to be raised by a single mother. I was a young man who had done my best to get by, to make my mother proud. I'd gone to law school, had become a good lawyer, and was making a decent living before Ben Clancy came along and upended my world by putting me in prison. Had that been the catalyst? Had the two years in prison hardened me that much? I didn't think so, but they'd certainly prepared me for what was to come. I'd become a killer when my mother was murdered. When I went to West Virginia and murdered those first two, I'd enjoyed it. Killing gave me a tremendous sense of power, and the power was like an addictive drug. I'd lost no sleep over killing those two, just as I'd lost no sleep over Ben Clancy or Big Pappy Donovan.

"I suppose I am a killer, Granny," I said. "It isn't something I consciously think about. It wasn't something I intended and I don't really regard myself as some kind of assassin, but I guess life doesn't always lead us where we intend to go."

"You obviously don't believe in the old adage that revenge is a dish best served cold."

"No, ma'am, I don't. I like mine hot."

There was an ornamental bridge over the creek just ahead of us. On the other side of the creek was a small clearing where someone had placed a picnic table. Granny walked across the bridge, and I followed.

"The boys built this bridge for me and cleared this little spot. I like to sit here and think sometimes."

She sat down, made a motion with her hand. "Take a load off."

"I will as soon as this is done," I said as I sat down across from her.

She smiled and shook her head. "I remember when I first met you. I thought you were as straitlaced as they come. And you were. But life has a way of taking a toll on people, and you've sure seen more than your share of sadness."

"I think about the Holocaust survivors sometimes," I said, "and I wonder if what I've been through is similar to what some of them went through. Being uprooted, hauled off to prison, losing everything, including my child, having loved ones killed. The difference between so many of them and me is that I've been able to strike back against those who have wronged me. Maybe some of them could have killed a few Nazis here or there but chose not to because they wanted to survive. Maybe some of them did kill a few Nazis and paid the price. Me? I'm in the second group. I don't care if I survive at this point. I want revenge, and I'm willing to die to get it. I don't necessarily want to die, but I'm not willing to go back into a cage. I'll die before I'll do that."

"What can we do?" Granny said.

"A few things," I said. "First off, I need a clean car, an SUV, one that can't be traced to anyone. Nothing fancy, around a 2008 model, but not so beat-up that it stands out. I can pay, so don't worry about that. Can you come up with something?"

Granny nodded. "Not a problem."

"I need a couple of clean IDs, different names, just in case I need to rent cars or whatever I have to do. I want the photos to have beards on my face. I also need a cop uniform, one that looks like a Knoxville patrolman. I could buy the stuff online, but that would leave a trail. Know any good seamstresses?"

"You're looking at a woman who has made more clothes than the fanciest New York designer, dead or alive."

"Good. You're hired. I also need a badge, a cop hat, and a cop blue light. The badge doesn't have to be perfect, but the hat needs to be pretty spot-on. I'm going to put the blue light on my dashboard. You can buy one of those at Walmart."

"We'll figure out where to get everything and send Eugene's oldest boy."

"I was also wondering whether you have some kind of tranquilizer you use on the hogs that I could inject him with. I'll get him unconscious, bring him up here, and spend a little time with him."

"You don't want Ronnie and Eugene to help you get him here?"

"I feel like they've done enough. No sense putting them in harm's way again. You guys had a reason to be involved with Clancy because of James, but this is my fight. What he did caused my girl and my baby to die. I'd like to handle it myself. What about the tranquilizers? Do you have anything like that?"

She nodded. "We have a couple of tranquilizers around I've gotten from vets over the years. One in particular might work for you, I think, but I need to tell you up front it might kill him. The drug works fine on hogs, but they don't use it on humans anymore. It's called ACP, acepromazine. Strong medicine. The vet told me it was developed as an antipsychotic drug for humans, but they've come up with better drugs since. It'll put a pig down in a hurry, though, I can tell you that."

"Do you inject it?"

"In a muscle. You could stick it in his backside or his shoulder."

"How long does it take the pig to go to sleep?"

"Seconds."

"Could you figure out the dose for a hundred-and-eighty-pound man and sell me a syringe full?"

"I suppose I can do that," she said.

Granny reached across the table and put her hand on my arm.

"Darren, after you do this thing, where will you go from there? This will be five people. Are you going to stay in Knoxville and practice law and act like nothing ever happened?"

I shook my head. "I'm getting out of Knoxville. I don't know where I'm going, but I'm not staying. Just too much pain everywhere I look. I only have a couple of cases going, but I'll just give them their money back and tell them to find another lawyer. I mean, what are they going to do? They can't force me to stay. They can threaten to disbar me, but I don't care if they do."

Granny took a deep breath. "We don't want them to disbar you."

"Why? What difference does it make?"

"Listen, Darren, I know I told you we went legit with the moonshine business, and we tried, but we couldn't make any money. With all the regulations and the competition, it's damned near impossible to get ahead legally. So we've picked up a few other sources of revenue, went back to some old ones, and I've been thinking about expanding.

I've thought about you a couple of times in that regard, and I've come up with something that would involve you if you're interested. It would be a complete turnaround for you, an about-face, but in exchange for us helping you out with this doctor, I'd like you to give it some serious thought. It's a big ask, but you've made some big asks of us, too. That last man you brought up, here, the one you called Big Pappy? That was a mess. And then I had to get the doctor to patch you up."

"I remember," I said. "And again, I thank you. You guys have been so good to me and done so much for me, I'd consider anything you ask me to do."

"Thank you, Darren."

"What is it? Do you need a lawyer?"

"I need to make a few phone calls first, work some things out. But if you're agreeable, I have some old friends who will be extremely helpful."

"I don't understand, Granny."

"Let's deal with your doctor first. If that works out, and I'm sure it will, then we'll talk about my idea. I think you're going to love it. It'll appeal to your sense of irony."

"I love irony."

"I know. This will be irony at its best."

"You're killing me, Granny. What do you want me to do?"

She sighed and tapped me on the arm.

"You're a persistent devil," she said. "Stephen Morris is up for reelection in November, correct? Didn't the legislature change the law and make the district attorney's term seven years?"

"Yeah, I believe that's right."

"I want you to run against him, Darren. And if you do, you'll beat him. I'm going to get you elected as the next district attorney general of Knox County."

I looked at her, stunned. "What's in it for you?"

"More than you know," she said as she stood up from the table and hooked her arm around mine. We crossed the bridge as my mind raced. District attorney general? Me? I was a murderer.

"The irony is blowing your mind right now, isn't it?" Granny said.

I chuckled. "I don't know if the irony of me becoming the district attorney general is blowing my mind as much as the fact that you just used the phrase 'blowing your mind.'"

"We're going to make a lot of money together, Darren," she said as we made our way back toward the house, "and we might even have some fun while we're at it."

CHAPTER 9

Granny had a car and my uniform in three days. They'd also gathered IDs, the hat, the badge, and the blue light. I went to a magic shop in the Old City, a place I'd visited more than a year earlier, and bought a fake mustache, a beard, and a small bottle of adhesive. I'd used them before, and along with a baseball cap and some sunglasses, the fake beard altered my appearance considerably.

During the three days it took Granny to make the uniform, I walked around the Portal's parking lot each evening at dusk, mapping out security cameras and looking to see whether Dr. Fraturra's silver Porsche was in the lot. It was always there, even on Sunday. I followed him home each of those evenings. My plan was to eventually follow him and then blue-light him right before he got to his house. I figured he'd pull into his driveway, thinking I was a cop, and I'd drug him and grab him up.

But something kept eating at me. It just wouldn't work. Fraturra lived on a fairly busy street in a wealthy area that overlooked the Tennessee River. His house was gated. The reason he drank so often at the Portal in Turkey Creek was that it was pretty much a straight shot from the bar to his house. The street was all four lane or five lane, and it was well lit. On the weekends, there was a lot of traffic until after midnight. I started thinking that if I blue-lighted him, the first thing he would do would be to call 9-1-1 and have them on the phone when I walked up to the car because Morris had warned him I might be coming after him. The dispatcher would know immediately that no real police officer in the area had called in a suspected DUI, and they'd be on me in a heartbeat. I was also afraid, because of the lights in the street, that the car I was driving might be noticed by someone. *I* might be noticed, even though whoever saw me might not be able to identify me. It was just too risky.

Besides all those things, there were other problems. From the limited time I'd observed Fraturra, he left the bar anytime between nine and midnight, depending on how the hunting was going, I supposed. He wasn't much of a hunter, though, because I'd only seen him leave with one woman. He took the same route home each evening, went through the gate, and then into the garage. Both the gate and the garage closed within thirty seconds of him pulling in. I needed to rethink the entire plan. I'd have to go back to Granny for more help. I needed a boat and three throwaway cell phones, and I needed Eugene and Ronnie.

In the meantime, I continued to watch and gather information. Fraturra's massive brick-and-stone home wasn't far from the Cherokee Country Club. If you were anybody in Knoxville, if you wanted to show you had status, you bought an overpriced house on the river. Fraturra's backyard led to the water, which was roughly two hundred yards wide at the spot where he lived. It was about fifty yards from his garage to his boat dock on the river. He'd ensured his privacy by lining each side of his yard with Leyland cypress trees that had grown to about thirty feet.

On the night we decided to make our move, which was ten days after my initial meeting with Granny, Ronnie and I pulled into Sequoyah Hills Park and backed up to the boat ramp. At sundown we unloaded a twelve-foot jon boat with a three-horsepower motor into the river. Eugene was outside the Portal, waiting for Fraturra to come out. Ronnie and I acted like we were fishing and floated on the current, making our way slowly downriver toward Fraturra's, which was just over a mile away from the park. When we got to Fraturra's house, it was dark, and Ronnie eased the jon boat up next to Fraturra's dock. I got out of the boat, sprinted for the cypress trees, and made my way along the trees in the darkness up to the house, about fifteen feet from the garage. I pulled a ski mask out of my pocket, Ronnie let the jon boat drift back out to the middle of the river, and we waited.

About ten thirty, my throwaway cell buzzed.

"He's coming," Eugene said when I answered, and I moved a little deeper into the tree branches.

Nearly fifteen minutes later, I heard the gate buzz, and it began to open. The garage door opened at the same time, and within thirty seconds, Fraturra's Porsche came rolling in. I sprinted through the opening in the garage door and slid beneath the back bumper like I was stealing second in a baseball game. I was wearing loose, black workout clothes, a pair of gloves, and the mask. The garage door closed immediately.

The engine cut off, and the car rocked as he opened the door and climbed out. I had the syringe in my hand. The cap to the needle was in my pocket. As soon as Fraturra closed the car door and started walking toward the door that entered the house, I came out from behind the car, took three quick steps, and jammed the syringe into his right hip before he knew what happened. He squealed like one of the pigs he would soon be meeting, turned, and tried to take a swing at me. I ducked it and backed away. I couldn't take a chance on him scratching me or punching me or pulling my hair. I simply couldn't leave any trace evidence behind. I knew the cops would most likely find footprints near the shrubbery outside, but they'd never find the shoes to match them. Even if they manufactured something and tried to claim they found the shoes, they were a size and a half too big for me.

Fraturra looked at me with a mixture of rage, confusion, and fear. He started toward the door leading to the house, then turned back and staggered wildly toward his car. Granny had been right. The pig tranquilizer worked quickly. Within ten seconds or so, he fell in a heap onto the concrete garage floor. I put the cap back over the needle and put the syringe in my pocket.

I stood over him until the automatic light that had come on when the garage door opened went off and I found myself shrouded in darkness. There was a locked door that led to the outside about ten feet from the garage door. It faced the backyard and the river. I called Ronnie and said, "Coming now."

I walked over, unlocked the door, and pushed it open. The warm night air was barely moving and smelled of freshly cut grass. I turned back and patted Fraturra's pockets until I found his cell phone and his car keys. I took them out and tossed them across the floor. Then I wrestled him onto my back in a fireman's carry. He was bulky and heavy, but I managed to get him out the door. I laid him down on the ground and relocked and closed the door. Then I knelt over him for a few minutes, gathering myself and listening for traffic, dogs, kids, anything. There was nothing but the sound of leaves rustling mildly in the trees and bushes.

I lifted him and threw him back over my shoulder, skirted his ridiculously expensive swimming pool, and started down the slope to the river. I stayed close to the trees. Ronnie had the jon boat tied to Fraturra's dock when I got there, and he helped me get Fraturra in the boat. We covered him with a canvas tarp, I removed the ski mask, and we untied the boat, fired up the small outboard engine, and headed back to the boat ramp at the park. We were there just minutes later.

"You're sure he won't wake up?" I said to Ronnie.

"No way," he said, and we pulled the boat onto the trailer with Fraturra still covered in the tarp. We put restraints on Fraturra's wrists and ankles just in case, secured the restraints to the supports beneath the jon-boat seats, strapped the tarp down, climbed into the truck, and headed for the mountain. I was confident we hadn't been seen by a soul.

When we got to the Tiptons' place, Eugene opened the barn door, and Ronnie drove the truck in. The three of us pulled Fraturra out of the back and dumped him onto the dirt floor, and Ronnie backed the truck and trailer out. By the time Ronnie returned, Fraturra was starting to wake up. He was moaning and trying to lift his head. Ronnie cut the restraints off him while I picked up a bucket near the pigpen, walked out back to the creek, and filled it with water. I carried the bucket back inside and dumped it over Fraturra's head. He started spitting and sputtering and shaking his head, and then he started cursing. I picked him up by the hair and dragged him to a post near the center of the barn. I had a fifteen-foot length of hemp rope, and Eugene and Ronnie helped me stand him up and tie him to the post. I wrapped him like a mummy. He was completely immobilized.

Then I went back outside and got another bucket of cold water. I threw that in his face, too. I wanted him awake, at least semi-clearheaded, so he would understand that he was losing his life for a reason. I wanted him to know that my brand of justice was being served upon him, that revenge was being taken, and that he'd brought this on himself by being an irresponsible, drunken piece of shit.

"You!" he said after the second bucket of water.

I nodded. "That's right, Doc. Me."

"What are you going to do to me?"

"I'm going to kill you, just like you killed Grace and my daughter."

"I didn't kill them!" he cried. "I didn't kill anyone!"

"Were you on call that night?" I said.

"I tried to get someone to cover for me. I'd been having a hard time. I called Bernie Weinstein, but he wouldn't cover my call. He's the one you should be after. Or Jenkins! Bill Jenkins! He's the one who actually botched the surgery."

"He didn't botch anything. He just didn't get there in time. And that's on you. You know the baby suffocated, right? And Grace? She bled to death. I can't kill you both ways, so I've decided to kill you a little at a time."

I was standing ten feet away from him. He looked pathetic with that rope wrapped around him.

He started to cry. "Please. I'm sick. I just need to get well. I have family that cares about me. I have an autistic child."

"To whom you pay zero attention, from what I understand."

"I'm sick! I have a disease!"

"And what disease would that be?"

"I'm an alcoholic."

"There's a cure for that, you know," I said. "Stop drinking."

"I can't. It's a disease, I'm telling you."

"My father was a drunk," I said. "Every time he lifted a can or a bottle or a glass to his lips, he was making a choice, and that choice was to drink. He used to beat the hell out of my mother and me. Then one day he didn't beat the hell out of us anymore because I grew up enough to beat the hell out of *him*. I kicked him out of the house, got rid of him, just like I'm going to get rid of you. A couple of years after I threw my father out, he got drunk and ran his car into a tree. And you know what? Nobody cared. Nobody missed him.

"You're just like him, you know. Every time you drink or snort coke or smoke weed or eat mushrooms or whatever the hell else you do, you're making a choice. The night you were on call and Grace died? You made choices that night, Doc. I know what choices you made because I went to that bar. I did what the cops should have done. I talked to the bartender. What's his name? Bud? Yeah, Bud. He thinks you're an asshole, by the way. I asked Bud what you did that night. I know what you drank, how much you drank. I know you were chasing a blonde named Danielle Davis. I know she ran like a scalded dog when you went into the bathroom. All those choices you made that night led to Grace's death and Jasmine's death, and now all those choices you made are going to lead to *your* death."

I looked over at Granny and Eugene and Ronnie. They were standing by the wall just inside the door, stone-faced. I'd fantasized about choking Fraturra into unconsciousness and then waking him up, choking him again and waking him up, just so he'd know what it felt like for Jasmine, although I had no idea what she'd really felt, if anything at all. I'd thought about waterboarding him. Then I was going to slit his throat and stand in front of him while he bled to death, the same way Grace had.

But in the end, I couldn't do it. I could kill, but I couldn't become a barbarian.

I reached into the pocket of my sweatpants and wrapped my hands around the Walther P-22 pistol that I'd used to kill Big Pappy Donovan less than a year earlier.

"You're the one who has a choice now," Fraturra said in a tiny voice. Snot was running out of his nostrils and over his lips. "You don't have to do this."

"You're right," I said. "I don't have to do it, and to be honest with you, Grace wouldn't want me to. But I choose to mete out justice myself when the circumstances warrant and the system fails me. Your buddy Morris isn't going to prosecute you, but he should. At the very least, you should become intimately acquainted with some extremely unpleasant animals behind the walls of a penitentiary. And since you're a doctor, they'd find ways to blackmail you, too, or bleed you for protection money. You'd be much poorer when you came out than when you went in. But that isn't going to happen, is it? Morris made that quite clear.

"Grace's parents could sue you. I could sue you. But in the end, how do you put financial value on a human life? I mean, that's downright sick. You took Grace's life at a certain age, and she made so much per year and the lawyers would say she would be expected to make so much per year for another certain number of years. Then her income would peak and begin to fall as she got older. Toward the end, she wouldn't be earning much, so the value of her life at that time would decrease. It'd be all about numbers, not about what Grace actually meant to other people. Malpractice defense lawyers place no value at all on that. It's just too vague, too uncertain. It's too *human*. You can't *quantify* it. So tell me, Dr. Fraturra. What's sicker? The way they do it, or the way I'm going to do it? At least with my way, you won't feel much pain, it'll be quick, and your family won't have to go through all the heartbreak of a funeral and a burial."

"What will my family know?" His voice was trembling, breaking. He was truly pitiful with the tears running down his cheeks and the snot running over his lips.

I felt nothing for him. I shook my head.

"Hear those hogs back there? They haven't eaten in a while. I don't think you'll last long once I toss you in there."

He began to scream, but I brought the gun up and silenced him with a shot to the forehead. Then I emptied the clip into his chest.

I shot him a total of ten times.

Granny brought me a mason jar filled with moonshine, and she and I and the boys took turns taking pulls from the jar while we waited for Fraturra's bleeding to slow. As the corn liquor warmed me, I felt satisfaction in knowing that I had ended the life of the man who, in my eyes, had killed Grace and Jasmine. I also got another dose of the addictive power that one feels when taking a human life. I basked in the glow of the power for a few moments; then I dragged Fraturra to the pigpen and dumped him over the railing while Granny, Eugene, and Ronnie set about cleaning up the rest of the mess.

PART II

CHAPTER 10

Eugene dropped me off three blocks from my place around two in the morning, and I moved carefully around the apartment building until I knew I could get in without anyone seeing me. I'd left my car there and a light on in my apartment. As far as any of my neighbors knew, I was home.

When I drifted off to sleep a little while later, I had a dream in which Grace was standing in the bedroom just a few feet away from me. Behind her was a veil of white mist that looked like a cloud. She was holding a baby wrapped in a pink blanket in her arms. I looked at her and reached out to her, but she shook her head and frowned at me.

"You could have made something worthwhile of our deaths, Darren," she said. "You could have resisted your urges, shown some growth, but you disappointed me again. Goodbye, Darren. You've disappointed me for the last time."

Then she turned, stepped into the mist, and disappeared.

I sat up on my elbows and reached toward the mist.

"Worthwhile?" I said. "How could I possibly take what Fraturra did to you and the baby and turn it into something worthwhile? Killing him wasn't an urge, Grace, it was a *necessity*. It was what I had to do to balance things. How could you fault me for that? What can I do, Grace? What can I do to make you understand? Come back, please. Come back and talk to me."

The white mist slowly darkened, and a fissure appeared suddenly. Mrs. Judge emerged with the silky red robe billowing around her and her thick, dark glasses. The scales were in her hand and the sword in its scabbard.

"Another one bites the dust at the hands of the assassin," Mrs. Judge said.

I lay back and covered my eyes with my forearm. "Go away. I don't need to justify myself to you."

"I'll get you eventually," she said. "Justice always prevails."

"That's a load of crap. Take your platitudes and shove them."

"Do you think you'll get away with this one, too, Mr. Street? Maybe someone saw you. Maybe you left something in that garage. Maybe you made a mistake. Or maybe your hillbilly friends will turn on you and rat you out."

"You'd love that, wouldn't you? Justice loves a rat. I'm surprised you don't keep a few of them around, maybe carry one on your shoulder. It'd be a good look for you."

She made a horrid sound, a sharp cackling that I realized was laughter. "You'll make a mistake soon. And when you do, I'll be waiting."

My eyes opened, and there was only darkness. I listened to the hum of the bedside fan and thought about what I'd done and the utter lack of emotion or empathy I felt when I was pounding rounds into Fraturra. It was like I had tried to tell Grace: I killed out of necessity, but I also had to admit that I took some pleasure in it. It wasn't like a duty. It wasn't like I was akin to a soldier who had been ordered to clean a latrine. I chose to kill.

I managed to drift off, slept fitfully, and climbed out of bed at five in the morning. I spent the next day cleaning the house and running errands—doing mindless tasks just to keep myself busy. I listened to newscasts all day, wondering when and if they would report Fraturra missing. That night, I drank a pint of bourbon and sat in front of the television. There was a baseball game on, but I had no idea who was playing and didn't care. I passed out sitting on my couch around eleven o'clock, woke up at four in the morning, and staggered into the bedroom. Grace and the baby didn't appear that night. Two hours later, at 6:00 a.m., I heard a loud knock at the front door, and I immediately thought to myself, *Cops.*

I looked through the peephole on the door. Someone was covering it, so I walked into the kitchen and leaned forward over the sink. I could see the front stoop. There were four of them standing out there, all men in ill-fitting suits and sporting bad haircuts. I was right. They were definitely cops. I went back to the door and said in a loud voice, "Who are you and what do you want?"

"Tennessee Bureau of Investigation," a deep, rough voice said. "Open the door."

"No, thanks," I said.

"Open the fucking door or we'll kick it down."

I walked back to the bedroom and grabbed up my cell phone, turned on the video recorder.

"Go ahead," I said as I came back to the door. "But just so you know, you're going to be on audio- and videotape. Got a warrant?"

"Open the door, Street. We're not dicking around with you."

"You didn't answer my question. *Do you have a warrant?* Because if you don't and you kick that door in, I'll sue all four of you and everyone else I can think of."

"You're wanted for questioning," another voice said.

I almost laughed out loud. "Wanted for questioning? That's nice. Wanted by whom? The TBI? And what would the TBI like to question me about?"

"We'll talk about it at our place."

"No, we won't," I said. "I don't want to be questioned by you or anyone else. Even if you had a warrant, which you obviously don't, I wouldn't talk to you. I have this constitutional right to remain silent. Maybe you've heard of it."

"We have reason to believe that you may be holding someone against their will in your apartment," the first voice said.

"Holding someone against their will?" I said. "Are you kidding? Don't take offense if I start laughing.

"Listen, guys, the intimidation thing didn't work, okay? It isn't going to work. I've been there, done that many times. And if you really had evidence that I was holding someone against their will, you would've already kicked the door in. You also would have brought a warrant and a tactical team. So just go on back to your office and tell your supervisor I wouldn't let you in and wouldn't talk to you. I'm going back to bed now. I have a headache."

"Morris isn't going to let you get away with this," the rough voice said.

"Get away with what?"

"You know damned good and well what I'm talking about."

And that's when I decided to drop it on them. Granny's suggestion. I knew it would freak them out, and I knew I'd get a kick out of it.

"Morris is up for reelection in November," I said through the door. "You guys go tell him he's finished. Tell him Darren Street is going to be the new district attorney general in Knox County, Tennessee."

I could almost feel the air being sucked through the door as I turned, walked into my bedroom, and closed the door behind me. I sat down on the bed and began to smile. I wished I could have seen the looks on the cops' faces when I said it. And seeing the look on Stephen Morris's face when they told him? That would have been priceless.

But as far-fetched as Granny's idea may have seemed at first, the more I thought about it, the more it appealed to me. I actually had some things going in my favor. Morris was smug, not well liked, and a lot of people thought he'd done a lousy job as the district attorney, including me. I'd had much more press than he had, and much of it was extremely sympathetic. I'd been wrongly convicted of a murder and managed to get myself vindicated. My mother had been murdered. My girlfriend and baby had recently died in what most people thought was an unavoidable medical tragedy. Practically everyone—or at least practically every potential voter in the county—had heard my name on television or read about me in a newspaper. And the thought of actually beating Morris and taking his job, making him experience the humiliation of being rejected by voters in his own county, was appealing. I'd read stories about how emotionally and psychologically devastating political losses can be to candidates. It occurred to me that beating him might even be better than putting a bullet in his brain.

On the other hand, the only time I'd been active politically was during Morris's campaign when he took down Ben Clancy. I'd done a lot of grunt work during that campaign, but I didn't really know anything about how to play the game. I had no idea how to run a campaign. I had no idea how to organize. I had no idea where to even start. And I didn't have a ton of money.

Still, I thought, *stranger things have happened.* The district attorney general was arguably the most powerful law enforcement officer in the district. The only people in law enforcement close to rivaling him were judges and the sheriff, because they were also elected, but if a judge or a sheriff told an elected district attorney to do something and he didn't want to do it, he could tell them to go piss up a rope.

Why not give it a shot? I knew I might take a beating in the press if the cops started feeding them stories that I was suspected in a bunch of murders, but the natural response to that would be: "Is that right? Why haven't they arrested me? Do they have a single shred of evidence?" It could backfire on them and put the cops in a terribly uncomfortable position, and it could backfire on Morris and make him appear vindictive and inept.

So again, why not try? I'd been bitching and complaining about the system screwing me for years. Why not become a powerful part of the system and see what happened? I didn't know exactly what Granny wanted in exchange for helping me get elected, and I didn't know how she planned to pull it off, but I was willing to give it a shot. Hell, I might even be able to do some good and start redeeming myself for all the killing I'd done. But if not, I'd just raise some hell and, like Granny said, have some fun.

I lay back on my pillow and stared up at the ceiling, a smile on my face.

"You're crazy," I said to the ceiling. "You belong in a loony bin."

CHAPTER 11

Eugene and Ronnie Tipton were brothers, both roughly ten years older than I was. They bore the look of men who had seen more than their share of pain in their lives. They appeared tired, but they were tough, independent men, far from defeated by tragedy and the lack of opportunity typical of so many of the people who lived in the mountains around Knoxville, Gatlinburg, Sevierville, and Pigeon Forge.

Eugene was the older and bigger of the two. I believed he was two years older than Ronnie, but I wasn't certain. Both were muscular and had dark, smooth complexions, black hair, and dark eyes. Their appearances, along with Granny's near-black eyes, made me wonder whether they were somehow descended from the Cherokee Indians who inhabited Tennessee before the whites either killed them or drove them out. Both men were wearing denim bib overalls over short-sleeve white T-shirts.

Granny was sitting across from me at her kitchen table, her white hair pulled back into a ponytail and a green scarf around her neck. She was sipping on a cup of hot tea. Eugene, Ronnie, and I were all drinking beer. Now that the task of ridding the world of Fraturra had been completed, she'd invited me up to flesh out her idea of putting me in the district attorney's office.

"I suppose you'd like to know *why* I want you to run for district attorney in Knox County," Granny said.

"I have a lot of questions," I said.

"You might say that law enforcement in Knox County is our enemy right now, but that could change very quickly, couldn't it?"

"I'm not sure I'm getting you," I said.

I looked at Eugene and Ronnie, both of whom had smirks on their faces.

"Knox County is as dirty as it gets," Granny said. "Everybody is on the take, including the district attorney, and there's plenty for the taking. The sex trade is strong in and around Knoxville, what with all the tourists coming in and out of Gatlinburg and Pigeon Forge. The drug trade is strong and growing every day. Opioids are taking over the country. Heroin is now the drug of choice again in a lot of areas because it's cheaper than OxyContin. Methamphetamine is everywhere in a bunch of different forms. It's just wide-open. The feds can sound their trumpets all they want about fighting a war on drugs. They're losing just like they always have, and they'll continue to lose until they do something about the root of the problem, which is poverty. But the members of the United States Congress don't care about helping people get out of poverty. They care about helping their rich friends and donors avoid taxes. They care about helping their rich friends and donors become richer. They care about making *themselves* richer. So it's never going to end. Which means there is always money to be made, and lots of it. Knox County is a big market, Darren, and we want in.

"There's also a ton of gambling. There's cockfighting, dogfighting, and bare-knuckle fighting, not to mention the run-of-the-mill sports gaming and backroom casinos. We're talking upward of fifty million a year, just in that county. The district attorney gets a small cut from everything, which doesn't mean he gets a small amount, and so does the sheriff."

"Stephen Morris takes dirty money?" I said. I thought about it for a second and decided it didn't surprise me.

"Do you know where he lives?" Granny said.

"Can't say that I do."

"Let's just say his living conditions have been considerably upgraded since he became the district attorney, and district attorneys don't make that much. And guess who set it all up originally? I didn't know this until a few months ago, but it makes sense now that I think back on it."

"Who?" I said.

"Ben Clancy. The very same man who framed you for murder and who we hanged in our barn and fed to our pigs."

"Son of a bitch," I said. "But Clancy didn't live an extravagant lifestyle. I mean, I did surveillance on him before we grabbed him up. Are you sure?"

"I have an old friend who operates in Knox County and who Morris has allowed to keep operating in exchange for a little piece of a big pie. She works in the sex trade, runs a big porn store out on the interstate and an escort service. She told me Clancy set things in motion many years ago, he and a sheriff named Joe DuBose. Did you know DuBose? She said he's dead."

"Yeah, he and Clancy were pals. I didn't care much for him. Doesn't surprise me that he was dirty."

"Certain people in Knox County are allowed to operate in exchange for money and protection. My friend is one of those people. They watch out for her and the others who have been chosen. If somebody new tries to come in, those who are protected serve them up to the police, the police make their arrests, the prosecutors prosecute them, the judges sentence them to prison, and it appears as though people are doing their jobs. But it's a selective process. The ones who are allowed to operate without interference get richer and richer. All they have to do is refrain from doing stupid things. They don't get to kill people, burn down houses, crazy things like that."

"Why haven't you gotten in before now?" I said.

"Because somebody beat me to it a long time ago. There's a man named Roby Penn who controls the gambling. Mean as a striped snake from everything I've been told about him. Wears this big, white handlebar mustache and military fatigues. They say he was some kind of Special Forces soldier in Vietnam. He's also related to the sheriff. He's got the gambling rackets locked down."

"How does the money work?" I said.

"That's set up out of the sheriff's department. Morris has an assistant who supposedly supervises special investigations, but I don't know of any special investigations they've done. He's also Morris's bagman. He collects Morris's piece from the sheriff, but the sheriff does most of the work. He keeps the accounts and sees to it that the money is collected every month. He makes distributions to Morris and whoever else gets paid. I don't know the full extent of it, but it's a big operation."

"I wonder why the feds aren't onto them," I said.

"The feds don't care about public corruption anymore," she said. "They're too busy worrying about terrorists."

"So it's the Wild West?"

Granny smiled. She looked at her grandsons and took a sip of her tea. "And it's about to get wilder. We've been wanting to get into Knox County for years, but we've been shut out. Now that we have you in the picture, it's a real possibility. We, along with some powerful friends I happen to have in Knox County, think we can get you elected. In exchange, you let us move in and do business. We don't care about prostitution and we don't fight animals, but we *are* interested in the drug trade and we'd like to open a casino near the county line, maybe two."

"And all I have to do is leave you alone?" I said.

She nodded. "You tell the sheriff you won't prosecute us. We'll stay in the county so the Knoxville city police won't bother us. If the TBI tries to sting us, you make sure it goes away."

"What do I do about the others? The cockfighters and the dogfighters and the bare-knuckle fighters and the pimps? What do I do about this Roby Penn you were talking about?"

"As far as Penn goes, we're going to have to figure out a way to take him out of the picture, and it isn't going to be easy. Especially since he's the sheriff's uncle. The rest of them? I don't care what you do about them except for my friend. I'll tell you her name when the time comes. Chances are you won't have to worry about it, though, because they've already made their deals with the sheriff. They've been around forever, so I don't really see anything changing. The sheriff isn't suddenly going to start bringing you dogfighting and cockfighting cases to prosecute. Your office won't be deluged with gambling and prostitution cases. The biggest obstacle is that you and the sheriff are going to have to figure out a way to get along. You're going to have to trust each other."

"Which means I'll have to go on the take with that carnival barker. He's a showboating redneck. I can't stand him."

The sheriff of Knox County was the kind of stereotype that I loathed—the big, fat, loud Southern county sheriff. Many local sheriffs in Tennessee operated quietly. They were powerful in their own fiefdoms and served eight-year terms, so their primary focus was usually to get elected and then get under the radar and stay there. Once a sheriff got himself elected in Tennessee, the voters rarely heard from him until he came up for reelection, and if he hadn't done anything stupid, they'd reelect him.

It was fairly easy to stay out of sight, too, because the truth of the matter was that nobody really cared about the criminal justice system. It was one of the bastard stepchildren of government. Politicians and taxpayers didn't want to fund it, nobody wanted to think about it unless they had to, and nobody outside the system really cared about the elections of criminal-court judges or sheriffs or district attorneys or public defenders. Sure, there was the prurient interest generated by murders and rape and violence and corruption, but the fact of the matter was that our society—like most societies—didn't give a tinker's damn about people who committed crimes. We wanted people who murdered, people who raped and robbed and assaulted other people, people who used or sold drugs, and people who ran whores or gambling operations, removed from society, warehoused, and forgotten. They were nothing more than short-term fodder for the news industry and a source of employment for those—prosecutors and cops and defense lawyers and judges and clerks and probation officers and all the others employed by the criminal justice system—who fooled themselves into believing there was such a thing as justice and wanted to be a part of that system. Once we were all done using the criminals for our own benefit, they became a dirty, forgotten little secret, and nobody really cared.

But the sheriff of Knox County, a larger-than-life, cowboy-hat-wearing, chain-smoking blowhard by the name of Clifford "Tree" Corker, preferred the spotlight. He didn't toil in silence or in private. There appeared to be nothing cerebral about him. The forty-two-year-old had been sheriff for eight years, having been appointed by the county commission for two years after the previous sheriff fell off a roof and broke his neck, and then having won another six-year term at the polls. He was up for reelection in November, but nobody was opposing him. Corker made sure he strutted onto the stage of every crime scene in the county that attracted a television camera or a news reporter. He held press conferences on a regular basis, touting his department's latest "drug roundup" or the apprehension of the latest "danger to the good people of Knox County" in a deep Southern bass. He vowed to "enforce the law of the land" and carried two pearl-handled, nickel-plated, ornately engraved .45-caliber Colt Python double-action revolvers in holsters he tied around his massive thighs with strips of rawhide. If the law of the land was broken and he needed to blow somebody full of holes, he was ready.

"Don't sell Tree Corker short," Granny said. "He's powerful, and he appears dangerous. He's got a boatload of laws that say he can do pretty much anything he wants, the FBI ignores him, and he has a thousand employees. Most of those employees are loyal to him just because he gave them a job. Five hundred of them are armed and trained to use their weapons. He has a jail he'd love to put you in if you cross him."

"I was in it for a year," I said. "It was a shithole, and I'm never going back."

"You'll have to figure out a way to deal with him," Granny said. "Telling him you're willing to turn the other cheek and go on about your business would be my suggestion. But there are some folks who are going to have to leave his county—his uncle, in particular—in order for us to come in, so that'll have to be worked out. We don't care if we pay him the same cut his uncle has been giving him, but we're not paying any more."

"How do you propose to get this Roby Penn out of the county?" I said.

"By upsetting his applecart," Granny said. "By making him extremely uncomfortable. He'll make a mistake when we do that, and we'll be waiting."

"Will I be involved in upsetting his applecart?" I said.

"We're going to run you into it like a Brahma bull," Granny said.

"How are you going to do this, Granny? How are you going to get me elected? You have to tell me."

"Soon. I'll tell you soon."

I looked at Eugene and Ronnie, then back at Granny. I nodded my head. "Fine. I'm in. You folks have put your lives and your freedom on the line for me more than once. You help me get elected district attorney, and I'll make sure you get to do whatever you want."

"We won't kill anybody unless it's absolutely necessary," Granny said.

"I suppose I appreciate that. So what's first?"

"I'm going to make a phone call or two and get you some real help," Granny said. "I'm talking real money and real advice and assistance. Bankers and legitimate businesspeople buy senators and representatives, not district attorneys and sheriffs. People like me usually put up the money for people like you, but I've got something else in mind."

"I can't say this surprises me," I said. "The corruption, I mean. I saw it in prison. The guards were in on almost all the hustles. I guess I hadn't really thought about it being here, though. I mean, Knox County specifically. And if it's here, it's everywhere."

"All over the world, Darren."

"That's depressing when you really think about it," I said. "What about the district attorney in this county? Do you pay him?"

"He was here last evening, sitting right where you're sitting now," Granny said. "Fine man. Think the world of him, and I pay him every month, like clockwork."

CHAPTER 12

Tree Corker looked down through an opaque window at the large crowd of men in the abandoned warehouse off Heiskell Road in the western part of Knox County. He was looking forward to watching two men do battle. He'd heard they were both good fighters with similar styles and that the odds were nearly even. It was a bright, sunny Sunday afternoon outside, but inside, the dark aura of bloodlust hung heavy in the dim light. Corker caught intermittent whiffs of dog and chicken dung, blood, man sweat, and fear. He knew the warehouse had stored many things over the thirty years of its existence: tobacco, car parts, water heaters, weapons, explosives, marijuana, and cocaine. He also knew it was now owned by a corporation formed by the heirs of the late Jess Plummer and leased through the heirs' lawyer on a month-to-month, handshake agreement to his uncle, a white-supremacist bookmaker, hustler, and maybe even a psychopath named Roby Penn.

Roby was standing ten feet across the room. He was a thin sixty-five-year-old former LRRP—Long Range Reconnaissance Patrol—in the Vietnam War. Roby was wearing short-sleeve khaki military fatigues. His arms were covered in tattoos, his head was shaved, and he sported a thick, white handlebar mustache. A gray scar crossed his nose like a small lightning bolt, the result of an argument with an ex-girlfriend with a bad temper and a beer bottle several years earlier. At least that's the story Tree had heard. He'd also heard the girlfriend had wound up in a dumpster.

"Should be a good fight," Corker said. "Who you betting on?"

"The marine," Penn growled. Roby Penn often didn't speak like other men. He chose to communicate more like a wild animal, in snorts and growls.

"Word is he's tough but doesn't have much experience," Corker said.

"He did three tours in Afghanistan, got shot four times, took a bunch of shrapnel from an IED, and is still standing. I know Shaker's a good fighter, but I'll take the marine anytime. He's like Sergeant Barnes from that movie *Platoon*. He ain't meant to die."

Corker knew the marine was Gary Brewer. He came from a wealthy family in Knoxville. His father and grandfather had both made fortunes in the insurance business.

"Didn't the Brewer kid go to college?" Corker said.

"Graduated from Tennessee with a business degree and then enlisted in the marines," Penn said. "Headed straight for Afghanistan."

"Why in the hell would he do something like that?"

"Some people just feel the need to serve," Penn said. There was an edge to his voice. "I felt that need many years ago. I wish I hadn't done it now, for a lot of reasons. Cost me half my left bicep, then I came home to people calling me a baby killer. Come to find out the whole reason we went into Vietnam was a ruse by the government. But fuck it, don't matter now."

Roby cast a sideways glance at Corker.

"I guess you never got the patriotic itch, did you? Never felt the need to serve your country."

"Never did," Corker said, "and I ain't the least bit ashamed. I never thought it would be a good idea to go to some foreign land and risk getting my ass shot off for a bunch of crooks in Washington."

Corker exhaled a cloud of smoke from the cigarette he was puffing on. "I don't see the politicians' sons going," he said. "And damned few of our representatives served in the military before they were elected. I always figured it'd be best for me to just stay right here and serve the people of my county."

"That seems to be working out pretty good for you," Penn said.

"It has since you and Clancy got me in this job," Corker said. "Who's Brewer fighting?"

"I told you earlier. Harley Shaker."

"Right. The bricklayer from Newport."

"Yeah."

"I've seen Shaker fight. Ain't ever seen him lose."

"Should be interesting," Penn said.

"The gate looks pretty good today."

"Be more than thirty thousand dollars. Once we figure up the vig on the bets, we should have a real good day."

Corker heard footsteps coming up the back stairs and turned to see Stephen Morris, the district attorney, walk into the room. Morris was wearing blue jeans and a black T-shirt.

"And there stands the last man I expected to see here today," Corker said. "What brings you out to our little playground?"

"Have you heard about Darren Street?" Morris said.

"The lawyer? The guy everybody thinks has killed a few folks and gotten away with it?"

"That's him," Morris said. "I think he just killed another one, but that's not the big problem."

"What is the big problem?"

"Can we have the room?" Morris said to Roby Penn.

"Fuck you. This is my place. You want privacy? Go outside."

"How about I just have the sheriff here arrest you and send your sorry ass off to prison for running an illegal gambling operation?" Morris said.

Corker quickly stepped between the two men. He knew Roby and Morris had met, but they'd had very little contact. Morris didn't know how truly unpredictable Roby Penn could be. He didn't know that something as simple as the empty threat he just made could send Roby off the deep end.

"I got no intentions of arresting anyone," Corker said. He smiled widely. "Especially my uncle Roby. He's paid you ten times more money than the government has over the past four years. You'd be biting the hand that feeds you."

"He ought to learn some manners," Morris said.

"And maybe you ought to take your happy ass right back down those steps while you're still able," Penn said.

"Did you just threaten me? Did you just threaten the district attorney general of Knox County?"

Practically before the sheriff could blink, a nickel-plated Colt 1911 .45-caliber semiautomatic pistol appeared from nowhere and was in his uncle's right hand. It was pointed at Morris's forehead.

"I'm not sure," Penn said. "Let's ask the sheriff. Did I just threaten the district attorney general of Knox County?"

"Easy, Roby," Corker said. "Go easy now. Me and the district attorney are going to walk down the stairs and have a little talk. When I come back, he won't be with me."

Penn nodded his head slowly, not taking his eyes off Morris.

"That sounds like a good idea," he said.

"We're going now," Corker said as he slowly took Morris by the arm and turned away. "Why don't you just go ahead and put that hand cannon away?"

Corker followed Morris down the steps and out a small door that led to a loading dock at the back of the warehouse. A rusted chain-link fence separated the property from a line of white oak trees a hundred feet away. Once they'd gotten outside, Morris spun. His face was pink with rage.

"What the hell was that?" he yelled. "I mean, I know Roby's crazy, but he just aimed a pistol at my forehead! You ought to arrest him."

"Calm down," Corker said. "That man is my uncle and a big part of your paycheck every month, and you know it. He is *not* getting arrested, unless you want to go back up there and try it yourself. But if you do that, you and I both know you won't come back. Besides, what would be your explanation for being out here at this warehouse in the middle of nowhere while cockfighting, dogfighting, and bare-knuckle fighting is going on—not to mention a shitload of illegal gambling? You're working undercover? You're looking for evidence in a case? Roby isn't one to be trifled with. He takes things to heart. And doesn't cotton to people coming onto his property and telling him what to do."

"I politely asked him to give us some privacy."

"Forget about it, all right? Water under the bridge. Just keep taking your money and let Roby be. So what did you want to talk about? What's the problem with this Darren Street?"

"He says he's going to run against me in the election. I don't know if he's bluffing. He hasn't picked up any qualifying papers, but he told four TBI agents who went to question him about a suspected kidnapping and murder that he was going to run against me."

Corker chuckled. "Be damned," he said. "If he does it, he's got some set of balls on him."

"It isn't funny," Morris said. "Street is smart and he's determined, and he's been a darling in the press because of all the bad shit that's happened to him. He'll get thousands of votes on sympathy alone."

"Hasn't anybody made any progress on any of those murders he's supposedly committed last year?"

"None. Nobody's even looking into them anymore. From what I've been able to find out, the files are closed. They're cold cases."

"And the latest? You said he told four TBI agents who went to question him about a possible kidnapping and murder that he was going to run against you. Is this kidnapping and murder a new case?"

"Yeah. The doctor who was supposed to be taking care of Street's girlfriend and baby when they died has gone missing."

"What do you mean, 'supposed to be' taking care of them?"

"He was on call, but he was drunk at a bar, trying to pick up a woman. Street's girlfriend had a rare medical condition. If the doctor had been there and been sober, he could have handled it, and she and the baby would have been fine. But he didn't show up until it was too late, and even when he did show up, he was drunk."

"Sounds like a case you should use to make yourself look like a white knight," Corker said. "Prosecute the doctor. What could you make? Reckless homicide? Criminally negligent homicide?"

"Can't do it," Morris said.

"Why the hell not?"

"Two reasons. First off, the doctor is a friend. We go way back. Besides, it's a civil matter, not a criminal case. All Street has to do is sue him. I told him as much."

"He came to see you about it?"

"Yeah. He came to the office. I turned him down. He pretty much threatened me. But that's not the worst of it. The doctor has pulled a Ben Clancy. He's disappeared into thin air. Vanished. No sign of him anywhere."

"Street?" Corker said.

"It's his modus operandi."

"Sounds like you've got a problem, Counselor. So what do you want from me? What are you doing here?"

"I wanted to give you a heads-up on Street, first of all. If he runs, he needs to be stopped. We've got too much at stake if he somehow manages to win."

"That ain't the way I see it," Corker said.

Morris's mouth dropped open. "What do you mean?"

"Nothing really changes for me if you lose," Corker said. "The worst thing I see happening is that there's one less finger in the pie."

"And what if I decide to go to the feds and tell them about your operation?"

"Then I'm afraid you and your wife and your children and your momma and daddy can expect a visit from Roby and some of his friends."

"Not even Roby would murder a district attorney general."

"I wouldn't count on that. If Roby gets wind that you're thinking of going to the feds, God knows what he'd do. Roby hates the federal government. His favorite nighttime reading is *The Turner Diaries*. Do you know *The Turner Diaries*?"

"Vaguely. Some fictional account of a radical who thinks the government wants to take his guns and his religion so he decides to blow up some federal buildings."

"That book has inspired a lot of radical white folks, Mr. DA, and Roby is one of them. I wouldn't mess with him if I were you, and I damned sure wouldn't go threatening to rat anybody out to the feds if you lose the election."

"So this is how it's going to go, then?" Morris said. "You're going to leave me hanging out on my own, fighting my own fight?"

"If I'm getting what you're saying, you're asking me to talk to my political base, maybe raise you some money, get some organizing done, that kind of thing. Maybe even come out publicly and endorse you. Is that what I'm hearing?"

"That's what you're hearing."

"I don't recall you helping me get elected," Corker said. "I don't recall you saying a word to help me or getting me a single vote. So I expect I'll just sit back and see which way the wind is blowing in a month or so. I'll probably have a sit-down with this Darren Street fella, though, see what's on his mind, see if he's willing to join the congregation if you have to leave. And then I'll decide what to do. Whatever my decision, you can bet it'll be in my best interests."

Scott Pratt

"Thanks a lot, Sheriff," Morris said. "It's good to know loyalty doesn't mean shit to you."

"A man who talks about loyalty in this line of work is a fool," Corker said. "I believe in the good Lord above, but I also believe in evolution. Only the strong survive around here. Now I'm gonna go back inside and watch this fight. I don't think it'd be a good idea for you to do the same."

CHAPTER 13

Corker watched while Morris stomped away, his shoulders slumped, muttering to himself.

"Some folks just don't have what it takes to last at this kind of thing," Corker said aloud as he turned and started climbing the back steps to Roby's observation room.

Up to that point, Corker knew of nobody who had announced they were running against Morris in the November election. It was a powerful job, but it was thankless. There were almost a hundred employees who brought all their personal baggage to work every day, and it paid less than a hundred and fifty grand a year without the illegal perks. If a murder was committed and went unsolved, the DA got the blame. If it was solved and the guilty party went to prison for life, barely anyone noticed.

Morris was unopposed in the August primary, which pretty much made him a slam dunk in November. But now this Darren Street apparently wanted in. Corker thought it might be difficult, though. Street had missed the primary election, so he would have to run as a write-in candidate. Write-in candidates were rarely elected, although it had happened on occasion. As he climbed the last step, Corker decided to just watch it play out. It might even be entertaining.

"You get rid of him?" Roby Penn growled as the sheriff stepped up to the window. The large crowd had circled two men below. Both were bare-chested and heavily tattooed, wearing only blue jeans and athletic shoes.

"You know, it probably isn't a good idea to stick a Colt .45 in the face of the district attorney general," Corker said.

"He's a pussy," Penn said. "I don't trust him."

"You don't trust anybody. I assume the marine is the one with the buzz cut?" Corker said.

"That's him."

"How much you got riding on him?"

"A couple grand."

"Who you betting with? Yourself?"

"I'm betting with Harley Shaker. Harley's got some money. Ain't afraid to bet on himself."

"Any man that wouldn't bet on himself has got no business down there," the sheriff said.

"How about you?" Penn said. "Care to make a wager?"

"I'm not much of a gambling man, Roby, you know that. I just like to pick up my cash at the end of the day."

Sheriff Corker knew the rules of bare-knuckle boxing were simple. No biting, no gouging, no head butting, no kicking, and no hitting a man when he was down. There were no time limits to the rounds. Once the referee said, "Fight," they fought until one man either quit or was knocked unconscious. The sheriff had heard people say that bare-knuckle boxing was actually safer—in terms of head injury—than gloved boxing because if the fighters hit each other in the head with as much force as they did with gloves, they'd break their hands. The two men downstairs were fairly evenly matched from a physical standpoint. Harley Shaker was a couple of inches taller than the marine, but the marine was thicker through the chest and shoulders. Harley's hair was long, black, and pulled into a ponytail. The marine's hair was sandy blond and less than a quarter inch long.

The vocal crescendo built as the betting intensified and money changed hands. The two men met with the referee in the center of the dirt floor, and he gave them last-second instructions. They touched fists, backed a few feet away from each other, and the referee said, "Fight!"

Shaker began circling to his left, and both men began throwing short, exploratory jabs. More punches were aimed at the bodies than at the heads. Shaker landed a solid right hook to the marine's ribs, and the crowd became even more excited. The marine backed away, gathered himself, and went back at Shaker with his fists close to his face. His left fist struck like a cobra and caught Shaker square in the temple. Shaker's knees buckled, and he nearly went down. As he gathered his balance, the marine swarmed him, striking him five times in succession. One of the blows was solid to the solar plexus and took Shaker's breath. He fell to the floor in a heap. The marine backed off as the men whooped.

"He's finished," Roby Penn said to the sheriff.

"I've seen Shaker take worse. Give him a minute."

The marine stood over Shaker and spit on him.

"Fucking cracker," he said. "Pussy-boy cracker."

It turned out to be a mistake. Shaker was on the ground for only a short time before he stood, staggered briefly before righting himself, shook his head, and let out a guttural yell.

"Looks like the marine shouldn't have spit on Harley," the sheriff said. "I don't think he's taking it well."

"Bring it, soldier boy!" Shaker yelled.

The marine waded back in on light feet, taking short steps, maintaining his balance. He tried to sneak an uppercut in, but Harley blocked it with an elbow and countered with a hard right that caught the marine flush across the bridge of the nose. Blood started pouring from the marine's nostrils, and he fell backward. Now it was Harley's turn to pounce. He began pummeling the marine with body shots and knocked him senseless with a precision blow to the chin. The marine went straight over on his back as half the crowd roared and the other half booed.

Shaker stood over the marine for a second, but then he suddenly jumped on him, straddled him, and began beating him with his fists, elbows, and forearms. The referee pulled him off, but Shaker knocked the referee out cold with a punch to the temple. He turned back to the motionless marine. Harley looked around, saw a piece of concrete the size of a brick on the ground a couple of feet away, picked it up, and bashed the marine's skull several times with the concrete. He finally stood, dropped the concrete, and raised his arms in victory.

"Spit on me, would you?" Shaker yelled. "Fuck you! I done killed me a soldier boy."

The crowd immediately began to disperse.

"Shit," Sheriff Corker said. "This ain't good."

"Get on down there," Roby said. "See if he's really dead."

"If he's really dead, I ain't here."

"Do you think I'm here? Do you think anybody was here? Dead or alive, we gotta deal with him. All I'm asking you to do is go down there and check it out while I deal with my boys and the money. I'll be along directly."

Sheriff Corker descended the two flights of steps to the fighting area. Harley Shaker was standing ten feet from the marine, a wild look in his eyes. Everyone else, including the referee, had left.

"What the hell, Harley?" Corker said. "You know the rules!"

"He spit on me! You seen it! He spit on me! Nobody spits on Harley Shaker and lives to tell about it."

The sheriff knelt and felt for a carotid pulse. Nothing. The marine's eyes were bloody, open, and lifeless.

"You killed him," Corker said, struggling to stand back up.

"Shouldn'ta spit on me."

"Do you know what kind of heat this could bring down on us?"

"I don't care. Bring the heat. He shouldn'ta spit on me. You gonna try to arrest me? 'Cause that won't go too good for you."

"No. Get on out of here."

"Not without my money. I want my money."

"Fine, you want your money? You can just hang around and collect from Roby. I don't know if he'll feel much like paying you, though, after what you've done."

A few minutes passed. Shaker paced in a circle, and the sheriff smoked a cigarette.

"Is he really dead?" a rough voice said. It was Roby Penn. He walked through a back door and sauntered into the abandoned warehouse space a few minutes later.

"Deader than four in the morning," Sheriff Corker said. Corker looked back down at the marine, who had somehow chosen to come to this place for a bare-knuckle-boxing match and wound up dead.

"Harley, you crazy son of a bitch. What'd you have to go and kill him for?"

"He spit on me, Roby. You seen it."

"And now we got a body on our hands that we have to get rid of. And this ain't just some redneck who lives with his granny, Harley. This boy's family has a bunch of money. They're gonna make sure people come looking for him."

"So? We make sure they don't find him," Shaker said.

"What do you think we ought to do with him, Tree?" Penn said to the sheriff.

"Shit, I don't know. We only got about three hundred people running around out there who know what happened here today."

"Yeah, and every one of them knows the code and the price for breaking it. They'll keep their mouths shut," Penn said.

"Bull. They drink and they flap their gums," the sheriff said. "Word'll get around."

"So what do you want to do with him?"

"Get a truck, a tarp, and some shovels."

"So you're gonna bury him?" Penn said. "Where?"

"I figure it's your place and your problem," the sheriff said. "Besides, you make the most money, you take on the worst problems when something goes bad."

"You want *me* to bury him? You don't give me orders, fat man."

"I'm not touching this, Roby. Make Harley help you. Maybe he'll think twice before he goes off on somebody again. And make sure y'all do it right. This guy needs to go away."

CHAPTER 14

A gleaming black Cadillac cruised slowly into the parking lot of a popular restaurant not far from Neyland Stadium and backed into a spot about twenty feet from where I was sitting. It was a new car, a sleek CT-6 sedan. It looked like it should be carrying a mob boss. The windows were tinted, so I couldn't see who was driving.

After receiving a phone call from Granny Tipton, I'd jogged from my apartment to a public park a couple of miles away, cutting through strip malls, doubling back, heading into and out of residential areas briefly, and then down Neyland Drive toward the restaurant. I had to make sure the cops weren't following me. After Dr. Nicolas Fraturra, I'd gone back into full paranoid mode. It was an exhausting way to live, but I was already becoming used to it. I got up off the bench I was sitting on and walked toward the car. I went to the passenger side, opened the door, and peered in.

The driver was a woman. She appeared to be about forty, a redhead with a creamy skin tone and barely noticeable freckles. Her eyes were clear and emerald green. Her hair was short and combed back from her forehead, held in place by mousse. Her jawline was taut and her cheekbones high. She had deep dimples in her cheeks. She smelled like a lilac bush and was nearly as pretty. She was wearing a black-and-white-striped silk blouse open at the neck and a tight black skirt that went to midthigh. Coming out of the skirt were legs that were long and slim and covered in dark hose.

"Nice car," I said as I climbed in and sat down in a plush leather seat.

"You're sweating on it," she said.

"Sorry. I'll wipe it off when I leave."

I stuck my hand out and she took it.

"Darren Street," I said.

"Claire Tate."

"It's nice to meet you."

"My father's good friend Elizabeth Tipton says you need some political advice and organization."

"I'm blissfully ignorant of the process of getting oneself elected to public office," I said. "Never dreamed I'd be doing this."

Claire pulled out and began to drive. "Well, I'm not blissfully ignorant," she said. "In fact, you might call me somewhat of an expert."

"Is that right? How many elections have you been involved in?"

"Close to fifty, I'd say. I've been sort of a hired gun at times."

I was surprised by the number of elections in which she'd been involved, given her age.

"What's your winning percentage?" I said.

She turned and looked at me with those emerald eyes. Damn, she was pretty.

"Ms. Tipton told me you have a strong personality. She didn't tell me you're a smart-ass."

"Legitimate inquiry," I said. "Do you at least win more often than you lose?"

"I rarely lose elections that I become involved in," she said. "When I do, it's usually because of my candidate. Candidates do stupid things and think nobody will find out, but when you run for a public office, you open yourself up to the microscope. Have you done anything stupid in your past, Mr. Street?"

I nodded vigorously. "I've done an incredible amount of stupid things in my past," I said. "I may be hopeless."

She gave me a look of disdain and fixed her eyes back on the road.

"At least you're running in a county that doesn't care much about local elections," she said. "Knox County is indifferent, for the most part. There are more than 330,000 adults of voting age, but only 225,000 of them have bothered to register to vote. On average, in a county election that involves the district attorney general, about 60,000 of those will actually cast a vote. So about twenty-five percent, one out of four, registered voters cares enough about the office to participate in the election."

"That's almost depressing," I said.

Claire Tate spoke with a Southern accent, but it was refined, a bit like the high-society Atlanta or Charleston accents I'd heard on occasion during my life. I wasn't really sure whether I liked it. It was pleasant enough, but it made her sound like a snob.

"It shouldn't be depressing to you, Mr. Street," she said, "because it means you only have to get about 30,000 votes to win, and since you missed the qualifying deadline and will be running a write-in campaign, the fewer votes you have to get, the better. I realize that 30,000 may sound like a lot, but like I said, we have 225,000 voters out there. It's doable."

She reached out and pressed her finger against the display on the dashboard. The glove compartment opened in front of me.

"There's a manila envelope in there," she said. "It's for you. It's a packet of materials you need to have filled out and in my hands in two days."

"What kind of materials?" I said.

"A qualifying petition, a petition to allow you to become a write-in candidate, some personal information needed by the election commission to make sure you qualify as a candidate. My understanding is there might be some things that would disqualify you, but we're going to keep those to ourselves."

"What kind of things are you talking about? What would disqualify me?"

"Let's just say that I wouldn't suggest you write down anything about harming anyone."

She was obviously talking about the murders, and I'd never laid eyes on this woman before. She said Granny sent her, but maybe a cop had intercepted a call or gotten lucky somehow. For all I knew, there could be a recorder running in the car or a hidden microphone transmitting what we were saying to cops in a surveillance van.

"Wait," I said. "Stop the car. I want out."

"Don't be silly," she said.

She was turning onto James B. White Parkway, and she stepped on the gas.

"I'm your friend," she said. "I shouldn't have said that. I apologize. Sometimes I just can't help myself."

She sounded sincere, but I wasn't going to give her anything at all.

"I don't have any idea what you're talking about when you mention harming people," I said.

"Of course you don't," she said. "Good for you."

I sat up in the seat and turned toward her. I raised my voice a little, made my tone edgier.

"Who the hell are you?" I said. "Really. Who is your father, and what is his connection to Elizabeth Tipton? Give me some facts I can check."

"You don't have to curse at me, Mr. Street," Claire said. "Nor do you have to take that tone with me. I told you. My name is Claire Tate. I'm a strong and intelligent woman who was fortunate enough to be born the granddaughter of Senator Roger Tate."

"*The* Senator Roger Tate? As in United States Senate?"

"That would be him."

I shook my head in wonder. Roger Tate was the senior US senator from Tennessee. He was the chairman of the Senate Appropriations Committee, one of the most powerful committees in the Senate.

"How does Granny know Roger Tate?"

"My grandfather grew up in the hills of Sevier County, not far from where Elizabeth Tipton grew up. They attended the same church. His family was poor, but he was ambitious, and he wound up getting out and doing some incredible things. He told me he was once very much in love with Ms. Tipton before she became Ms. Tipton, but that she didn't want to leave her beloved mountains. She wound up marrying another man and staying in the mountains while my grandfather went in another direction. But he remains fond of Ms. Tipton and is more than willing to help her any way he can, anytime he can. He's also willing to turn a blind eye to some of the things she's done to provide for herself and her family. She reached out to him on your behalf, and here I am, my grandfather's emissary and your brand-new campaign manager. I earned a bachelor's in political science from the University of Tennessee, a master's from the University of Virginia, and a law degree from Yale, and I'm a veteran of many political wars. If you want to become the next district attorney general of Knox County, you will do what I tell you when I tell you. Are we on the same page, Mr. Street?"

"Call me Darren," I said. "I hate being called Mr. Street."

"Maybe later," she said. "Right now I'd like to keep things on a professional level. You're Mr. Street and I'm Miss Tate."

"Okay," I said. I'd calmed down and decided to mess with her head a little, just for some amusement.

"Are you single?" I said.

"Why would you ask that? Didn't I just say I want to keep this professional?"

"Just curious," I said. "No offense intended."

She glanced over at me and sighed. "Single. Never been married."

"Lipstick lesbian?"

"Why is it that anyone over twenty-five who isn't married must be a lesbian?"

"I'm guessing you're mid to late thirties, and you're extremely attractive. It was just a question. You don't have to answer."

"Why would you even care?"

"I don't. I'm just testing your limits. You'll find that I enjoy doing that on occasion."

"I'm not a lesbian. I just don't like men much. I find them boorish and boring, and you just proved my point."

"Thanks," I said.

"You're welcome. Now, if you're finished with your inquiries into my sexual preferences, maybe we can get on with some productive discussion."

"By all means, productively discuss," I said.

"You need to hold a press conference in the near future."

"Okay," I said. "How do I go about getting the press to come?"

"Leave that to me. You will undoubtedly face some questions about certain crimes some people believe you have committed. I'll coach you how to handle those questions."

"You don't have to coach me," I said. "I may be boorish and boring, but I'm not stupid. I haven't committed any crimes. I'll just deny it."

"Some methods of denial are more effective than others, Mr. Street," she said.

"Seems pretty simple to me. I didn't do it. I've never committed a crime in my life, and anyone who says I have is a liar."

"'Misinformed' or 'mistaken' are better. 'Liar' is too combative."

"Fine."

"Are you always this prickly?" she said. "You'll need to be nice to people if you want them to vote for you."

"I can be nice when I want to," I said. I was enjoying the back-and-forth. She was bright and quick, and she smelled so damned good. But I didn't know her from Adam. I'd been burned in the past, so I wasn't going to trust her blindly.

"Good. Try to want to right now."

"I get upset when people accuse me of committing crimes I haven't committed. What made you mention it, anyway?"

"I believe Ms. Tipton may have said something to my grandfather about you having some skeletons in your closet."

"Granny would never say anything like that about me," I said.

"My grandfather doesn't like surprises," she said. "I'm sure Ms. Tipton knows that. He would want to know everything he could about you before he agreed to something as unusual as what we're about to do. He's going to personally endorse you, you know. That in itself will go a long way toward beating Morris. He's also going to request that some money be discreetly transferred from his treasury to yours."

"Damn," I said. "Granny must have something on him that's pretty embarrassing."

"I'm sure she doesn't *have* anything on him," Claire said. "There's still such a thing as loyalty, you know. My grandfather is extremely loyal to his old friends."

"Whatever," I said. "But like I said, I don't have any idea what you're talking about as far as skeletons in my closet. I think I'm ready to go back now. Will you take me back to the park?"

"You're as ungrateful as you are insolent," she said.

"Not ungrateful, and I don't mean to be insolent. I'm just extremely careful."

She turned the car off I-40 and headed back in the direction of the park where she'd picked me up. We rode in silence for a while before she spoke again. Her tone was gentler, almost kind.

"I know you've been through some incredibly difficult things," she said. "I'm genuinely sorry for your losses, all of them, and so is my grandfather. You've seen more than your share of pain."

I didn't quite know what to say, so I said nothing for several seconds.

"Why are you really helping me?" I said as she pulled into the parking lot at the park.

"Because my grandfather asked me to help you," she said. "Because Ms. Tipton asked my grandfather to help you. And because I think it'll be fun. I can't wait to see the look on that weasel Stephen Morris's face when he finds out Roger Tate is backing you and Claire Tate is your campaign manager."

"You know Morris?" I said.

"Went to the University of Tennessee at the same time he did. We had a political science class together. One day, he got it into his head that it would somehow be a good idea to kiss my neck and pinch me on the posterior."

"Really? And how did that go over?"

"He lost a tooth."

She handed me a card and a prepaid phone as I opened the door to get out.

"My number's on the back. Always call me from that phone. I have a prepaid, too. The number is already programmed into yours. I'll return calls and call you from my prepaid. We'll get new ones every couple of weeks. And get those papers back to me within two days."

"Will do," I said, and I climbed out of the car. To my surprise, she climbed out on the other side and walked around the car. It was the first time I'd seen her standing up, and it was an image I knew I wouldn't ever forget.

"Mr. Street, just one more thing before you go. I think we should get this out of the way right now. I don't care what you've done in the past. I've heard the circumstances and the allegations, and if they're true, I want you to know I don't judge you. I probably would have done the same things you did. There's a part of me that admires you, not only for what you did but also for getting away with it."

"I didn't do anything," I said. I wondered whether what she'd just said was genuine. If so, I thought I could come to like her very much. If not, well, I'd deal with that when the time came. Still, she seemed genuine, and I'd developed a strong bullshit detector over the years.

"I know," she said. "I just thought you needed to hear that."

I stood there watching as the Cadillac drove away.

This woman is different from Grace, I thought to myself. I didn't know whether that was good or bad.

CHAPTER 15

I called Granny Tipton the morning after I took a ride with Claire Tate. She told me vaguely what it was she knew about Senator Roger Tate that would allow her to get him on the phone and agree to help me win the district attorney general's election in Knoxville.

I was right about it being something embarrassing. She told me Senator Tate had possessed an affinity for drinking moonshine whiskey and having sex with multiple women at the same time when he was building his wealth and political machine. With a young wife and baby at home, he'd needed a discreet place to indulge those affinities. Granny's husband just happened to have opened a tavern outside Sevierville that the young senator—he was a state senator then—would drive all the way from Nashville to visit from time to time. It afforded him an opportunity to visit his parents and family and, while doing so, scratch an itch. She mentioned there might have been photographs involved.

Still, she said, their friendship was strong.

"Roger has a genuine affection for me," she told me over the phone. "And he will have until he knows the photographs can no longer be used against him. Which means he will have a genuine affection for me until the day he dies, because I've told him that if I die, I'll simply pass them along to my grandchildren with very specific instructions on how to use them. They're in remarkably good condition. We've been extremely careful with them over all these years."

"Have you ever asked him for anything else?" I said.

"I use the leverage very sparingly," she said.

"Thank you for using it now," I said.

"It isn't all for you, Darren. It isn't an act of generosity. We stand to make a great deal of money in Knox County once Roby Penn is gone and we can move in."

"Is Penn really that bad?"

"A very unpleasant fellow. I'm sure you'll meet him at some point. In the meantime, Senator Tate wants to meet with you. I haven't told you this, but he does have some conditions for helping you. I think they're reasonable, but they could put you in some danger."

"Danger? What does he want?"

"I think you should discuss it with him."

"When does he want to meet?"

"He said he can fly in day after tomorrow. We'll talk here, at my house."

"Sounds like a plan."

The senator was seventy-one years old, Granny told me, and had grown up about two miles from her house where his family scratched a living out of the mountain on a farm, raising cattle and tobacco. She knew him from both church and the one-room school in which they were educated. He excelled at academics, was charming and personable, and she knew early on that he was destined for things far beyond the Smoky Mountains.

They were also attracted to each other, she said.

"It was physical," she told me. "The kind of thing that happens when people are young and hormones are raging."

They'd sneaked off on occasion and spent time together. I would never have been so impolite as to ask Granny whether they ever had sex, and she didn't volunteer any information on that front. They'd drunk moonshine together, which Granny's father had made, and "fooled around some." That was as far as she would go.

Granny's father had taught her his recipe, and she believed herself to be one of a very small number of young women in or around Sevier County, Tennessee, who'd known how to make corn liquor. When the time came for Roger Tate to go off to the University of Tennessee in Knoxville, he'd proposed to her, but her parents had been in ill health and she hadn't wanted to leave them or her mountains. She'd turned him down, and he'd left.

"He wrote me letters over the years, and he stopped by to see me a couple of times," she said. "He worked his way through college in only three years and then went to law school at Vanderbilt in the late 1960s," she said. "When he graduated, he got a job as general counsel at a medical supply company that was being started by one of his friends. They didn't have much money, so he took most of his salary in stock options. They built the company steadily, and five years later it went public. Roger became an instant multimillionaire that day. He eventually bought controlling interest in the company and still owns it, I believe. He's one of the richest men in the United States Senate, if not *the* richest."

"Where did his political career start?" I asked. "Did he represent Sevier County?"

"No, he was beyond us at that point. He had established a home in Nashville by then, where his business was, so he ran for one of the Nashville district seats. Won big, too. He served three terms in the Tennessee Senate and then ran for the big time, the United States Senate. By that time, he had more money than any of his competitors. He basically bought the seat, which is how it's done routinely these days, from what I understand."

"And he's been in the United States Senate for what, forty years?"

"I suppose that'd be about right."

"Wow, people think these little local offices are powerful," I said. "Head of the appropriations committee? Control over the purse strings? That's *real* power."

"It hasn't gone to his head," Granny said. "I think you'll like him."

"I'll see you in a couple of days, then," I said. "What should I wear?"

"Just be yourself," she said. "Roger doesn't much care for fancy."

CHAPTER 16

I spent about an hour filling out the forms for Claire Tate after I hung up the phone. They were routine questions that asked whether I'd ever been convicted of a felony, whether I owed a bunch of money to the government, how old I was, how long I'd been a resident of the state and the city/county, and whether I was a licensed attorney.

When I was finished, I went for a run. I'd found that the running did me a lot of good. It helped me clear my head, and it made me feel better. I talked to Grace a lot during the runs—not out loud but in my head—and I would try to imagine her answering. I hoped she approved of the direction I was headed, and I hoped she thought I'd make a fine district attorney. But Grace hadn't appeared since she'd stepped through the veil. I had the feeling she'd abandoned me, that she'd moved on to another plane and had put me behind her. I tried talking to my mother, too. I also imagined that she seemed pleased about me going after the district attorney's job, but like Grace, my mother had faded far off into the distance.

I ran for an hour and got back to the apartment, intending to take a shower and then go get some lunch. Something felt wrong as soon as I entered my apartment. I couldn't quite grasp what it was, but I felt it the second I walked through the door. I stepped through the foyer, and there, sitting at my kitchen counter, was a large man in a uniform wearing a cowboy hat. I recognized him from television and from the few times I'd seen him in court: Sheriff Clifton "Tree" Corker. I stopped and stared at him.

"I believe it's a crime to break into people's homes without their permission," I said.

"You gonna arrest me?"

"You pick the lock?"

"Never met one I couldn't."

I walked to the refrigerator and pulled out a bottle of water. "You want one?" I said.

"Nah. Don't drink much water. You got a beer in there?"

I grabbed a beer. I walked over and set it down on the counter in front of him while I took a seat across from him. "What can I do for you, Sheriff?"

"I hear you're considering a run for the district attorney's office," he said.

"You heard wrong."

"That right? How so?"

"I'm not considering it. I'm doing it. Come November, there'll be a new DA here in Knoxville."

"Damn, boy, they didn't tell me you were so cocky."

"What do you want?" I said.

"This is a nice little place you got here," the sheriff said as he popped the cap off the beer bottle and took a drink. "Nice and cozy."

"Either tell me what you want or get out of my apartment. I don't give a shit who you are or who you think you are, you don't break into my house without a damned good reason."

"And if I don't have a good reason?"

"Let's just say there could be consequences."

"Damn!" Corker said. "You *are* a rooster, ain't you? What're you gonna do? Kill me like them other five?"

"No idea what you're talking about."

"Of course not. So what are you going to do?"

"I'm going to give you about ten seconds to tell me what you're doing here. After ten seconds, I'm going to kick your fat ass all over this apartment. I'll give you hundred-to-one odds I can get across this counter before you can get one of those pistols out of the holster. If I'm wrong and you kill me, I'm sure you'll get away with it, but I won't care, will I? I'll be dead."

"Are you telling me you're not afraid to die, boy?"

"Not in the least, and don't ever call me 'boy' again. Now what's it going to be?"

I felt my body beginning to tense as I prepared to leap across the counter and commence pummeling the pink-faced bastard. I was looking him straight in the eye, and I saw him give in. I knew right then that at his core, this huge pistol-toting redneck was a coward.

"Take it easy," he said, holding up both of his hands. "Stephen Morris came to see me and wanted me to talk to you."

"About what?"

"Maybe reconsidering? He'd make it worth your while to stay out of the race."

"Really? How much?"

"I don't know exactly. I'm thinking somewhere in the neighborhood of fifty to a hundred grand, I'd imagine."

"Damn," I said. "His salary isn't much more than a hundred grand a year. Why would he want to pay me so much?"

"Let's just say it's possible he makes a little on the side."

"Yeah, I've heard," I said. "I've also heard it's more than a little. Let me see if I've got this right: You and your department turn your backs to cockfighting, dogfighting, bare-knuckle fighting, prostitution, gambling in several forms, and drug distribution. In exchange, you get a cut of the action. The district attorney gets a cut, too, because he isn't up your ass all the time about bringing cases for him to prosecute. You let a select few people operate with impunity, and whenever somebody new and stupid comes along and tries to set up shop, your select few operators—who also double as informants—help you set them up and bust them. You run them through the system, send them off to jail, and look like a real sheriff instead of the corrupt asshole you really are. How am I doing?"

"Nearly good enough to get yourself killed," the sheriff said.

"Relax," I said. "You don't have to worry about me. I don't have any intention of getting in the middle of your business. I'll have some minor demands, but I don't think you'll have a problem with them. If I win, you can keep going, business as usual, with a couple of small changes."

"What kind of changes?"

"Like I said, minor changes. There may be someone I want you to let in, which means someone will have to go. Is that going to be a problem?"

"Probably not. Depends on who's coming in and what they want to do."

"It'll be someone experienced. Somebody who knows what they're doing. They'll agree to the terms that are already in place, whatever they are."

"Who's gonna have to go?" Corker said.

"I think I'll keep that to myself for now," I said. "But we can work something out. We're reasonable men, right? We can find mutually beneficial solutions to problems, can't we?"

"Don't know if I can trust you yet," Corker said. "If you ain't with us, you're against us."

"The truth is I don't give a shit about you and what you do or don't do. The sheriff's real job is supposed to consist of three things if I'm correct. One is to maintain the jail, and I know from firsthand experience that you do a lousy job of that. The second is courthouse security. Last is law enforcement, and for you guys that's mostly domestic violence and meth heads. Your guys don't even write speeding tickets because it costs you votes when they do."

"We enforce the law," Corker said.

"No, you don't. You get in front of a television camera every chance you get to give the appearance you're enforcing the law. But that's okay with me. I don't care. Keep faking it. My office will crack down on homicides, armed robberies, gangs, home invasions, things like that, most of which happen in the city. I'll concentrate on making the city and the county—where I can—safer. Now if you let things get out of hand and the drug trade gets violent or people start pulling out guns at the cockfights, things will change. You and I will have a problem. But as long as you and your operators keep a low profile, see no evil, hear no evil."

The sheriff rocked back and forth in the stool he was sitting on for a few seconds, sizing me up.

"I don't like Morris," he said. "He's like a damned whiny child, and he lives like a king. He might as well put a sign out front of his house that says, 'Screw you, FBI. I'm on the take, and there's nothing you can do about it.' You, I maybe could get to like, but I'm not sure. You've got that look in your eye, that I-don't-give-a-damn look."

"I don't," I said.

"A man who doesn't give a damn is dangerous."

"Maybe Morris will beat me and you won't have to worry about anything."

Corker shook his head slowly. "Somehow I just don't see that happening. I've seen you do some pretty incredible things in the past. If you want this badly enough, and it appears as though you do, it'll happen. And when it does, I'm afraid you and me are gonna butt heads somewhere down the road."

"I hope we don't," I said. "But if we do, it'd probably be best if you wear a helmet. Now if there isn't anything else, get out of my apartment. You can take the beer with you."

CHAPTER 17

I have to admit I was a little nervous as I drove through the switch-backs on the steady climb up the mountain to Granny Tipton's to meet Senator Roger Tate. The plan, I'd been told, was to have lunch and later discuss the things that needed discussing. I could ask whatever I wanted—except I was forbidden to mention the dalliances of the senator's youth—and he could ask whatever he wanted. If he brought up the people I'd killed, Granny told me to deny it. No sense giving him any leverage he didn't need to have. If he asked about Ben Clancy specifically, she said she'd handle that one herself.

It was a hot and humid day as I moved slowly past the rhododendrons and mountain laurels, stands of old oak and elms, and skirted the creeks that rushed down the mountain, swollen from the unusual amount of rain we'd had that summer. When I got to Granny's, I was shocked to see a helicopter in the field between her driveway and the creek. The senator obviously traveled in style. Two men I assumed were a pilot and maybe a security guy were walking near the chopper.

When I walked into Granny's house, the first person I saw, after Granny, was Claire Tate. She was standing in the living room looking at photographs on the wall, pictures I'd looked at several times. She was wearing tight black jeans and a pale-blue silk shirt. She was incredibly striking. Granny led me through the house and into the kitchen, and there, looking out the kitchen window above the sink, was the senior senator from Tennessee and one of the most powerful men in the country.

He turned as he heard us walk in and smiled broadly, revealing perfect white teeth. Senator Tate was a little over six feet tall with silver hair and bright-sky-blue eyes. He was fit and trim and looked like he could run a marathon. He may have had some bad habits in his younger days, but the man standing before me took excellent care of himself. His skin was as smooth as any seventy-year-old I'd ever seen, and his grip when he shook my hand was like a vise.

"I've heard much about you, Mr. Street," he said, looking me squarely in the eye. "Some of it was good."

He smiled and released my hand. It was a Thursday afternoon, but the smell of fried chicken filled the house. Fried chicken was usually reserved for Sundays in the mountains.

"I hope you brought an appetite," Granny said. "These Washington folks said they usually eat salad, but this is Tennessee, I'm entertaining, and I'm putting on the dog."

"Smells great," I said.

The senator, Claire, Granny, and I sat down to a meal of fried chicken, biscuits and gravy, mashed potatoes, green beans, fried okra, fresh tomatoes and onion slices, couscous, and chocolate pie. We washed it down with sweet tea. Claire, who looked like she'd prefer raw tuna, took it in stride. She didn't eat much, but she ate. The senator let it rip, and so did I. It was delicious.

When we were finished, the four of us walked outside, and Granny led us down the path to the small clearing where she and I had talked once before. She was carrying a small cooler, and I took it from her hand and carried it until we sat down. She opened the cooler and produced a pitcher of iced lemonade and four plastic cups.

"This is beautiful," Senator Tate said, looking at the surrounding mountains, the creek, and the meadow beyond. "Brings back a lot of fond memories of being outdoors. My understanding is that you were raised in the city, Mr. Street."

"Sort of the outskirts of the city, over by Farragut before it developed the way it has now."

"Do you like to get outdoors? Hunt or fish?"

"Love to camp, and I've done a lot of fishing in my day. Not to say that I'm any good at it, but it clears my head. I used to take my son a lot."

"Yes, your son. That would be Sean, correct?"

"I see you've done your homework."

"Your first wife cheated on you, if you'll forgive me for saying so, with an older man. Very rich man. She moved with him to Hawaii and took your son with her."

I didn't really see what my ex-wife, Katie, screwing an older man had to do with anything. The senator mentioning it stung a bit, but I let it go.

"That's right," I said.

"Do you have any contact with him?"

"He comes every summer. I stay in touch by calling, but it's difficult to get past his mother sometimes. She's not exactly what I would describe as a kind person."

"I want to extend my condolences for the death of your mother and for what happened recently with Miss Alexander and your daughter. That was a terrible thing, from what I understand."

"Thank you, and, yes, it was terrible. The doctor had some serious substance-abuse issues that people were aware of prior to that day. He had no business practicing medicine."

"I've been told that he's gone. Nobody has heard from him in a couple of weeks."

"That's what I hear."

"What's your theory on his disappearance?" Senator Tate said.

"My theory? I don't really have one, but if I did, it would probably be along the lines of he knew a huge lawsuit would be coming down the pike and that the medical licensing board would be taking a close look at him, so he ran away to avoid the beating he knew he was about to take."

"So you don't think any harm has come to him?"

"I don't know, Senator, but if harm did come to him, it couldn't have come to a more deserving person."

"So Elizabeth tells me you'd like to be the next district attorney general in Knoxville," Senator Tate said. "Tell me, if you don't mind, why you would want such a dirty job."

He spoke with a slow mountain drawl, a baritone that was almost mesmerizing. It was the kind of voice that could hypnotize an unsuspecting person into believing damned near anything he said. I was certain that his voice had played a major role in his political success. It was a voice of persuasion.

I wondered briefly whether I should give him some flowery bullshit answer to the question he'd just asked me or just tell him the truth. Then I thought about how many times he'd probably asked people questions just like the one he'd asked me. Thousands, I guessed. No point in trying to dress it up. I looked him in the eye.

"Because I can't stand Stephen Morris. He's gutless, and he doesn't deserve the job. Because I think I can help Granny and her family in certain ways. Because the system has let me down more than once, and I'm hoping maybe I can do better. And maybe I think I might be able to atone for some things I've done in the past, set some things right, at least in my own mind."

"You're trying to forgive yourself for the killings you've done," he said.

"If I ever killed anyone, sir, and I'm not saying I have, they deserved it."

"Sometimes the system fails us," Senator Tate said. "It failed you by allowing you to be locked up for a crime you didn't commit and subjected you to things I can't even begin to imagine, and it failed you when your mother was killed. Although, to be perfectly frank, I don't believe you gave the system much of a chance when your mother was killed. You acted hastily."

"I don't really remember how I acted, sir," I said. "I have very little recollection of that time in my life."

"You were far more methodical with Ben Clancy," he said.

"With all due respect, sir, I'd rather not discuss Ben Clancy."

"I'll discuss him," Granny said. "He was a psychopath in a suit with the power of the federal government behind him. We did the world a favor when we got rid of him."

"We?" Senator Tate said.

"I've never lied to you, Roger. We're old enough now that there isn't really any point in starting. We hanged him in my barn and fed him to my pigs. Darren was there. He played a major role in Clancy's death, as he should have. There isn't a trace left of Clancy, and I'm not the least bit ashamed of it."

I felt a sudden wave of nausea run over me as I listened to the words coming out of Granny's mouth. I couldn't believe she'd just admitted murdering a former assistant US attorney to a US senator. I looked at Senator Tate. He just smiled and shook his head.

"I've always admired your candor, Elizabeth," he said. "So good riddance to Mr. Clancy, and don't worry, your secret is safe with me."

"As is yours with me," she said with a wink.

The senator cringed, and his face flushed. It was the only time that day I saw him lose his composure, even though it was only for a second.

"Yes, and I appreciate that more than you know, Elizabeth," he said. "Now, down to business. I'm prepared to do what it takes to get Darren elected to the office. Claire has already started setting up an organization. We're calling in favors from old friends, and believe me, because of my position on the appropriations committee, I have plenty of old friends. Money won't be a problem. We'll outspend Morris ten to one if we have to, absolutely drown him. You'll have to do the dog-and-pony shows, the rubber-chicken circuit. You'll have to speak to Ruritan Clubs and veterans' organizations and neighborhood associations. You'll have to speak to the press, but only under tightly controlled circumstances. Claire will advise you on all that. I don't even think we'll have to do a smear campaign on Morris. I hate doing that, for one thing, but he just seems to have done such a poor job, I think we can beat him without it. We can keep him busy putting out fires, start rumors and things like that, so he won't have time to pay much attention to you. Originally, I would have done these things just for Elizabeth, but something has happened, and I want your word that you'll do everything you can to investigate and, if a crime was committed, hold those responsible accountable, including the sheriff of Knox County."

I shook my head slowly. It was an involuntary movement.

"Am I to take that as a no?" the senator said.

"I'm sorry . . . no . . . it's just that when you mentioned the sheriff, it threw me for a second. He showed up at my apartment yesterday. Broke in. He was sitting at my kitchen counter when I came back from a run."

"What did he want?"

"He was trying to intimidate me. It didn't work out for him."

"Good. My hope is that he's going to wind up behind bars where he belongs. But back to what has happened. A good friend of mine, Art Brewer, contacted me a few days ago. He lives here in Knoxville and has been extremely successful in the insurance business. He has a grandson, Gary, who graduated from the University of Tennessee and then joined the marines because he wanted to join the fight against ISIS. He wound up leading combat platoons in Afghanistan and Syria, did three tours, was wounded several times, and was highly decorated. But he came home a changed young man. Art said he was haunted by nightmares, was paranoid and restless, had no interest in holding a job, and had turned to drugs and alcohol to medicate himself. Art also said that his son, Gary's father, told Art that Gary had gotten into bare-knuckle box-ing, which I think is something akin to cockfighting using men instead of roosters. Gary's sister, who is the closest in the family to him, said he went off last Sunday to do a fight somewhere in the western part of the county, and he didn't come back. He hasn't been seen since. Art called the sheriff's department and, as you would expect, has received no help. The Knoxville police say it's out of their jurisdiction if it didn't happen in the city, District Attorney Morris has not asked the TBI to help with the investigation, and the FBI says they have jurisdictional problems as well."

"Not if official misconduct is involved," I said.

"Exactly," the senator said. "If a public official is engaged in corrupt practices, the FBI has every right, in fact they have a responsibility, to investigate."

"So why don't you pull a few strings?" I said. "Seems to me that you could get the FBI in Knoxville to do pretty much anything you want."

"I can, but they're going to need an in," he said.

"You mean an informant."

"Call it what you like."

"You want me to get elected DA, act like I'm on the take like Stephen Morris and the sheriff, and help the FBI bust them all."

"And find out what happened to Gary Brewer," the senator said. "That's the most important part. Find my good friend's grandson."

My stomach began to churn even worse than it had earlier.

"I have to tell you, Senator Tate, I hate snitches. The thought of becoming one makes my skin crawl."

"But you'll do it," he said. "You'll do it for me, and for Grace, and for your own redemption."

I downed the last of the lemonade in my glass and looked at him.

"If you get me elected, I'll figure out a way to find out what hap-pened to Gary Brewer and hold people accountable," I said. "I give you my word. But I have to draw the line at becoming an FBI informant. I just can't become a snitch for them. I've seen people do it, and it always turns out badly for the snitch. It's a deal-breaker, sir. I'm sorry."

The senator looked at me sternly. He obviously wasn't used to people saying no to him.

"You'll find Gary Brewer," he said. "Dead or alive. You'll make it your mission."

"I will."

"Very well. Let's get this done."

CHAPTER 18

Sheriff Tree Corker squeezed off another round as gunshots echoed off the surrounding hills. The sheriff and Roby Penn were firing at rats that scurried around a garbage pile fifty yards away. They were on Roby's land, a forlorn, forty-acre patch of woods and weeds about seven miles northeast of Knoxville. The garbage heap had grown over the years as Roby had piled everything from old tires to rotted food, empty paint cans, and crumbling lumber. The rats had settled in about five years earlier, and now they were everywhere.

"You can't shoot for shit," Roby said as yet another blast emanated from the barrel of one of the sheriff's Pythons. Dirt shot up about ten feet to the right of a rat that sat on its haunches, chewing on something it was holding in its paws.

"That wasn't even the one I was aiming for," the sheriff said. "He ducked down behind the pile just before I pulled the trigger."

"Yeah, right, and the Pope's a Buddhist," Roby said.

It was ten in the morning on Sunday, and the heat and humidity were already starting to rise. The sheriff's cruiser sat nearby, a shiny black Ford LTD with large gold stars on the hood, the trunk lid, and both sides. "The High Sheriff of Knox County" was airbrushed in gold on each front quarter panel. The sheriff pulled a handkerchief from his pocket, lifted his cowboy hat, and wiped his forehead.

"Gonna be hotter than a three-peckered billy goat today," he said.

He holstered his Python and sat down on the tailgate of Roby's pickup truck as Roby took aim and fired with an illegal, fully automatic M16 chambered in .556 millimeter. Roby squeezed the trigger, and a rat did a backflip as the round tore his head off.

"I hate rats," Roby muttered.

"Then why don't you clean up this damned mess?" the sheriff said. "All it'd take is some kerosene and a lighter."

"Because then I wouldn't be able to come out here and kill the little bastards. I said I hate rats. I didn't say I don't like killing them."

"So what're we gonna do about this Darren Street?" the sheriff said.

"I don't like it," Roby said. "Him just showing up out of nowhere like this. You think he might be a plant?"

"A plant? You mean some kind of informant?"

"Yeah, you think the NSA or the CIA might have sent him down here?"

"To do what?"

"Spy on us, you dumbass!" Roby yelled. "Take us out. Maybe send us off to one of those supermax federal pens I've heard about that's underground and you don't ever see any light or hear any kind of noise."

The sheriff had noticed Roby getting stranger over the past year. Conspiracy theories such as the one he was spouting were becoming more common. He'd also noticed that Roby never seemed to sleep or eat. He drank whiskey like a town drunk, but the sheriff didn't remember the last time he'd seen Roby eat a sandwich.

"Nobody sent him here to spy on us," Tree said. "Relax. He just hates Morris."

"You said you talked to him?"

"Yeah. I broke into his apartment and surprised him."

"Talk about money?"

"It didn't come up. I didn't get the sense he was interested."

"Well, then, we just keep making our money. Hell, maybe he won't even want a cut."

"I just don't know," Tree said. "I mean, it isn't like he's spick-and-span Mr. Clean or anything. He's supposedly killed five men, and he had this look in his eyes when I talked to him. Like he wasn't afraid of anything or anybody. Like he didn't give a shit."

"He ain't killed no five men," Roby said. "He'd be in prison or dead."

"He's been in prison, but they sent him up for a murder he *didn't* commit, and he got out of it after a couple of years. There are a lot of stories about him. He's supposed to be a tough man. He makes me nervous."

Roby picked off another rat as the assault rifle cracked. He lowered the weapon to his side, turned to the sheriff, and said, "If he bothers you so much, if you really think he's going to cause us problems, then take care of him."

"Take care of him how?"

"Figure something out. Make him have an accident."

"What kind of accident?"

"Dammit, Tree, do I have to figure everything out for you? You're the damned sheriff of Knox County. You got as much power as God Almighty. You got deputies that'll do anything you ask them to do without batting an eye or asking a question. If you think he's going to be a problem, fuck him up. Kill him."

The sheriff hated it when Roby spoke to him about killing people as though it were nothing. He couldn't imagine taking a life, and he was afraid of and didn't understand people who thought nothing of it. Roby was one of those people, and the more the sheriff was around him—especially within the last year—the more he feared him. Roby had always been an angry man, but his anger had escalated.

"Killing people isn't really my style, Roby. You know that."

"I ain't killing him for you, not unless he gets into my business. Wait a minute. I take that back. I might kill him just for sport."

"Don't kill him, Roby. He hasn't done anything to you. Let's just see how it goes."

"See how it goes. Like it did with that marine. I got stuck getting rid of him. You should've taken care of that."

"You gonna start that up again? It happened at your place during one of your events. It was your responsibility. I'm dealing with the fallout, and believe me, there's plenty of it. His granddaddy and his daddy have been wearing me out."

"What have you told them?"

Roby turned to face the sheriff, and his eyes were like lasers, flashing heat and anger.

"Same old same old. We're investigating. We're on it. We're doing everything we can, but we don't have any leads. From what I understand, the marine had gone pretty psycho lately. I'm trying to convince them that he's walking the Appalachian Trail or headed for the Grand Canyon or something. I keep telling them he'll pop up soon."

"He won't," Roby said. "He ain't never gonna pop up. As a matter of fact, he's in a barrel six feet under that garbage pile right there. Put him there myself with a front-end-loader attachment to my tractor."

"I wish you hadn't told me that," Tree said. "I didn't want to know what you did with him."

Roby walked over to the bed of the truck, removed the clip from the rifle, cleared the round from the chamber, and laid the rifle in a case.

"I gotta go, Tree," he said. "There's a fight up in Hawkins County I want to see."

"Bare-knuckle?"

Roby nodded. "I ain't promoting, but I have a pretty good idea of who's gonna win. I know the boy that runs the fights up there real well. One of the fighters is going to put on a good show and then take a dive. I'll take home enough money to make it worth the trip."

"Give some thought to what we ought to do about this Street," Tree said.

Roby shook his head. "I think it'd be better to do something about Morris. I wouldn't mind being rid of him once and for all."

"You can't kill a district attorney, Roby," Tree said.

"Didn't you tell me he said if he lost he might go to the feds and tell them what we've been into for all these years?"

The sheriff had let it slip and had regretted saying it the moment the words passed his lips. "He did say something like that, but I don't think he was serious."

"Well, from my way of thinking, better to deal with him before he goes to the feds than after."

"I don't think the feds really give a damn about us, Roby."

"Maybe they don't, but you know how much I hate them. I hate them, I hate the TBI, I hate the police, the tax man. Anything to do with the government, I hate. Hell, I'd hate you if you weren't my nephew, and sometimes I hate you, anyway. If the feds came nosing around, the bodies would start piling up pretty damned fast."

"They'd just kill you," Tree said. "You can't fight them. Remember Ruby Ridge? Waco? And the boys out west at that Malheur wildlife refuge last year didn't fare too well. One of them is dead, and a bunch of them are in jail."

"I ain't Randy Weaver or David Koresh or any of them others," Roby said. "Feds, state troopers, TBI, I don't give a damn. They come messin' around here, they're gonna die."

CHAPTER 19

I looked around at the trees full of bright-green leaves, the calm water, and the sky dotted with high cumulus clouds as the pontoon boat made its way slowly eastward on the Tennessee River. We'd already passed Thompson-Boling Arena and the cavernous Neyland Stadium and were headed for the fork where the Tennessee River split into the French Broad and Holston Rivers. I was at the wheel of a pontoon boat that had been rented by Claire Tate. Also on board were Claire and a reporter from the only daily newspaper left in the city, the *Knoxville News Sentinel*. The conversation had been sparse and felt forced.

The reporter's name was Janie Schofield. I'd been reading her stories for years since she covered the criminal courts. She was around fifty, a quiet brunette who wore glasses and stayed in the background most of the time. She didn't sensationalize and seemed serious about her work. I'd talked to her a few times over the years, but I couldn't say I knew her well.

Janie was wearing a yellow sundress. She had a nice tan, and the color went well with her brown skin. Claire was covered in sunscreen. She was wearing a two-piece purple swimsuit with a pink wraparound cover-up and a pink broad-brimmed hat. Both of them were wearing sunglasses. I was wearing blue swim trunks and a white tank top. We looked like a few friends out for an early-afternoon cruise. All three of us had a can of beer in our hands, but nobody was drinking quickly. I stopped the boat about fifty yards off the shore of Island Home Park and dropped the anchor.

"I suppose you're wondering what we're doing out here on this lovely day," Claire said to Janie.

"I think I might have a couple of educated guesses, but you certainly have my curiosity piqued," Janie said.

"Darren is going to run against Stephen Morris for district attorney general. I'm his campaign manager. My grandfather is supporting him openly. He'll be coming to Knoxville in late October to appear with Darren at a rally."

Janie looked at Claire, then at me, then back at Claire again.

"I'd heard a rumor that Mr. Street was planning a huge lawsuit against the doctor that was involved in the death of his little girl and that he had asked your grandfather to intervene with the Tennessee Medical Licensing Board," she said. "My source was obviously mistaken."

"Obviously," Claire said. "We're giving you an exclusive, a scoop in the old journalistic parlance, I believe."

"Yes, you are," Janie said. "What's the catch?"

"No catch, but I do have some other information I'd like you to check into through your own sources. If it turns out to be true, you may have a prizewinner of a story on your hands."

"Is that right?" Janie said. She looked skeptical, which, I was sure, came with the territory in journalism, just like in law. "What kind of information might that be?"

"What do you know about Jim Harrison?" Claire said.

"Jim Harrison? The Jim Harrison who works for Morris?"

"Right. He supposedly handles special investigations for the district attorney, but he never brings any cases. Have you ever seen him in a courtroom trying a case or conducting a hearing?"

"Come to think of it, no, I haven't."

"That's because his real job is, for lack of a better term, bagman for the district attorney."

"Bagman?"

"You're familiar with the term, correct?"

"Of course I'm familiar with the term. A bagman is a collection boy, a courier. He picks up money from one place and delivers it to another."

"Dirty money," Claire said.

"And he picks this money up from whom and takes it to whom?"

"He picks it up from the Knox County sheriff and gives it to Stephen Morris. I'm sure he keeps a small piece for himself."

"And where is the Knox County sheriff getting this money?"

"Various people. Pimps, operators of gambling establishments and strip clubs, cockfighting and dogfighting promoters, bare-knuckle-fighting promoters, human traffickers."

Janie looked startled. She quickly drained her beer and asked me for another one. I reached into the cooler and pulled one out, popped the top, and handed it to her. I was as confounded as she was. When we left the boat dock earlier, I had no idea the conversation was going to go this way.

Janie took a long drink of the second beer, wiped her mouth, and said, "Forgive me, Miss Tate. I have all the respect in the world for you and for your grandfather, but what you're telling me is explosive stuff. Do you have any evidence that any of it is true?"

"We've only recently become aware of the extent of the corruption in Knox County involving the sheriff and the district attorney. We were hoping that you might be able to develop some sources and expose what's going on."

"Just in time to get your candidate elected," Janie said.

Claire's eyes flashed, and I saw Janie cringe. Claire was definitely the more formidable of the two women.

"My candidate will be elected by a landslide whether you do this or not," she said.

"Then why are you telling me this? Why don't you get the TBI or the FBI involved?"

"The TBI is tricky," Claire said. "They work very closely with the district attorney. As a matter of fact, they won't even investigate a case unless the district attorney asks them to, and obviously, Morris hasn't asked them. If we tried to go around him, we're afraid someone close to Morris might tip him off and he'll shut everything down before we can prove anything.

"The current presidential administration has changed the FBI's mandate. Their primary task is counterterrorism. They don't care much about whether a redneck sheriff and a DA in Nowhere, Tennessee, are shaking down vice peddlers and drug dealers. So that leaves it to someone like you. You can work quietly, be cautious and inconspicuous, but you'll have to work pretty quickly. We'll help any way we can. When the time is right, pounce on them and print your story."

"And wind up in a landfill somewhere," Janie said as she drained the second can of beer and tossed it at me. I pulled another out of the cooler and handed it to her.

"You certainly don't have to do a thing," Claire said. "I'm just making you aware of a situation. You can do what you wish with the information. If you think some harm might come to you, then by all means, stay away from it. Darren, of course, will do everything he can to put a stop to the corruption on his end after he takes office. Perhaps, down the road, he can deal with the sheriff."

"Maybe he ought to just kill him," Janie said. She was taking large gulps of the beer.

"Beg your pardon?" Claire said.

"The word around the cop campfire is that your candidate has bagged a few," she said.

"Not true," I said.

It was the first time I'd opened my mouth. Claire had told me to let her do the talking, and up until that moment, I'd done so. I had often heard that criminal defendants, after telling themselves and everyone else they didn't commit a crime over an extended period of time, actually began to believe it. I knew exactly what I'd done, but it had become instinctive to deny I'd killed anyone.

"How much more beer you got in there?" Janie said as she took a long drink from the can.

"There's one left." I looked at Claire. "You want to head upriver and get some more? I only brought six."

"I like beer," Janie said.

"I don't think we'll need any more," Claire said. "Why don't you pull up the anchor and let's start back? Janie can drink the last one on the way."

I did as Claire requested and started the boat back toward the dock.

"So you've never killed anybody?" Janie said.

"No," I said.

"Swear?"

"I swear." She obviously didn't drink much.

"Pinkie swear?"

"I've never killed anyone. The questions you should be asking are why nobody was ever arrested for my mother's death, why Ben Clancy has never been found, and what happened to the doctor who killed my daughter and girlfriend. All of those things happened under Morris's watch."

"I don't let people tell me what questions to ask, thank you very much," she said. Her words were becoming slurred now, and she was getting louder.

"Sorry," I said. "No offense."

"I don't suppose you know anything about that marine that went missing recently," she said. "I wrote a story about it a few days ago. Did you read it?"

"I did read your story, and, no, I don't know anything about what happened to him."

"You're responsible for everyone that goes missing around here, you know," she said. "Just ask the Knoxville cops. I know a bunch of them. It's a standing joke with them. Somebody disappears, they say it must've been you that made them go away. They call you The Reaper."

"Is that right?" I said. I said the words silently a couple of times and imagined myself in a black hooded robe, carrying a scythe. I wouldn't have admitted it, but I liked the image.

"You're not planning to print that, are you?" Claire said.

"No, I think that might be borderline libelous since I've never seen a shred of concrete evidence that Mr. Street has ever harmed a soul."

"That's good to know," Claire said.

"It's strange, though," Janie said. She was looking at Claire, but she sounded as though she might be talking to herself. "Nobody even seems mad at him. I've heard a lot of cops say if he did kill those two guys in West Virginia, they deserved it, and if he killed Clancy, he deserved it, too. This doctor? He's a hot topic of conversation right now. Nobody knows all the details, so nobody knows quite what to think. Our so-called medical reporter has been looking into it, but he's an idiot. He won't come up with anything. What happened at the birthing center, Mr. Street, if you don't mind me asking?"

"I don't think he should answer that question," Claire said. "I'm sure there will be litigation. The court file will be public record. You'll be able to find all the information you need there."

We cruised back to the dock at a much faster speed than we'd cruised out. I tied the boat off while Claire and Janie gathered their purses and towels. I picked up the cooler and climbed off the boat. Janie was already walking to her car.

"What just happened?" I said to Claire. "Was that a disaster?"

"Not at all," Claire said. "Let me deal with it."

"I thought the plan was for me to get into office and then take down the sheriff. When did you decide to bring her into the picture?"

"After you left Ms. Tipton's. My grandfather and I stayed and talked some more with Ms. Tipton. We decided it might be best to change the plan then."

"By bringing a reporter in? Why?"

"Because Granny thinks if the sheriff presses you, if he backs you into a corner, if he tries to do harm to you somehow, you'll kill him. And we don't want you killing anyone, especially the sheriff."

I was a little surprised that Granny would express such an opinion to the senator and Claire, but given my history of showing up at her house with bodies, I could understand to some degree.

"I promise I'll try not to kill anyone," I said.

"Don't let it hurt your feelings. We can use this woman."

"She appears to be a drunk, which makes her unpredictable."

"Again, I'm sorry to say this, but we think that even though she drinks too much, she's not as unpredictable as you. She's been working at that paper for twenty-five years. I knew she was a boozer, but it doesn't affect her work."

"Are you going to talk to her again?"

"Of course. I'll be at her front door this evening. We'll have a chat. She doesn't have a husband, so it'll just be us girls and her cats."

"You know she has cats?"

"I do my homework, Mr. Street."

"And what will you chat about?"

"Her future. Or rather, her lack thereof if she doesn't treat us fairly. We have a lot of friends in the newspaper business, including the company that owns the paper she works for. Try to behave yourself, Mr. Street. I'll call you tonight."

CHAPTER 20

The press conference was an interesting experience. Claire organized it, and it was held in a meeting room at a hotel in downtown Knoxville. Three television stations showed up—all the major networks that still did evening newscasts—and three print reporters. Janie Schofield was one of them. Claire had coached me for hours the day before, and I did fine.

It was a blonde from one of the network TV affiliates who asked the question: "Mr. Street, I'm sure you're aware that there have been allegations that you've committed at least one, and perhaps several, murders over the past two years," she said. "Would you care to comment?"

I did what I'd always done. I denied the allegations. I also went on the offensive, hammering on the fact that there was absolutely no evidence against me and not a single witness had come forward. I questioned Stephen Morris's abilities, given the fact that he had several unsolved murders in his district (the ones I'd committed weren't the only killings that had gone unsolved during his tenure). I also cited some facts Claire had given me about the unusually large number of cases pending in the criminal courts of Knox County because the district attorney's office was unorganized and continued cases on a regular basis. I told people that I had been on the wrong side of the criminal justice system, that I had been falsely accused and convicted, and that I wanted to do everything in my power to see that false accusations and imprisonments became a thing of the past. I ended by pointing out that the murderer or murderers of my mother had never been brought to justice. I never said a word about Ben Clancy other than to deny I had anything to do with his disappearance.

They seemed to buy it, and the whole thing lasted less than a half hour. The resulting stories were generally positive, and Claire seemed pleased.

Then, over the next several weeks, I learned the true meaning of humility. Not humiliation—I'd suffered plenty of that at the hands of Ben Clancy and the many prison guards I'd known—but humility. I learned to be humble. And I did it visiting with groups like the Ruritan Club, the Daughters of the American Revolution, the Veterans of Foreign Wars, the Rotary Club, and the dozens of other community organizations in and around Knoxville. I would usually speak briefly after we'd eaten chicken or spaghetti or lasagna or whatever the group happened to be serving that evening, but I quickly found that the most valuable part of the interaction was listening. I'd always been a fairly good listener, but when I was hearing stories of children throwing their lives away to methamphetamine or opioids, stories of children and old people neglected and beaten and treated like animals, it affected me deeply. I heard stories of victims of rape and murder and armed robbery and how those incidents traumatized not only their victims but also spread through entire families like the ripples from a rock being thrown into a calm country pond. Those stories changed my perspective on the nature of crimes and those who commit them. It also made me want to help protect people. Even if I didn't get elected, I knew I would never again defend a criminal.

As September rolled into October and the election grew ever closer, I found myself walking in the door at night, exhausted, thinking about the families of the people I'd killed. I knew one of the boys in West Virginia, Donnie Frazier, had had a girlfriend. He'd probably had other family as well. I didn't know whether his mother and father were alive, whether he had aunts or uncles or cousins or nieces or nephews who may have been affected by his death, but he probably had. It was the same with Tommy Beane, the other man I'd killed in West Virginia, and Ben Clancy and Big Pappy Donovan and now Dr. Nicolas Fraturra. How had my committing the ultimate crime—the taking of another human being's life—affected those around my victims?

It was the first time I'd ever thought in those terms, and the only reason those thoughts entered my mind was because of the stories I'd heard while campaigning. I'd really never given a damn about the families or friends of my own victims. They had done terrible things to me or to people I loved, I'd made the decision to kill them, and I'd done it and moved on without reflection. I couldn't exactly describe the feelings I was experiencing as guilt, but for the first time there were at least the beginnings of some regret.

On a Wednesday evening, I'd just settled in at my apartment after meeting with a group of particularly cantankerous members of MADD, Mothers Against Drunk Driving. Many had had loved ones killed or maimed by drunk drivers, and some had been seriously injured themselves. They'd wanted to make damned sure that I knew how they felt about prosecuting drunk-driving cases. Claire was standing in the back while I was peppered with questions.

I told them the truth. I told them I'd prosecute drunk drivers to the extent the law would allow. There were always new laws being proposed in the state legislature to make the penalties for DUI harsher. Tennessee, in fact, had some of the toughest laws in the United States, but some of the members of the group would be satisfied with nothing short of the death penalty.

The doorbell rang around ten, and I immediately popped off the couch and headed into the bedroom, where I pulled my Walther P22 pistol from beneath the mattress. I held the pistol in my hand as I walked toward the door. There was a small foyer and a short hallway leading away from my front door. I didn't want someone to shoot me through the door, so I stopped where the hallway opened onto the kitchen and said loudly, "Who is it?"

"It's Claire."

"One second," I said, and I jogged back to the bedroom and put the pistol back under the mattress. I walked back quickly and opened the door.

"Catch you at a bad time?" she said.

"Nope. Just had to put my gun away. Figured you wouldn't appreciate being greeted that way."

"How considerate of you. Why do you have a gun?"

"For protection."

"From whom?"

"People who might want to do me harm."

"Can you give me an example of someone who might want to do you harm?"

"Oh, I don't know. The sheriff, maybe, or one of his cronies. The sheriff's nephew. Stephen Morris or one of his cronies. Family members of people who may have heard ugly rumors about me. Old friends from federal prison."

"I see," she said. "Long list. Have I come at a bad time? Can you talk?"

"No, not at all. It's fine. I was just unwinding. Tonight was pretty intense."

"I don't see any alcohol anywhere. How do you unwind?"

"I was just sitting on the couch thinking. I have a couple of beers in the fridge, maybe a bottle of wine in the cupboard. Can I offer you something?"

"A glass of wine would be nice," she said.

I rarely drank wine and didn't even know what I had in the cupboard. As it turned out, there were two decent bottles in there, one of them Grace's favorite.

"Grace loved this stuff," I said, holding it up. "Will this do for you?"

"Perfectly," Claire said.

I uncorked the bottle and poured two glasses. Claire took one and sat down on the couch. I sat at the other end.

"You did a good job tonight," she said. "That was a tough crowd and you handled them beautifully."

"Thanks," I said. "I'm trying to get better at it."

"You're a natural. You've gotten some confidence and people are drawn to you."

"So how do you think things are going?" I said. "Do I have a chance?"

"All of our information shows that you're going to beat him by at least five thousand votes. And we're not even finished with him yet. Do you know he bullies the principals at the schools his children attend? He threatens to sue them if they so much as breathe in the direction of one of his children. And his children, from everything I've gathered, are entitled brats. His wife slapped a male teacher across the face a month ago, and he refused to allow the police to do anything about it. He has a thirteen-year-old girl who was texting in class. The teacher took her phone, gave it back to her at the end of class, and within an hour, Mrs. Morris was in this teacher's face, screaming at him. When he told her he understood why her daughter acted the way she does, she slapped him. He had a handprint on his face for three days. Once that gets out, along with a couple of other things we have planned, you'll be home free. And that doesn't even take into account my grandfather's endorsement. That will be a spectacle. Wait and see."

"This is all great. Thank you. I really appreciate everything you're doing. I mean that. The only problem is that I'll have absolutely no idea what I'm doing when I go into the office. I mean, I wonder how many of the lawyers will quit, how many of them will give me a hard time, how many of them will have had problems with Morris and expect me to remedy them immediately."

"He's run a pretty loose ship," Claire said. "You'll have some work to do. Have you been studying how other district attorneys organize?"

"I have. I think I'll figure it out pretty quickly. I just don't think that part of it is going to be much fun."

"Delegate, delegate, delegate," she said.

"Need a job?" I said. "I'm going to fire the bagman the first day if he doesn't quit. You can take his place and get things organized."

"Thanks," she said. She had a beautiful smile. "I think I'll head back to Washington when I'm finished here. I miss the swamp. Listen, Darren, there's something we need to talk about."

I set the glass down on the table and looked at her.

"Do you realize that's the first time your stuffy ass has managed to chill out enough to call me Darren?" I said.

"I think it's time we can become a bit more familiar," she said. "Not *too* familiar, of course. And I don't appreciate you calling me a stuffy ass."

Not that I wanted to become *too* familiar with her. Grace was still too close, her memory too fresh. Claire was attractive, though. Damned attractive.

"I apologize," I said, "but I'm glad you've decided to call me Darren. Mr. Street makes me feel old. What do we need to talk about?"

"Gary Brewer."

"The marine? I thought I had been deemed too unstable for that assignment."

"Janie Schofield is terrified. She's making absolutely no progress. Grandfather wants you to get involved."

"Okay," I said. "What do I need to do?"

"Meet with the US attorney."

Stephen Blackburn had been the US attorney for the Eastern District of Tennessee when the feds put me in jail. But Blackburn was gone. There had been a presidential election, and the new president, as was his right, had fired all the US attorneys. Blackburn had been replaced with a man named Thomas Henshaw. I knew nothing about him other than he was well connected, like all US attorneys, and he had a reputation for enjoying old Scotch and expensive cigars. Henshaw was to the feds what I would be to Knoxville, only he had a hell of a lot more on his plate. He oversaw the office that prosecuted all the criminal cases in federal court in forty-one counties in Eastern and part of Middle Tennessee. He also had many other duties. I didn't envy the man at all.

"When are we supposed to meet him?"

"Tomorrow at two, his office."

"So you've already made the appointment. You coming?"

"Wouldn't miss it."

CHAPTER 21

I could tell US Attorney Thomas Henshaw was unhappy that I was in his office. He was unhappy that the granddaughter of the chairman of the Senate Appropriations Committee was in his office, and he was unhappy that a deputy director from the FBI office in Washington and a deputy director from the Department of Justice had gotten him on a conference call and basically ordered him to meet with us and devise a plan to end the corruption that was going on in Knox County, and to find out what happened to Gary Brewer in the process.

Henshaw was a husky man, around sixty, with silver hair, brown eyes, and bushy, dark eyebrows. He had the jowls of a bulldog. An unlit cigar dangled from his lips, and deep lines etched his forehead. He was scowling. His eyebrows were arched and his thin lips were tight, almost pouty.

The office was typical of a US attorney—a framed photograph of the president hung on the wall behind his desk, American and Tennessee flags stood in the corners, there were shelves of law books, photos of dignitaries, and a large seal of the Department of Justice with its *Qui Pro Domina Justitia Sequitur* motto, which means "who prosecutes on behalf of the Lady Justice" on the front of Henshaw's desk. I looked at the seal for a few minutes, studying it. It depicted a bald eagle rising above a shield of red, white, and blue and holding an olive branch in its right talon and thirteen arrows in its left. I supposed the significance of the olive branch and the arrows had something to do with tempering justice with mercy.

Also in attendance was Bradley Kurtz, Special Agent in Charge of the FBI office in Knoxville. All the agents who were there when I was framed and convicted of murder had been reassigned to other parts of the country. Kurtz was around forty-five, tall and lean, and looked like his face should be on a recruiting poster for the Gestapo. He had crystal-blue eyes, blond hair, and a face that was all sharp angles and thin lines.

"Thank you for meeting with us," Claire said after everyone settled in and it became obvious that Henshaw wasn't going to say a word.

"I didn't vote for your father, Ms. Tate," Henshaw said. "I hold this office by appointment of the president, but I've been told that you need our assistance and that I am to be at your service. I'm not accustomed to being at anyone's service."

"We don't want you to be at our service," Claire said. "You serve the people of the Eastern District of Tennessee, correct?"

Henshaw snorted.

"They need your service because their public officials are allowing criminals to ply their trade unmolested, with one very important exception: the public officials extort money from the criminals in exchange for allowing them to operate."

"So?" Henshaw said. "Did you see what the United States Supreme Court did last summer, Ms. Tate? You live in Washington, right? I'm sure you read the Bob McDonnell case. The governor of the great state of Virginia took a hundred and seventy-five thousand in bribes from one man, was convicted by a jury, and the Supreme Court reversed the case. They said the trial judge's interpretation of a 'political act' was too broad. In my opinion, what they did was give elected officials the right to do whatever they want and charge whatever they want to do it."

"This case is far different," Claire said. "And I think you know it."

"I don't know a thing about your case. We live in a dangerous world right now," Henshaw said. "Mr. Kurtz here concerns himself with things like terrorism and making sure some crazy person with a gun doesn't go into a school and shoot a bunch of kids. He deals with all kinds of human trafficking, people selling babies, people selling young girls for sex. He deals with cybercrime, which is probably the fastest-growing area of crime in the world right now. He deals, on occasion, with large amounts of narcotics. And he does this in not one, but *forty-one* counties. I help and advise him. I prosecute the cases he and his agents bring. We're all very, very busy. And now you're asking us to . . . What exactly do you want us to do?"

"Build a case against the sheriff of Knox County, the district attorney general of Knox County, and their associates. Prosecute them and put them in prison."

"For what?"

"Official misconduct. They're extorting money from criminals. Are you deaf?"

"I hear quite well, Ms. Tate, and you can keep the sarcasm to yourself. How much are we talking about?"

"I don't know exactly, but they're getting a piece of the proceeds from illegal gambling on cockfights, dogfights, bare-knuckle boxing, and unlicensed casinos. They also get a cut of all the prostitution that goes on in the county and almost all the drugs that are sold in the county. My understanding is that it started when a former employee of this office, Ben Clancy, was the district attorney, so it's been going on for quite some time. I'm sure we're talking about millions of dollars."

Henshaw looked over at me like I was an insect. "Forgive me," he said to Claire, "but why is this man here?"

"Because he's going to be the next district attorney, and he wants to help."

"You're sure he's going to win the election?"

"Are you a gambling man, Mr. Henshaw?"

"Just tell me what you have in mind."

"Mr. Street has already been approached by the sheriff. He was just feeling Mr. Street out, trying to discern whether he would allow things to continue as they are if he were to be elected."

"And what did Mr. Street tell him?"

"Nothing, really. He doesn't trust the sheriff. But my grandfather would like to get Mr. Street involved in this case, and that's where you come in. After he's elected, Mr. Street is going to approach the sheriff and tell him he wants a full share of the protection and extortion money that's flowing to law enforcement in Knox County."

"I am?" I said. This came as a complete surprise.

Claire ignored me and kept talking. "He's going to record every conversation, turn all the money over to the FBI, and let you gentlemen do what you do. He'll do most of the work, and you can be the heroes."

"I'm not really comfortable with this," I said.

Kurtz cleared his throat. "There will have to be an agent, probably two, nearby every time he talks to the sheriff. We'd have to be there in case a dangerous situation developed and to authenticate the tape recordings if the case goes to trial. We have to transcribe the tapes. We have to log and store everything. It's actually a great deal of work, Ms. Tate, and you're mistaken when you say he'll be doing most of it. It's offensive."

"My apologies," Claire said. "I certainly didn't mean to offend you."

"This isn't something new to us, you know," Kurtz said. "We've been aware of the accusations and innuendo for quite some time."

"It goes far beyond accusation and innuendo, I assure you," Claire said. "May I ask what you've done with the information you've received?"

"No, you may not. I'm not at liberty to discuss investigations," Kurtz said.

"So there is an investigation," Claire said.

"I didn't say that."

"So there isn't an investigation," Claire said.

"I didn't say that, either. I'm not going to discuss any investigation with you, Ms. Tate. And as for Mr. Street, there would be concerns. He's suspected of killing several people, including Ben Clancy."

"I didn't kill Clancy or anybody else," I said.

"Well, you've also been charged and convicted of murder. You served two years in prison."

"And I was exonerated, and Clancy was arrested and eventually put out to pasture."

"The point is, let's say you were able to make a case on the sheriff and perhaps some of his associates. If the sheriff doesn't buckle and plead guilty, if he goes to trial, Mr. Street will face a vicious attack from the defense. They'll go after him with both barrels blazing. His credibility will be destroyed, and that doesn't make for much of a witness."

"I can handle it," I said. "Besides, that's a long way off."

"I think it's a big waste of time," Henshaw said. "Let's say you manage to take this sheriff down. You think it's going to stop gambling and prostitution and drugs? People have been doing those things since they've been walking upright. And what about the district attorney? You say he's involved? How are you going to get to him if he's no longer the district attorney?"

"He lives large," I said. "Shouldn't be much problem to prove that he couldn't have financed his lifestyle on his salary."

"You're chasing your tail. As soon as you take the sheriff out of the picture, the vice trades you're talking about will just open up. There will be competition. People will get hurt."

"So you condone what he's doing?" I said.

"I'm not condoning him taking money, but a lot of law enforcement officials allow select people to operate so they can keep some form of control over things. It's less violent that way."

"Fine," I said, "but let's at least get the corruption out of the sheriff's office. And there's another part to this that I'm surprised you haven't mentioned. Gary Brewer?"

"Ah, yes, Gary Brewer," Henshaw said. "The junkie gambler who took up bare-knuckle fighting to pay for his habits. Probably got himself killed in a fight. We're supposed to feel sorry for him, though, because he was a marine and his family is wealthy."

"Wow, you are one compassionate son of a bitch, aren't you?" I said.

"Watch your mouth," Henshaw said.

I stood up and looked at Claire. "Let's go," I said. "We don't need these guys."

The meeting reminded me of the one I had with Stephen Morris about Dr. Fraturra. Both Henshaw and Kurtz had made up their minds they weren't going to help us before we'd walked into the room. The only reason they'd met with us at all was because of Roger Tate.

"Sit back down, Darren," Claire said. "We can work this out."

"Do what your master tells you," Henshaw said to me. "I don't like any of this, but I have bosses, and my bosses tell me I have to work with you. So sit down, shut your mouth, and let Mr. Kurtz, Ms. Tate, and me figure out how we're going to go about it."

"Tell your bosses I told you to go to hell," I said. "I don't want your help. I'll take the sheriff and the rest of them down myself after I'm elected. Then I'll go to the paper and tell them what a huge help you boys were."

And with that, I walked out the door.

CHAPTER 22

Claire sounded furious over the phone, although I thought I detected a tone of reluctant respect in her voice.

"I don't know whether I've ever met anyone as pigheaded as you are," she said.

I was driving toward my apartment, and she'd just left Henshaw's office.

"They're not interested," I said. "Don't you understand? If they're not interested, if they feel like they're being forced to help us, they'll screw it up. They won't be committed. And if they screw up, there's a good chance I wind up dead."

"But you don't just talk to a US attorney and the Special Agent in Charge of the Knoxville FBI the way you did," she said.

"I didn't start the insolence," I said. "Both of them were disrespectful to you and to me, and I'm not wired to put up with that kind of crap. I don't care who they think they are or what their titles are. To me, they're just men in suits who have the power of the US government behind them. How they use that power is up to them, but I hold them to a higher standard than they obviously hold themselves."

The thought crossed my mind that what I'd just said about holding them to a higher standard was pompous, considering what I'd done in the past, but I let it go quickly.

"So what are you going to do, Darren?" Claire said. "How are you going to get to Corker and these other people? Do you even know the full extent of what's going on?"

"I have other friends who will help me."

"Who? Ms. Tipton?"

"That's a pretty good start. Those are solid people, Claire. They don't have any political agenda. They're reliable and do exactly what they say they'll do. They don't have bosses and they don't judge. They're not afraid. But I have some other ideas, too. I spent years tearing the government's criminal cases apart. I can figure out how to build one."

She paused for a few seconds. I heard her sigh.

"What?" I said.

"I'm just afraid you're going to find yourself beating your head against the wall if you try to go after them the traditional way," she said.

"Why? What makes you say that?"

"It's been going on for a long time. Something just isn't right. Believe me when I tell you, Darren, I've been around these wars for a long time, and something stinks here. You're not going to get to these guys using informants and wiretaps."

"So what, then?" I said. "Should I just start killing people?"

"I don't know. Maybe."

I paused for a long minute before responding. This woman was different from Grace. Far different.

She changed the subject by saying, "Are you ready for tomorrow?"

Her grandfather, Senator Roger Tate, was flying into Knoxville to make a personal appearance with me at the Knoxville Civic Auditorium.

"Will anyone be there besides us?" I said.

"I've told you, Darren, it will be packed. People will come from hundreds of miles around just to see my grandfather, to shake his hand, to hear him speak. He's brought billions of dollars into this state through the appropriations committee, people genuinely like him—or at least most of them do—and they'll want to make a connection. They won't care much about you at first—no offense—but when Senator Roger Tate tells them he's flown all the way from Washington because he has such strong feelings about you and what a good job you'll do as district attorney general, people will pay attention. The story about Morris's wife slapping the teacher in the face is going to hit the streets in the morning, and then we'll have the rally tomorrow night. We'll cruise from here, and then you'll be in a position to deal with Morris and the sheriff and to find Brewer."

Claire had been pretty much spot-on with everything she'd told me up to that point, so I decided to trust her.

"How about dinner tonight?" I said. "We can talk about tomorrow and plot against Morris and the sheriff."

"Where?"

"My place. I'm a good cook."

"I don't know if that's such a good idea," Claire said.

"C'mon, I'm not going to hit on you. We're doing this very unusual thing together. You've been a huge help to me, and I'd like to cook dinner for you. I don't see why we can't at least be friends."

She paused for several seconds.

"What are you going to cook? I'm a vegan." I thought I detected a hint of pain in her voice, as though I'd perhaps hurt her feelings when I said I wasn't going to hit on her.

"Figures," I said. "What would you like?"

"I don't know, maybe some kind of roasted brussels sprout skewer with a dipping sauce?"

Brussels sprouts. There wasn't a dipping sauce in the world that would make brussels sprouts appealing to me. My stomach turned at the thought.

"Sounds great," I said. "What time?"

"Seven thirty?"

"Wine?"

"I'll bring the wine," Claire said.

"Perfect. See you tonight."

CHAPTER 23

Claire showed up right on time, looking chic in designer jeans and boots and a peach silk blouse. The more I was around her, the more I noticed how striking she was. She turned the heads of both men and women everywhere we went, and she carried herself with an air of confidence that was just shy of haughty. She had a beautiful smile, though, which I was seeing more and more of, and she was relaxing around me more often. We joked with each other, made wisecracks. I liked her sense of humor.

I'd found a recipe for roasted brussels sprouts with a lemon-thyme dipping sauce and had done a test run before she came to the apartment. The texture seemed fine, but to me, the taste was disgusting. But one of the first things she said when she walked in the door was, "Something smells divine."

"Really?" I said. "You think that's divine?"

"You don't like brussels sprouts?" she said.

"I'd rather eat canned cat food."

"Well, I hope you're not going to. It won't go very well with the wine I brought."

I'd made some Chicken Marsala for myself, and since she was a vegan, I'd mixed some prosciutto in with it just to taunt her. It turned out really well, and I was hungry. I gave her a corkscrew, she opened the wine while I plated the food, and then we sat down to eat.

"You haven't told me much about Grace," she said about a minute into the meal.

The sound of Grace's name surprised me, and I stopped chewing for a second.

"I'm sorry," Claire said. "If it's too painful, just forget I mentioned it."

"No, no, it isn't that. I just hadn't heard anyone say her name in a while. When she first died, I thought I'd die, too, but something unusual happened. She came to me in a dream—it was like it was real—and she told me she was disappointed in me. She basically said goodbye, she slipped through this veil of mist, and I haven't dreamed of her since. I don't feel her presence; I don't feel as though she's watching over me. I feel guilty about it, but to be honest, I've thought very little about her. I can barely remember her voice. I have some photos, but I put them away. I just don't want to look at her every day and revisit all of it, and if she's abandoned or given up on me, which I think she has, then there isn't much point in torturing myself."

"Why would you think those things?" Claire said. "Why would you think she's abandoned you or given up on you?"

"She was a gentle soul who wouldn't harm anyone. She was truly a wonderful human being. She was as smart as they come, she was kind and considerate, and she was even-tempered. She loved her work. She loved people. She hated injustice. She was as close to perfect as anyone I've ever met."

"That's a tough legacy to follow," Claire said.

"Grace defended criminals and never once gave any thought to the crimes they'd committed. I used to be able to do that, but I changed. She didn't."

"And you think she abandoned you when Dr. Fraturra disappeared?" Claire said.

"I didn't say that."

"It doesn't matter. You don't have to. For what it's worth, I think differently than she did. *If* you did something to Fraturra, I wouldn't condemn you for it, just like I wouldn't condemn you if you did something about what happened to your mother or if you evened the scales with Ben Clancy."

"You're hard-hearted," I said.

"Violent crimes are basically acts of terrorism," she said. "I've been taught, and I choose to accept the philosophy, that there is only one way to fight terrorism, and that is with violence."

I smiled at her, and although I agreed and could have continued talking about violence, I tried to change, or at least soften, the subject.

"It's different with my mother," I said. "I can remember her voice, but her face has faded some from my memory. When her house was blown up, they used so much dynamite that it practically vaporized everything. There wasn't a single photo of her that survived the explosion and the fire, and since I was living there at the time, all my photos burned up, too."

"Again," Claire said, "an act of terrorism. Did Grace love you? I mean, toward the end?"

"You don't beat around the bush, do you?"

"Is there any point? Answer the question, please."

I shrugged my shoulders. "Grace loved me very much at one time," I said. "After my mother's death, I became difficult and I tested her limits. We were back on the mend when she died, so I suppose the answer would be yes, I think she loved me toward the end."

"And you loved her?"

"I did. We would have married not long after the baby was born, I feel pretty certain about that. It's like you said the other day, I've been through some difficult times. I can become moody and distant. But she was patient with me. She was good to me. When I think about her, I miss her very much. When I think about what we might have been if some of these things hadn't happened, it saddens me."

I felt a tear slide down my cheek and wiped it away with my napkin.

"I'm sorry, Darren," Claire said.

"It's all right. Really. I'm not ashamed to show emotion when I talk about Grace. I feel cheated that we didn't get to raise Jasmine together. I think we would have done very well raising a child."

"I'm sure you would have."

"So what about you? How about a little quid pro quo? I don't know anything about your personal life. You told me you don't like men. I think you said they were boorish and boring, but I find that hard to believe."

"Why do you find that hard to believe?"

She took a sip of wine, and I noticed the pale-red imprint of her lips left on the glass by her lipstick.

"Because of the way you carry yourself, because of the way you dress. You want men to be attracted to you. Do you do it so you can swat them away like flies?"

"I have to admit you surprise me quite often," Claire said. "You're far more perceptive than you want people to believe."

"So you don't hate men."

"No, I don't hate men. I find them deliciously attractive, if you want the honest truth."

"That's one of the reasons I love to see a woman drink wine," I said. "Half a glass down the hatch and the truth starts bubbling up. Are you attracted to any particular type of man, or just men in general?"

"I like macho guys," she said. "I like men who do things. Who live for something. They have to be intelligent, of course, and I mean *extremely* intelligent, but they can't sit on their asses. They have to be physically fit, maybe a little bit dangerous, and they have to believe in a cause or an ideal and live to promote that cause or ideal. And I'm not talking about just any cause. It has to be something I consider noble."

"I would never have taken you for a Guinevere. You're a hopeless romantic in search of a king or a prince."

She winked at me. "Maybe."

"Ever dated a soldier, one of those officer-and-gentleman types?"

"I did," she said. She didn't seem to want to discuss it.

"Come on, now, Claire, you can't just leave me hanging. I opened up to you. It's your turn."

I was getting to know her better, but she was still a mystery to me. I wanted to know what made her tick, how she felt about certain things. I wanted to know what kind of man she was interested in, because, whether I wanted to admit it or not, I was becoming interested in her.

"He worked at the Pentagon when I met him," Claire said. "He was a major in the army, a Green Beret who wanted to move on to Delta. He was a good man, very dedicated to his work."

"Did you love him?"

"I did, and he loved me. But he loved his work more, so I suppose the old adage that one must be careful what one wishes for is true. I found and fell in love with a man dedicated to protecting and serving the country he loved, but there wasn't enough room in his life for his career and for me. He ultimately chose the career."

"How long since the breakup?"

"Last year in November."

"Ah, so it's still pretty fresh."

I reached across the table and patted her hand. "I won't say it gets better with time, but it changes. The pain eases just a fraction each day that goes by. You learn to cope. And who knows? Maybe you'll find another knight one day."

"Maybe," she said. "I don't think I'll ever find anyone like him, but I guess there's always a chance."

"And in the meantime, you get to work with new and exciting people like me," I said.

She smiled and pointed her fork at me. "You are not boring," she said. "I'll give you that. The way you went off on Henshaw and Kurtz this afternoon was a complete surprise."

"That was for you," I said. "The first words out of his mouth were, 'I didn't vote for your father.' What an asinine thing to say. I knew right then it wasn't going to go well. Besides, I don't have much use for the feds. They framed me and put me in jail. They dieseled me. They tried to break me, turn me into a robot."

"They dieseled you? What does that mean?"

"They handcuffed me with the black-box cuffs that they can practically break your wrists with, they shackled me, and they put me on a bus. I stayed on the bus anywhere from sixteen to twenty hours a day for three months straight. They'd feed me once a day—a bologna sandwich, a piece of fruit, and some milk—and they just rode me from prison to prison. There was no bathroom on the bus, so I had to be careful about what I ate and drank. If I lost control of my bladder or bowels on the bus, I was going to take a bad beating. Took a shower maybe once a month, didn't shave or cut my hair. They call it diesel therapy. It was torture. They do it to people they deem 'disciplinary problems.'"

"Who does it?" Claire said.

"The US marshals. US attorneys or prison wardens usually pick out the people who get dieseled, but the marshals do the dirty work."

"That's unconscionable. I'm going to tell my grandfather about it."

"He knows," I said. "There have been congressional hearings where it's come up. They turn their backs to it so they aren't accused of meddling in how the federal criminal justice system operates. Nobody wants to appear soft on crime."

"How did you get through it?" Claire said. "I mean, mentally?"

"About halfway through, I just made up my mind they weren't going to break me. And I thought a lot about Grace. She was my lawyer then, but I was already in love with her."

"Amazing," she said.

I raised my glass and she clinked hers against it.

"To never getting dieseled again," I said.

"To becoming the next district attorney of Knox County," she said.

"Excellent," I said. "Now tell me everything that's going to happen tomorrow."

CHAPTER 24

The event, which was held at the Knoxville Civic Auditorium, was billed as a political rally and had been well publicized. I had to hand it to Claire. She really knew her stuff when it came to running political campaigns. I had a huge organization of volunteers, envelope stuffers, sign distributors, and people who would make cold calls on my behalf. There were billboards all over Knoxville. I'd seen my name on at least ten buses and six billboards.

"Darren Street for District Attorney General. A Man of Integrity," the slogans beneath my face said. I found it horrifyingly embarrassing at first, but after seeing the images over and over, I got used to it. I didn't believe it, but I got used to it. Had it said, "Darren Street for District Attorney General. A Dangerous Man of Occasional Integrity," I would have liked it better.

The rally was held in late October, just two weeks before the election. Claire, as always, was right. The auditorium held twenty-five hundred people, and it was packed. They weren't there to see me. They were there to see and hear a man who was an icon in Tennessee, Senator Roger Tate. Several dignitaries came—state representatives and senators, the lieutenant governor, and the speaker of the Tennessee House of Representatives. They all sat up on the stage with us. About five minutes before the proceedings were to begin, the sheriff made his entrance, dressed in his uniform and his cowboy hat and carrying his signature

Colt Python revolvers. He took a seat on the second row on the stage, right next to the county clerk. I sat next to Senator Tate. It was a surreal scene and a surreal feeling, thinking I was about to be endorsed for a local political office by one of the most powerful men in the United States. The thought actually ran through my mind, *My God, my mother would be so proud.*

The mayor of Knoxville opened the rally by welcoming everyone and introducing a pastor who said a few words and then led everyone in the Lord's Prayer. A beautiful young child, a girl perhaps eight or nine years old with long blonde curls and wearing a pale-blue dress, sang a rendition of "The Star-Spangled Banner" that gave me goose bumps and had everyone in the place on their feet yelling when she was finished.

The lieutenant governor introduced Senator Tate, and Tate gave a forty-minute, mini–State of the Union address, combined with a State of the State of Tennessee address. He spent the last five minutes talking about me and what a fine gentleman I was, how I had seen hard times and overcome them, and how I would make a fine district attorney by protecting the people of Knox County and ferreting out corruption and aggressively prosecuting criminals.

And then it was my turn to speak. I was spiffed up to the max. Claire had bought me a charcoal-gray tailored suit with a shirt and tie and socks and shoes to match, and she'd ordered me to go to a spa in Knoxville that morning that she said was the best in town. They were waiting for me, and they pampered me for two hours, including giving me a haircut and a shave. Prior to the rally, there was another barber waiting backstage who put hot towels over my face, gave me a close shave, and made me smell the way I would imagine a high-dollar corporate CEO would smell.

There was a teleprompter in front of me, and I stuck to the words Claire had written. I thanked everyone for coming. I said I was honored and humbled to be endorsed by a man as revered as Senator Tate, and that I would bring honesty, integrity, and organization to the district attorney's office. I didn't say I'd bring those things "back" to the office, because it had been occupied by Ben Clancy for so long before Morris was elected that there hadn't been honor or integrity in the district attorney's office for a long, long time. I kept it short, around eight minutes, and then I began to thank everyone again.

Just as I was about to finish, a man holding up a large placard came walking down the aisle against the wall to my right. The placard said, "Where is Dr. Nicolas Fraturra?"

"Did you kill my brother?" the man yelled. "What did you do to him?"

I didn't know whether the man was really Fraturra's brother or a Morris plant. Maybe he was both. Security started to move toward him, and people started booing. I raised my hand to quiet the crowd as the man reached the bottom of the steps. He was about thirty feet away.

"What's your name?" I said.

"Michael Fraturra."

"And Dr. Nicolas Fraturra is your brother?"

"*Was* my brother! Until you killed him!"

"Who told you that, Mr. Fraturra?" I said.

"Stephen Morris told me you killed my brother."

"Did he offer you any proof?"

"He said Nick didn't save your girlfriend and your baby. That you lost them both because of a rare medical condition and that you tried to get Mr. Morris to arrest my brother."

"That's true, Mr. Fraturra. I went to Stephen Morris and asked him to arrest your brother for reckless homicide. He was on call the night my girlfriend and baby died, and he was too drunk to care for them. He could have saved them, but he arrived late and he was drunk. By the time another doctor got there, it was too late. They were gone."

"And Mr. Morris wouldn't arrest him so you killed him! What did you do with his body?"

"If something has happened to your brother, Mr. Fraturra, I'm sorry for your loss, just as I'm sure you're sorry for the loss of my girl-friend and daughter. But I didn't harm your brother. If he's gone, I had nothing to do with it."

"Liar! You're a liar and a murderer! I hope you rot in hell, you miserable son of a bitch!"

At that point, a security guard took Mr. Fraturra by the arm and led him out the door. I noticed Claire, flanked by two Knoxville police officers, follow them out.

"I'm sorry," I said to the audience. "I've been falsely accused before. There isn't really anything I can do other than deny the accusations because they aren't true. I hope you believe me. Thank you again, and I wish all of you the best, no matter who wins this election."

Roger Tate got up and spoke for another ten minutes, controlling any damage that might have just occurred. As he was finishing up, I saw Claire motion to him from the corner of the stage. He said, "Excuse me for just a second," and walked over to her. She whispered in his ear briefly, and he returned to the microphone.

"Ladies and gentlemen, the man who just claimed to be Dr. Nicolas Fraturra's brother is really a gentleman named Ronald Blair. After he left the arena, a Knoxville police officer asked him to provide some identi-fication. After a couple of minutes of questioning, he admitted that he was paid one thousand dollars to put on the show we all just witnessed. We've decided not to press charges."

I breathed a deep sigh of relief as people yelled their disapproval. Then I started to wonder about the $1,000. He said he'd been paid $1,000, but he didn't say *who* paid it. Between the release of the infor-mation about Morris's wife, the revelation about the plant at the rally, and the endorsement of Roger Tate, Morris was as good as dead in the water. My money was on Claire. I was betting she'd paid the guy, and it had worked perfectly.

Damn, she was good.

CHAPTER 25

Sheriff Corker was nervous. He and Harley Shaker had been summoned to the small trailer where Roby Penn lived on a Tuesday evening. Cigarette smoke hung heavy in the kitchen. The three men were sitting at the table, drinking beer and playing Texas Hold'em. Sheriff Corker had shown up at the allotted time. Harley had shown up ten minutes late, which caused Roby to go off on a five-minute, profanity-laced rant about respect and wasting other people's time. Roby had even threatened to shoot him. The sheriff had finally calmed Roby down. They'd settled in and were about five hands into the game, but the sheriff knew this evening wasn't about playing cards and strengthening male bonds. Something was troubling Roby. He was fidgety and even more irritable than usual.

"We got something we gotta do," Roby said after he polished off his second beer and followed it with a shot of tequila.

"Yeah," the sheriff said, smiling. He was doing his best to keep things light. "We need to deal some better cards my way."

"Shut up, Tree," Roby snapped. "I'm serious. I've got it all planned out so you won't have to strain that pea brain of yours. Harley, you're in because you killed that marine and put us all at risk. You gotta put in some work to make up for that."

"Work? What kind of work?" Shaker said. "I already helped you get rid of him."

"That could have blown up in our faces, but what I have in mind is going to settle things down once and for all. We need to do some wet work."

"Wet work?" the sheriff said as he sipped a beer slowly and sucked on a cigarette. "You're talking about killing people, Roby. I don't kill people. You know that."

"You don't have to kill anybody, you damned gutless little girl," Roby said. "But you're going along. I need somebody I can trust to help me and Harley get away. And you're right. Some people need to get dead."

The sheriff looked over at Shaker, who was staring down at his cards.

"I got no dog in this fight," Harley said. "Y'all got your scams going over here. All I do is fight once in a while."

"But you killed that Brewer kid. Brought a lot of pressure down on Tree and a lot of pressure on me. I figure you owe us."

"I don't figure the same," Harley said.

The sheriff could feel the tension building in the air. It was dangerous to stand up to Roby, and Harley was making him angry.

"Tell you what," Roby said. "Either you do what I want you to do or I'm gonna come to your house in the dark of night, and I'm gonna slit your throat, I'm gonna slit your wife's throat, and I'm gonna kill all three of your children. Then I'm gonna go over to your momma and daddy's and kill them. I'll finish up with your brother, your sister, and their families. Hell, I'll wipe out the whole damned Shaker line. Do you have any doubt I'll do what I say?"

Harley was obviously shaken by the threat. As he lifted his cigarette to his lips, the sheriff noticed his hand was trembling. Roby noticed, too.

"You better be scared, because I ain't fucking around here. Stephen Morris is going to get beat in this election. He's already told Tree he might go to the feds and cop to some kind of deal to save his own ass. If he does, we're finished, and I don't intend to allow that to happen. He's gotta go, and so does his wife, and both of you are going to help me."

"Why would you want to harm his wife, Roby?" Tree said. "She ain't involved in all of this."

"Don't be a damned fool. You think she hasn't asked him where all this extra money has been coming from? You think he hasn't told her? And do you think for a second that she's going to want to give up the fine lifestyle they enjoy now? She'll be right by his side when he goes to the feds."

"But she doesn't know anything other than what he's told her."

"Exactly," Roby said. "My guess is he's told her everything. She's dead, Tree. She may be breathing right this minute, but she's dead. I've made up my mind."

"I think it's a mistake. It's overkill. It's bad enough that you're thinking about killing a sitting district attorney—"

"Who's about to get his ass whipped in an election."

"Doesn't matter. You're gonna murder a sitting district attorney *and* his wife? What about his kids, Roby? You gonna kill them, too?"

"If I have to. And his fucking cat or dog or whatever. Anything that gets in the way gets killed."

"I'm not gonna be a part of killing kids," the sheriff said. "If you're planning to kill his kids, I'm out."

"You ain't out unless I say you're out."

"I'm serious, Roby. No kids. You can pull that .45 of yours out and blow my brains out right now, but I'm not going to live with the deaths of children on my conscience. I won't do it."

The sheriff and Roby engaged in a staring match for several seconds. The sheriff could feel his heart beating hard inside his chest. He hoped Roby couldn't hear it.

"Fine," Roby finally said, "but the wife's gotta go. Harley, you're gonna take care of her."

"You're going to bring every city, state, and federal cop within fifty miles down on us," the sheriff said.

"Shut up," Roby said. "I ain't finished. There are two more that have to go besides Morris and his wife."

"Who's that?"

"Morris's bagman, that asshole named Harrison, and Morris's junkie girlfriend, the one he takes drugs to so she can sell them and get high for free."

"And you're planning on doing this when?" Tree said.

"Saturday night. I've been working on it for weeks. Got it all planned out."

Roby reached to his left and picked up a pad of paper and set it on the table in front of him.

"Set the cards aside," he said. "Here's the plan."

The sheriff's mind was racing as the three men huddled deep into the night. He had to prevent Roby from doing what he was planning to do, but if he did, there was a good chance his cover would be blown.

Screw the cover, he thought. *It's been way too long, anyway.*

CHAPTER 26

Sheriff Corker pulled his personal vehicle, a ten-year-old red Dodge pickup, into the darkened barn next to the blue Ford Mustang. The car belonged to an FBI agent named Ron Wilcox. Wilcox had been Tree's FBI "handler" since the sheriff had gone to the agency looking for a way out of the jam he'd gotten himself into.

Corker had approached the FBI a few months after Ben Clancy was fired and thrown in jail. He'd wanted to go to them sooner, after Clancy was beaten by Stephen Morris, but Clancy had immediately moved into the US attorney's office and maintained his lock over the county's extortion and protection rackets. He was in that job for two years before the Darren Street frame job blew up in his face and he was fired and sent to jail to await trial for conspiracy to commit murder.

Clancy was out of the way after that, as far as the scams were concerned. He couldn't threaten to expose what was going on without exposing himself to a federal RICO prosecution on top of the conspiracy prosecution. But Roby immediately demanded that the sheriff talk to Morris, who had been in office for two years. Roby hated the government and hated prosecutors, but he hated jail more, and he wanted to ensure the protection would continue. So the sheriff approached Morris about the scheme, found Morris to be self-immersed and greedy, and it was an easy sell from there.

But once Morris came on board, Sheriff Corker had had enough. He was tired of being a bagman, a go-between, and an arbiter for the corrupt players in Knox County. He'd been naive when he first took office. He knew now that he had been handpicked by Ben Clancy and Roby precisely because he was so naive, but he was ready to put a stop to the things that were going on and become a real lawman. His problem? His hands were dirty. He'd done Clancy's bidding for two years, and although he hadn't spent a dime of the money he'd taken, he knew he could be convicted as easily as Roby and Clancy and Morris.

Sheriff Corker had no wife—he'd always been awkward around women; he was terrified of them—and no one he could trust enough to talk to about his dilemma. He was afraid to go to a lawyer because he'd always heard lawyers gossip among themselves and were notorious barhoppers. But he could no longer look at himself in the mirror. He'd gone into depressions that had caused him to consider taking his own life, but he'd picked himself up and decided to find a way out. When Ben Clancy went to jail, the sheriff had seen a glimmer of hope.

He'd first arranged a meeting with Stephen Blackburn, who was still the US attorney at the time, and spilled his guts. Blackburn, in turn, had put him in touch with Bradley Kurtz, the new Special Agent in Charge of the Knoxville office. Kurtz had handed him off to the young agent Wilcox, and ever since, the sheriff had worn wires, collected names and evidence, and turned over every dime of what was supposed to be his share of the extortion money from the rackets in Knox County.

The investigation had grown like a baby octopus, its tentacles stretching out with each passing month. Wilcox wanted tapes on Morris, of course, and on Harrison and Roby. Wilcox said he'd placed wiretaps on Morris's home and cell phones. Then Wilcox brought in a DEA agent named Higgins, who'd wanted the name of every drug dealer, what they were dealing, how much they were dealing, and who their suppliers were. The agent said he wanted tapes and he wanted to develop informants, but after about six months, he said he'd become involved in a much larger investigation and had to back off for a while. Corker hadn't seen him since.

It had been the same with the cockfighting, the dogfighting, the bare-knuckle. Wilcox demanded more and more information each month. He was building a case that he said would catapult his career to the top echelon of the FBI, and he guaranteed the sheriff complete immunity from prosecution. Wilcox wanted the sex traffickers, the pimps. He wanted to know where the women came from, how much they cost, who was buying them, and where they wound up. There was no way for the sheriff to gather everything, but he'd tried to get all he could. Wilcox also wanted to know about the organizations who ran the strip clubs, where their girls came from, how they rotated girls in and out, who the major players were. It became a seemingly never-ending series of questions without answers.

But nobody had ever gotten arrested, and as the sheriff walked toward the farmhouse where he met Wilcox every month, he knew that had to change, and it had to change now.

It was nearly one in the morning, and Corker was tired and irritable. Wilcox was in the kitchen, where he always was, with his feet up on the table. He was typical FBI—lean and athletic build, short hair, square jaw. Wilcox was in his early thirties, a pup compared with most of the other agents in Knoxville. He was drinking a cup of coffee.

"What's the big emergency, Tree?" Wilcox said. "My wife raises hell every time I leave at this time of night."

"I hate that for you," the sheriff said sarcastically, "but it's time for you to get off your ass and be a real agent. You need to do something with this case."

"Watch your tone," Wilcox said.

"You say you've been building this thing for years. I try to get you to move on people, and you won't do it," the sheriff said. "Well, Roby

Penn is out of control. He's going to kill four people on Saturday night. You need to stop it."

That got Wilcox's attention, and he took his feet off the table and sat up.

"What the hell are you talking about?" Wilcox said.

"Roby's got it in his mind that Stephen Morris is going to lose this election, which he is, and that he's going to come straight to y'all and start flapping his gums about what's been going on for years."

"Why would he do that?" Wilcox said. "He'd go straight to jail."

"Roby thinks the new guy, Darren Street, will crack down on everything. He thinks Morris will come to you and the US attorney to try to make a deal before everything caves."

"I'm not ready," Wilcox said. He looked almost frantic. "I mean, I haven't even taken anything to the grand jury. It'd be weeks, maybe months, before I could get any indictments."

"After all this time? What the hell have you been doing, boy?"

"Screw you," Wilcox said. "You have no idea the scale of this investigation, what's going on, what's at stake."

"I know I've been feeding you good information with a spoon for years, I've been giving you tapes, names, dates, phone numbers, addresses—whatever you asked me for I've tried to deliver. I've been giving you money every single month, and you haven't done a damned thing with any of it. Well, now it's time to shit or get off the pot. People's lives are at stake."

"Who's he planning to kill?" Wilcox said.

"Morris, his wife, Jim Harrison, and Morris's girlfriend, Leslie Saban."

"Christ," Wilcox said. "And he's going to do it Saturday? Do you know what he has planned?"

"I know everything," Corker said. "He wrote it down and showed it all to Harley Shaker and me just a couple of hours ago."

"Harley Shaker . . . that name seems familiar."

"He's the guy that killed Gary Brewer!" Tree said. "Don't you pay any attention?"

"And Gary Brewer is?"

The sheriff sighed and shook his head. How did Wilcox ever get into the FBI? How did he manage to stay?

"A soldier that went missing. Shit, Wilcox, are you going to protect these people or not? He's planning to kill Morris and his wife at Morris's house around eleven on Saturday night. He's going to call Harrison to an abandoned warehouse on Route 19 at midnight, and then he's going to break into Leslie Saban's apartment around 3:00 a.m. You and a SWAT team need to be at Morris's house, waiting for them."

"Them?"

"Shaker will be with him."

"What kind of weapons will they be carrying?"

"Pistols."

"Okay, Sheriff," Wilcox said, taking a deep breath and pushing himself back from the table. "You've done good. This is good. Just leave it to me. We'll take down Roby Penn and Harley Shaker on Saturday night. It'll be a big break in this case."

"So you promise you'll be there and you'll be ready?"

"Damn right. They won't stand a chance. We'll ambush them."

"You'll probably have to kill Roby."

"We'll do what we have to do. By the way, where are you going to be while all this is going on, Sheriff?"

"I'll be in a speedboat in the river. I'm supposed to pick them up after they kill Morris and his wife."

CHAPTER 27

Stephen Morris was getting on my last nerve. He apparently liked his life of luxury and wanted to keep it, because he certainly wasn't going down quietly. Claire kept assuring me that we were leading by a large margin and were going to bury him, but he kept going on the offensive. To everyone who would listen, he was saying I was a suspected murderer. Since I was now running for public office, and since he was telling the truth when he said I was a "suspected" murderer, there wasn't anything I could do about it. One of the weekly newspapers ran a story and quoted Morris as saying I was suspected in "two, and perhaps up to five" murders. That, the story said, qualified me as a "suspected serial killer," and those three words appeared in the headline. Two days after the reporter, whose name was Jon Brooks, ran his "suspected serial killer" story, I called the newsroom and asked to speak to him. I wanted to know why he hadn't bothered to call me and get my side of such a sensational story. I was told he no longer worked for the paper. Claire again. She didn't mess around.

I continued to brush off the accusations every chance I got. "Where is the evidence?" I would say when asked. "Show me one shred of evidence they have against me."

There wasn't any, of course, and I knew it. I turned it on anyone who brought it up.

"He's pointing the finger at me because he never found the person who killed my mother," I would say. I was careful not to mention or criticize the police, the sheriff's department, or the TBI. After all, I would be working with those people if I was elected, even after I got rid of the sheriff. I knew it would be difficult enough, given the circumstances and all the rumors, but I was confident I could gain their trust over time. Besides, despite the fact that I was occasionally feeling some regret, I still didn't think I'd ever killed anyone who didn't absolutely deserve killing, and I would have bet that nearly every cop in Knoxville would have agreed with me.

Morris's constant railing, however, was taking me to a dangerous place. It was still there, that caged lion inside of me, and Morris was beginning to represent fresh meat. Even if I was a killer, I believed myself to be more honorable than an extortionist thief who betrayed the public trust every day of his life. And as far as I was concerned, Morris was responsible for many more deaths than I was. People died every day from drug overdoses in Knox County. He protected drug dealers. People died in the sex-trafficking industry all the time. He protected them. Gary Brewer was most likely dead. He protected the bare-knuckle fighting. And that didn't even begin to take into account the countless animals that had died in the cockfighting and dogfighting rings. After watching him attack me on television one evening with a week to go before the election, I decided to pay him a visit and tell him that if he didn't shut his mouth, he'd be my next victim. I decided not to ask Claire for permission.

As always, I had to be careful. I didn't want anyone else to see us together or hear anything I might say to him. I also wanted to make sure he wasn't wired. So I went into my old Darren stalk mode where I used disguises and rented cars from shady operators for cash. The next morning, I drove almost a hundred miles away and bought a pair of infrared binoculars for cash from a large sporting goods store. In order to get close enough to him to have the conversation I wanted to have,

I figured I would need to confine him for a little while, so I wanted to do things in such a way that nobody but Morris himself could say I ever got near him. That meant surveillance. If I did it right, even if he did go crying to the press or the cops after I had my talk with him, I'd just say he was desperate and call him a liar.

I followed Morris from his home to his work and from work back home three days in a row, looking for an opening, and I watched his place on several occasions during those three days, both from the water and from a ridge I could hike to from a nearby park.

On the third day I followed Morris, I learned something that Claire probably already knew. Morris had a squeeze. She was young, brunette, extremely attractive, and she came out of her apartment and planted a kiss on his lips as soon as he got out of his car. He was carrying a box about the size of a shoe box. They disappeared into her apartment, and he came back out about forty-five minutes later. I didn't try to look through the windows to see what was going on. I just laughed out loud when she planted that big kiss on him. *Gotcha again,* I thought. I wondered when Claire was planning to release the news of his extramarital affair. I supposed she was saving it as a surprise. The bomb would most likely drop the day before the election.

I did some research on the address and the apartment number Morris went into and found out the young woman's name was Leslie Saban. There was very little information about her on the Internet, and since she looked so young, I assumed she was a student, maybe a law student he had met while doing a guest lecture. Or maybe she was an engineering student or a stripper. Who knew?

Morris didn't just have a girlfriend. He also had a six-thousand-square-foot mansion that sat right on the river. It was surrounded by at least twenty acres. There was a barn that housed two thoroughbred horses, a white rail fence that enclosed most of the property, a Lexus, a Mercedes, a BMW convertible, two children, and a wife. His estate was gated and named Serenity Ridge. The yard and the landscaping were immaculate, the barn looked to be nicer than most people's homes, and there seemed to be a constant influx and outgo of workers and helpers and nannies and house cleaners. Someone was always working in the yard or painting or working with the horses. The place was a buzz of activity, but Morris was rarely there. Unless his wife was independently wealthy—and I hadn't heard anything about her being so—he would have an extremely difficult time explaining how he managed to accumulate all these material goods on a district attorney's salary. I was looking forward to hauling him in front of a grand jury and asking him all about his goodies.

On Saturday night, three days before the election, I rented a pontoon boat from the same dock where Claire had rented the boat we took Janie Schofield out on. I paid cash, wore a fake beard, and used a false ID. I took the infrared binoculars, some fishing gear, and a six-pack of beer along with me. I eased the pontoon west until I came to Morris's estate and dropped the anchor in the middle of the river. It was early November, but the night was warm and clear, around sixty-five degrees with a slight breeze. Orion was directly over the boat.

There were a few other vessels around me, all fancy bass boats with lots of horsepower, trolling motors so they could get close to the riverbank and move slowly. They were illuminated by neon running lights. They stalked the shorelines in search of fish while I sat in the middle of the river and pointed the infrared binoculars at Morris's house. They'd cost me more than $500 and were surprisingly powerful.

The house was within fifty feet of the water, the river wasn't particularly wide at that point, and I could see the inside of his house clearly. Morris's wife, Gwyn, was in the kitchen, chopping vegetables. I scanned the house, and movement outside caught my attention. I trained the binoculars on the movement and could clearly see Morris sitting at a high table on his patio. He appeared to be texting someone on his phone. On the table in front of him was a water pipe, and when he put the phone down, he picked up the pipe, flicked a lighter, and took a deep pull off the pipe. I didn't know what he was smoking, but I assumed it was marijuana. I smiled to myself. There he was, the district attorney general, catching a weekend buzz on a fine November night on his luxurious patio. I didn't see any sign of his kids. Maybe they were out for the evening.

I watched him for a few minutes and saw him begin to fool with his phone again. Suddenly, country music filled the air. He liked it pretty loud, because I could hear it clearly from where I was floating out in the river. The song that was playing was "'Round Here Buzz" by Eric Church. *Perfect,* I thought, but I wished I'd bought one of the sets of binoculars I'd seen that had a video camera with audio capabilities. It would have been great to have a video of the district attorney smoking dope on his patio and listening to that particular song by Eric Church.

A few seconds later, I heard a small dog begin to bark excitedly, and I saw movement to Morris's left. A figure approached him carrying a handgun with a silencer attached to it. It was so clear through the binoculars, it was like watching a movie, and it played out as though in slow motion. Morris started to rise from the table, but the handgun belched a small amount of fire and smoke about a foot from his face, and Morris went straight over on his back.

"Oh, shit," I said quietly. *"Oh, shit. Somebody just shot him."*

I watched the figure who shot Morris in the head run straight toward me. At the same time, I looked back to the kitchen to see whether Morris's wife had heard or seen anything when another figure in dark clothing and wearing a mask walked up behind her and shot her twice in the back of the head. The second figure turned and disappeared. I trained the binoculars back to where the first person was running and noticed a large bass boat with no running lights sliding along the water from my left. It pulled up beside Morris's dock just long enough for the person who shot Morris to jump into the boat. That person was followed about five seconds later by another I assumed to be the one who had shot Gwyn Morris. The bass boat's engine roared to life, and they were gone. There was one other person in the boat, the driver. It had to be a man because I'd never seen a woman that large. I'd also never seen a woman who wore two pearl-handled pistols in holsters tied to her thighs. All three of them were wearing ski masks, and there wasn't a single thing about the boat I could identify, other than it was *fast*. It took off with a deep-throated roar and was out of sight in less than a minute.

I sat there, stunned, not knowing what to do. I'd just witnessed the murder of the district attorney and his wife. I was almost certain the sheriff was driving the boat, both because of his size and because of the pistols, but I couldn't tell anyone. If I called 9-1-1 and reported it, even from the prepaid cell I was carrying, my voice would be on the tape, and someone would recognize it because I was certainly about to become a suspect. I sat there and looked at the patio for several more seconds. The dog continued to go crazy, and pretty soon a neighbor's porch light came on and I heard a voice call out.

I pulled up the anchor and headed back toward the dock where I'd rented the boat. I knew it wouldn't be long before the place was crawling with cops.

CHAPTER 28

I drove home quickly and sat down on the couch. I was trembling and my mind was racing. I knew I'd be at the top of the list of suspects, and I figured the cops would come knocking around 6:00 a.m. I turned on the television and watched it mindlessly for a couple of hours. My phone ringing brought me out of the trance.

"Have you heard?" It was Claire's voice.

"Heard what?"

"Stephen Morris is dead."

I knew it, of course, but I had to act like I didn't, so I didn't make a sound. I wanted her to think I was in shock.

"Darren, are you there?"

"Yeah, yeah, I'm here. Did I just hear you say Stephen Morris is dead?"

"You did. And so is his wife."

"His wife?"

"Yes. Where were you tonight?"

"Here. I've been here going over these organizational charts and working on the acceptance speech you wrote for me. Hold on a second, Claire. Why are you asking me where I've been? How did they die?"

"The best information I have, and it comes from a solid source, is that somebody shot Morris while he was sitting outside his house on the patio. They shot his wife in the kitchen."

"So they were murdered, which means I'll be a suspect."

"That would be my guess, yes."

"Fantastic. What effect will this have on the election?"

"Unless they indict you and convict you by Tuesday, I guess you're the new district attorney general."

"I didn't want it this way."

"Neither did I. How will you handle the police when they come?"

"I'll be more cordial to them than I've been in the past, but I won't tell them much."

"They're going to be all over this, Darren. It's embarrassing for them."

"Morris lived in the county, didn't he? He had twenty-five acres out on the Tennessee River."

"You're right," Claire said. "The city won't even have jurisdiction. The sheriff's department will be investigating."

"That's just perfect."

"Why do you say that?"

"Because that's like the fox investigating who killed the hens. I'd bet my right arm the sheriff had something to do with this."

"Why? Why would the sheriff want Morris dead?" Claire said. "It seems to me he'd want to keep him on so they could keep their games running."

"You saw the sheriff at the rally. He knew Morris was beaten. Maybe Morris knew it, too. Maybe he threatened the sheriff somehow, or maybe they just wanted to tie off loose ends."

"Be careful, Darren. If they're capable of this, who knows? They might come after you, too."

"I can take care of myself. Besides, they can't just kill everybody who occupies the office. This was a warning to me, though. They want me to know they're serious. They want me to stay away."

"You won't, will you?"

"Not a chance."

"Let me know how it goes with the sheriff or his investigator or whoever he sends," Claire said.

"I can't wait to hear what they have to say. Good night, Claire."

CHAPTER 29

Sheriff Corker banged on the front door of Special Agent in Charge Bradley Kurtz's home at six on Sunday morning. Corker had just gotten away from Roby and Shaker a couple of hours earlier and had gone straight to the office. It took him a little time, but he was finally able to get Kurtz's home address. He drove straight there, looking and feeling haggard and dirty. After several minutes of banging, Kurtz opened the door wearing a black terry-cloth robe.

"Where the hell were you guys?" Corker demanded. "You let four people die!"

"You could get shot, beating on my door at this time of the morning. Don't ever do it again."

"Fuck yourself," Corker said. "I asked you a question. Where were you? Four people died. You were supposed to be there to prevent it."

"I have no idea what you're talking about," Kurtz said. The look in his eyes told Corker he might very well be telling the truth.

"Where is Wilcox?" Corker said. "Get him on the phone. I met with him late Tuesday night and told him Roby Penn and another man named Harley Shaker were going to kill Stephen Morris, his wife, Jim Harrison, and Leslie Saban. I told him it was time to start wrapping this case up. He said the FBI would prevent the murders and start indicting people. Did you know anything about any of this?"

"Keep your voice down," Kurtz said sharply. "I got a call a few hours ago that Morris and his wife were dead. And what did you say about Wilcox? You told him this was going to happen?"

"Tuesday. I told him Tuesday night."

"This is news to me. And what was that about wrapping up a case?"

The sheriff's eyes widened. Could it be possible? No . . . surely not.

"The case I've been feeding Wilcox for years. The RICO case he said he was going to use to send himself right to the top of the FBI's food chain."

Kurtz opened the door and invited Corker in. "Let's go to the kitchen. I'll make some coffee. You look like you could use it. Just keep your voice down, okay? My wife went back to bed, and my daughter is sleeping."

Corker followed Kurtz through the house to the kitchen.

"How long have you been meeting with Wilcox?" Kurtz said as he began to brew a pot of coffee.

"What? You're the one that assigned him to me."

"So you've been meeting with him ever since? Where?"

"At the safe house in Strawberry Plains. We've met once a month."

"And you've provided him with what?"

"What the hell?" the sheriff said. He felt like his head was about to explode. "What is happening here? He didn't give you anything?"

"Calm down and just answer the question. What have you provided to Agent Wilcox?"

"Anything he wanted. Tapes, mostly, and money. Video and photographs. I can't tell you how many times I put my life on the line for you guys. I did the same for that DEA guy Wilcox brought in."

"DEA? What's his name?"

"Higgins. But I haven't seen him in quite a while. He came in and acted all gung ho, but then he said he had bigger fish to fry and he left."

"Hang on a minute," Wilcox said. He picked up his cell phone and left the room. He returned a few minutes later, scowling.

"I'm afraid I have some bad news," Kurtz said. "There is no case, and Wilcox is AWOL. He's in the wind. Nobody has heard from him since Tuesday night. We talked to his wife Wednesday, and she said he went out to meet an informant and didn't come back. We thought maybe he was dead. And I just talked to the DEA. There is no Higgins around here. Never has been."

"I don't understand. How can there be no case? How is any of this possible?"

"Wilcox came to me not long after I put the two of you together and said Morris had refused to get into the protection racket. Without the district attorney, we didn't have an official misconduct case, and we'd promised you immunity. He said he was closing it down, and I didn't have any reason to believe otherwise. He's been working bank robberies and counterterrorism. He never mentioned you."

"So he just spent an hour with me once a month and collected the money? It was all a ruse? But what about Roby Penn and all the others? What about the lawyer in Nashville?"

"What lawyer in Nashville?"

"The one I take money to every month. Same cut as me and Morris. He gives it to somebody down there. I don't have any idea who it is, but I thought maybe it was the governor. He's obviously some big shot."

"We'll just have to get into it," Kurtz said. "Like I said, Wilcox told me he was no longer running a case with you, but that's obviously changed. He's gone from a potentially missing agent to a thief and a traitor to the bureau. We'll deal with him, and we'll check into this lawyer you're talking about."

"I can't believe Wilcox took that money," the sheriff said. "He took all the money I'd given him for these past three years and all the money that was supposed to be my share when Clancy was running things. I wouldn't spend it, so I wound up just burying it. When I came to you guys, I dug all of it up and gave it to Wilcox, too."

"How much did he take, total, assuming he really did this?"

"Oh, he did it all right, and he let four people die in the process. He had upward of six million."

"Shit," Kurtz said. "He could be anywhere with that kind of money."

"But you'll find him."

"I don't know what will happen. We'll most likely go after him with everything we have, but the bureau doesn't like to be embarrassed. We'll do it quietly. We don't like the public thinking one of our agents could be capable of something like this."

"What about whoever is taking money in Nashville? That'd be your responsibility."

"That's a little above my pay grade," Kurtz said. "I'll have to get back to you on that."

The sheriff slumped his shoulders and shook his head. "Man, Wilcox sure had me fooled. I'd like to snap his neck like a twig. What do you reckon he did with all that evidence I gave him?"

"Best guess? It's all up in smoke. I'll bet he burned every bit of it out there in back of that safe house."

"I guess these murders are on me now," the sheriff said. "I have to figure out a way to arrest my uncle and the man that was with him without getting myself killed."

The sheriff decided not to tell Kurtz he was the driver of the boat, but the thought of arresting Roby terrified him. And Harley wouldn't come in easy, either. The Shakers and the Penns were cut of the same cloth, and it was rough.

"I wish we could help you," Kurtz said, "but it's out of our jurisdiction."

The sheriff knew that was bullshit. Gambling was against federal law, too, as was transporting men and dogs and chickens across state lines for fights and for the purpose of gambling. But when the feds didn't feel like fooling with something, they always just said, "Sorry, out of our jurisdiction."

"You'll at least handle your end?" the sheriff said. "You'll tell your superiors at the FBI what Wilcox did and start tracking him down? And you'll start looking into Nashville?"

"I will," Kurtz said. "And I'm sorry for what Wilcox did. It isn't my fault, but it also isn't typical of the FBI. I think you know that."

"I'm gonna go now," the sheriff said. "Thanks for the coffee."

He got up and walked out of the house. The cup of coffee remained on the counter where Kurtz had set it down. It was still steaming. Corker hadn't touched it.

CHAPTER 30

I didn't sleep that night. The images of the masked man walking up to Gwyn Morris and shooting her at point-blank range in the back of the head kept running through my head, over and over and over. The images of Morris being shot would follow in a seemingly endless, bloody loop. I was reminded, once again, of how fragile life is and how quickly it can be taken. I felt bad for Morris's children and wondered whether they even knew. Who would tell them? What would they say to them?

I got out of bed at 5:00 a.m. and went for a run. My legs were heavy because of the lack of rest, and I struggled the entire way. I got back to my apartment at six, fully expecting the sheriff to be waiting for me, but there was nobody there and nobody came. As the morning went on, I kept a close eye on the news reports that were updated fairly regularly on the *News Sentinel*'s website. As it turned out, there had been four other murders in Knoxville that night. Two of them appeared to be gang related, but two others were not. Jim Harrison, Morris's bagman, was found dead in his car near an old warehouse just south of Knoxville. He'd been shot twice in the head. The other was Leslie Saban, Morris's girlfriend. She was shot in her apartment sometime during the night. The paper didn't say anything about the murders being related, and Sheriff Corker and his investigators weren't saying anything. I knew better, though. Sheriff Corker was definitely tying off loose ends. If Morris was going to be out of office, then Corker was making sure nobody would be going to the FBI or the TBI. Dead men—and women—tell no tales.

I called Claire at noon.

"Four of them in one night," I said. "These people are a lot nastier than I thought. Did you know about the girlfriend?"

"Of course I knew about the girlfriend."

"Why didn't you use her?"

"Because the information we had on her wasn't exactly something you put on a billboard or whisper in a newspaper reporter's ear unless you're willing to share definitive proof, and we weren't willing to share. We had some excellent photos and some very clear video- and audio-tape, but they were gathered by people we don't want anyone to know about. It didn't matter, though. We were going to beat him by a landslide, anyway."

"I've always heard that all is fair in love and politics," I said. "Do you mind telling me what you didn't want to put on a billboard?"

"Our people had tape and video and photos of Morris giving her drugs. She had a habit before they met that escalated. She wound up getting busted by the Knoxville cops. She asked him to use his influence to get her out of the jam, but these cops wanted money. So Morris apparently got the sheriff to start sending a fairly large amount of pills his way each month, and he gave them to Leslie Saban. She sold them and gave two vice cops a cut. Her charges were dropped."

"You just can't make this stuff up," I said.

"How did *you* know about her, come to think of it?" Claire said.

"I might have followed Morris one day and just sort of stumbled across her."

"And why would you have been following him?"

"No particular reason. I was just curious about how he went about his day."

"What else did you know about her?"

"Not much. The paper said she was a third-year law student at the University of Tennessee."

"She'd done an internship at the district attorney's office," Claire said. "That's how they met."

I remembered thinking she was probably a law student, but I didn't say anything to Claire about it. And I thought about the shoe box Morris was carrying the day I saw him go into her apartment. The box must have been full of drugs.

"Has anyone from the sheriff's department been in contact with you?" Claire said.

"No, not a peep."

"I guess no news is good news as far as they're concerned."

"I just hope they don't try to pin any of these killings on me."

"There's no way they could, is there?"

"I don't think so, but it's happened to me before. So what now? Who takes over at the district attorney's office?"

"Generally, if an elected official dies in office, someone is appointed to replace him until the next election. But since the next election is only two days away and you're obviously going to win because you're now unopposed, there won't be any point in putting someone else in the office. Normally, you wouldn't take over until the first day of January, but under these circumstances, I think my grandfather will call the governor and persuade him to appoint you to replace Morris immediately."

"So I'll start when? Wednesday?"

"They'll have a criminal court judge swear you in first thing Wednesday morning."

"Are you serious? I don't think I'm ready."

I wasn't ready. I'd never done anything remotely similar.

"You don't have any choice. You wanted to be the district attorney general, and now you've gotten what you wanted. It's time to hit the ground running."

CHAPTER 31

The cops finally did show up, around three o'clock in the afternoon. There were two of them, both men, one younger and one older. I didn't recognize either of them as they flashed their badges at me, but there was a sleaze factor about them I noticed immediately. One introduced himself as Detective Henry Scott. He was a black man, about forty-five, with a potbelly and a closely trimmed goatee. He was wearing a brown leather jacket and tinted wire-framed glasses. He also smelled like a teenager on his way to the prom, the result of entirely too much repugnant cologne. The guy reminded me of someone straight out of the seventies. The other man was early thirties, an acne-scarred kid named Josh Pence with long, scraggly, sandy-blond hair, a beard, and a screw-you attitude. I'd cross-examined guys like them dozens of times in court and had learned that to them, lying was a second language. I knew before they put their badges away they were vice, most likely narcotics.

I invited them in, which seemed to surprise them, and offered them bottles of water. We sat down at my kitchen counter, and I said, "What can I do for you gentlemen?"

"Looks like you might be the new district attorney," Henry Scott said.

"Wednesday morning, from what I'm told."

"Heard about the murders last night?"

"Is that a rhetorical question? Of course I've heard. Does this place look like a cave to you? I hated to hear it, too. I didn't like Morris, but I didn't want him dead. I was looking forward to putting him in jail after I beat him."

"That's funny," the young detective said, and he let out a short chuckle. "The thought of you putting people in jail."

The smirk he wore on his face was something that definitely needed to go, and I was in just the right mood to remove it.

"Oh yeah, Pence? Was that your name, Pence? Why would you say that?"

I already knew the answer, but I just wanted to bait him.

"Because everybody and his brother knows you should be *under* the damned jail if not on death row."

"That right, wiseass? You got proof of that?"

"You got some stones, man," Pence said. "Everybody's talking about it. I mean, running for district attorney after all the shit you've pulled and gotten away with? You're a legend in your own mind."

"And you're a punk with a smart mouth. I'd be careful about who I judge, especially when you're nothing but a phony who goes out on the street, does drugs with people, gets them to trust you, and then busts them for trusting you. You're worse than most of the criminals out there, as far as I'm concerned. You're a professional snitch. A rat with a badge."

"Fuck you, man," Pence said. "Maybe me and you should step outside."

"You go outside if you want. If you talk me into coming with you, you'll just wind up in the hospital. You also might want to keep in mind that it won't be long before you're going to be bringing cases to my office for me to present to the grand jury. I'm sure you know the district attorney makes all the calls on all those cases. So before you open that piehole of yours again, you might want to try thinking things through a little."

"Whoa, now, whoa," Scott said. "We're getting off on the wrong foot here."

They were definitely getting off on the wrong foot. All I'd done, as far as I was concerned, was let them into my home. I was beginning to regret that decision, and they were extremely close to being rudely ejected.

"What do you want?" I said.

"Mind if I ask you where you were last night?" Scott said.

"Yeah, I mind. I don't talk to cops. I exercise my right to remain silent as a matter of principle. Why do you want to know?"

"We're investigating the death of Leslie Saban."

I thought about it for a second. Morris and his wife were killed in the county, which made the case Sheriff Corker's jurisdiction. Harrison was killed at an abandoned warehouse in the county. Also Corker's jurisdiction. But Saban lived in an apartment in the city.

"You guys are vice," I said. "I think we've already established that. You're not homicide, so why are you out investigating a murder?"

"We do double duty when one of our informants gets popped," Scott said.

Shit. The cops Claire had told me about were sitting in my kitchen. Two dirty cops, having taken advantage of both Leslie Saban and Stephen Morris. I couldn't resist having a little fun at their expense.

"Leslie Saban was an informant? So you know she was sleeping with Morris."

Scott's eyebrows raised, and his mouth dropped open a little. He looked over at his partner, then back at me. "What makes you think she was sleeping with Morris?"

My patience was running thinner by the second, but I really wanted to mess with their heads. Instead, Scott had apparently decided to play some mind games of his own.

"Doesn't matter," I said. "She was sleeping with him. You know it and I know it."

"We didn't know she was sleeping with him," Scott said.

"Man, you guys are in way over your heads," I said. "Was everything Stephen Morris touched corrupt? The way I understand it, you two got lucky and popped Leslie Saban on a possession with intent to resell, a felony, and she got her boyfriend, Stephen Morris, to ask you to back off. But you guys had no doubt heard that Morris is a corrupt prick, so you decided to shake him down a little. In exchange for agreeing to drop the charges, you got Morris to agree to get yet another member of the law enforcement community to provide Leslie with enough pills so that she could sell them and make a good profit. You two took a percentage of that profit. Ring a bell? I know what you're wondering right now. Where is this man getting his information? Especially because the information is accurate. Am I right? Do you feel like you've taken a hit of LSD right now? Are your minds absolutely blown?"

Both of them looked like they were about to vomit.

"You, Detective Scott, probably needed a new leather jacket or a nice car for your girlfriend. Detective Pence probably has a really serious Viagra addiction. So you set it up, and you probably let the other dealers around know that Leslie was protected so nobody robbed her or killed her. But somebody obviously didn't get the message. I swear, this whole town is a cesspool. The county is bad, but I didn't know until recently that Morris had scams in the city, too. So why did you come by here, really? Why would you even think I killed Morris's girlfriend?"

"Because it's what you do, man," Pence said. "You wiped out your competition, his wife, his girl, and his best friend all in one night, and we intend to prove it."

He was trying to act tough, but the bravado wasn't working.

"Yeah, well, good luck with that one," I said. "You can go now. In the meantime, I suggest you both resign before I get settled into the office Wednesday and start looking around at corruption in the city's narcotics division. You might even want to leave the state."

CHAPTER 32

I hit the ground running just a few days later. There were thirty-five lawyers in the office besides me—thirty-six until Jim Harrison was murdered. There was a support staff of thirty-six that included receptionists, victim-witness coordinators, a legislative liaison, three investigators, grant writers, and several others who performed a variety of jobs.

The first couple of days I was in office, courts were in session all over the county so I couldn't just shut everything down and meet with everyone. I had a secretary call Morris's father and ask where his family wanted the things from his office moved. Then I asked her to hire a moving company to take Morris's things where his father directed. I know it must have appeared hard-hearted to those in the office, but the space was already tight and there really wasn't anything else I could have done. Meanwhile, I watched the news reports very closely. Sheriff Tree Corker said they were all over this investigation, that they would find the killer or killers of Stephen Morris and his wife and Jim Harrison if they had to chase them to the gates of hell.

All you have to do is chase yourself into the bathroom and look in the mirror, I thought.

That Saturday morning, a week after the murders, at seven, I rented a banquet room at a hotel in Knoxville out of my own pocket and made sure everyone in the office knew that attendance was mandatory. Claire came with me. I'd asked her to stay on a couple of extra weeks

Justice Lost

to help me get things organized, and she'd agreed. She already had an organizational chart for the office prepared. All we had to do was fill in the boxes with real people.

I also rented a suite in the motel where I could interview people privately while Claire talked to the group. She outlined the organizational chart and informed them how things would be run in the future. The dockets would be tightened up. Cases wouldn't be continued without a legitimate reason. If a police officer was subpoenaed to court and didn't show up for his or her case, it would be dismissed and his shift commander and the police chief would be notified immediately. It was the same with the sheriff's department. If officers were going to arrest people and bring cases, they had to show up for court.

I started interviewing the lawyers who had been with the DA's office the longest, and I asked them four questions: What did they think about Morris? What did they think about Jim Harrison? What did they think about Ben Clancy when he was the district attorney? And what did they think about the job the investigators in the office were doing? I encouraged them to be open and honest and promised their answers would remain confidential. They were leery of me, of course, but one of them, a salt-and-pepper-haired, fifteen-year veteran named Tom Masoner who prosecuted violent crime in criminal court and didn't seem to care much about what anybody thought of him, spoke right up.

"Morris was spineless, and I think he was a criminal," Masoner said. "I hate to speak ill of the dead, but he had to be skimming money, and a lot of it, from somewhere. Go take a look at his house and how he lived. I knew him when he was an assistant DA, before he beat Clancy, and he lived very frugally. Maybe he inherited a ton or maybe his wife hit the lottery, but he invited me to his house about six weeks ago and I was stunned. Luxury everywhere."

"I know," I said. "It's one of the things I became aware of during the campaign. What about Jim Harrison? What did you think of him?"

"A secretive weasel whose only purpose seemed to be to follow Morris around with his nose up his ass."

"Clancy?"

"Don't get me started. What he did to you was terrifying. If my wife hadn't just given birth to our second child, I would have quit over that."

"What do you think happened to Clancy?"

Masoner smiled and winked at me. "I think someone he railroaded—and you weren't the only one he railroaded—removed him from the gene pool. And if someone removed him from the gene pool, that someone did the rest of us a favor."

"Do you know the investigators who work in the office?"

"Of course. Their real names are Colton, Peete, and Dufner, but I call them Wynken, Blynken, and Nod. You know the poem? They're sleepy children in search of fantasy fish. They never catch a thing. They do nothing. Have you seen them?"

"As a matter of fact, I haven't."

"They go about nine hundred pounds between the three of them. I guarantee you they're sleeping through the meeting downstairs right now and they wiped out half the pastry table before the rest of us got near it."

"So they don't get out and investigate? They don't make cases?"

"Didn't you hear me? They eat doughnuts. If you want to find them at nearly anytime during the day, you can go to the break room. There'll be about a ninety percent shot they'll be stuffing their faces."

I smiled at him, leaned toward him, and reached my hand out. "You're my guy," I said.

He shook the hand and said, "What do you mean?"

"You're going to be second in command in the office. I need someone I can trust, and although I've known you for only about ten minutes, I think I can trust you. You're going to decide which lawyers get assigned to the criminal courts. I want aggressive litigators and trial lawyers, not pussies who plea-bargain everything on the docket. If there's deadwood, figure out a way to get rid of it and recruit some real lawyers. I'll find a way to get you a raise. You up for that?"

Masoner nodded and smiled back at me. "Finally, a man who recognizes true talent when he sees it."

I thought Masoner might, eventually, come to the realization that I was a man who operated in the gray areas of the law, that things weren't always rigid. But I also thought he might be okay with it, as long as I was able to keep him from knowing too much. Besides, I wasn't planning on running a dirty office. It would be clean, and I was sincere about getting aggressive trial lawyers and litigators into the criminal courts. I just hoped he'd be able to deal with my affinity for the Tipton family—and maybe certain other things—if the need arose.

"I think we're going to get along well," I said. "And I'm going to have some stuff coming down the pike I think you'll enjoy."

"What kind of stuff?"

"Can't tell you yet. I think I trust you, but not enough."

"Sounds like fun. When do I start this housecleaning?"

"Monday, but before you do, I need to ask you another question. How well do you know the TBI agents in the Knoxville office?"

"I know all of them pretty well."

"I need an intro. And it needs to be a good one."

CHAPTER 33

At Granny's request, that Saturday night Claire and I made a trip up the mountain to visit the Tiptons. Granny hadn't told me she was planning a party, but that's exactly what it was. A victory party for the new district attorney of Knox County was being held on top of a mountain in Sevier County by a woman who had committed plenty of criminal acts during her lifetime and would no doubt commit more. It was cold on the mountain that night, so the extended Tipton family, several people I didn't know, Claire, and I ate in Eugene's house, which was much larger than Granny's. It was one of those grand-scale log cabins, and it was beautiful. Once we'd eaten and the table was cleared, four guys started pulling musical instruments out of cases, and before I knew it, a full-blown, knee-slapping bluegrass concert was going on in Eugene's living room. People spilled out onto the wraparound deck, and Eugene and Ronnie built a huge fire about a hundred feet from the cabin. I tried to stick with beer, but when the Tiptons were involved, moonshine inevitably became a part of the party. Even Claire gave in to Granny's persuasion, and it wasn't long before I saw her loosen up and look at me in a way that made me think I'd best keep my distance from her or we'd wind up doing something we'd later regret.

The people at the party were the Tiptons' friends and employees. A few of them looked vaguely familiar—I'd probably seen them at the last party I'd attended at Granny's—but for the most part I didn't know a soul outside of the Tipton family and Claire. Granny had made an impromptu speech before we ate and announced to everyone that I was the new district attorney of Knox County and that some very lucrative new opportunities were going to be opening up for their family "business." Everybody seemed to be in a fine mood, and I was definitely the guest of honor and the man of the hour.

There was something I wanted to talk to Granny about, though, and I was worried about how she would react. The Tiptons had made a great deal of money selling prescription drugs over the years. The market was huge and growing by the day. I didn't know exactly how their operation worked, but Granny had obviously figured out a way to secure a reliable supplier because I hadn't seen any signs that they were manufacturing the drugs. I figured the Tiptons then sold the pills to distributors, who sold to dealers, who sold to users. That was the way other operations I'd seen throughout my career worked, and they were probably the same. Granny had mentioned moving into Knox County when I was elected, but I didn't want her dealing drugs in the county where I was the DA.

When I was doing the rubber-chicken circuit, I'd heard of all the devastation prescription pills were causing: the suicides, the overdoses, the breaking up of marriages and alienation of extended families, the extremely ugly damage the drugs had inflicted on innocent children. I'd decided I couldn't condone it. I wanted to spend time and resources going after the people who brought drugs into the county and ruined people's lives. I wanted to shut down doctors who operated pill mills. District attorneys around the country were banding together and beginning to file lawsuits against the drug manufacturers who made billions and didn't give a damn about the carnage their products caused. I could handle the gambling, but I didn't want to stand idly by and look the other way while Granny and her family imported drugs into Knox County.

I walked over to Granny, who was standing by the fire wrapped in a heavy coat and wearing a stocking cap on her head.

"Can we talk for a little while?" I said.

"Sure, let's take a walk."

There was no snow on the ground, but it was in the thirties, with a slight, damp breeze blowing. The ground was firm beneath my feet, and the fire cast a warm glow and caused shadows to jump along the ridges and trees that looked like ancient spirits who had come out to dance at the edge of the forest.

"Have you gotten started at your new job?" Granny said.

"I have. Didn't have any choice, really, and I haven't gotten much done. But I went in Wednesday and have been pretty much nonstop ever since. We even met with a bunch of employees for most of the day today."

"Terrible what happened to Morris," she said. "I suppose I could understand if they thought Morris would turn rat on them, but his wife? That wasn't right."

"They didn't just kill his wife. They killed his girlfriend, too."

"That young girl that was in the news that got murdered the same night? That was Morris's girlfriend?"

"Yeah. Morris apparently gave her drugs to sell and to take. Talk about dating the wrong guy at the wrong time. And the lawyer who got shot in his car was Morris's bagman. They definitely wanted to shut everybody up."

"You got any ideas on who might have done it?" Granny said.

"I have suspicions. I was hoping you might help me out."

"It was probably Roby Penn," Granny said.

"Could have been," I said. "I've been hearing about him for months, and none of it has been good."

I didn't know why, but I was uncomfortable sharing what I'd seen when I was sitting on the water the night Morris was killed. I didn't want to tell her about the pearl-handled pistols. Besides, I couldn't positively identify anyone. I hadn't gotten a look at a single face.

"From everything I know about Roby Penn," Granny said, "he's a bad *hombre* and getting worse by the minute. He has to go, and soon."

"How?" I said.

"We're counting on you, Darren. You'll figure something out."

I was beginning to wonder whether I really could do anything about Roby Penn. He seemed so deeply ingrained in what was going on in the county, and he was so violent, that I didn't know whether I could take him on. I decided I'd worry about it later. "Do you by any chance have any idea what happened to that marine? You've heard about him, right?"

"Yeah, I've heard, and I think I know what happened. There's a big network of men who attend those bare-knuckle fights in counties all over the Appalachians. They send out mass text messages when the fights are going to happen. Eugene and Ronnie know more about it than I do, but they've told me some things. The mass text seems like a stupid way to operate because it seems to me the cops could come in, grab up one phone, and they'd have everybody on the list. But the police just aren't interested in what they're doing, because they do it in counties where they know they can pay people off."

"Right, but back to the question. Do you know who killed Gary Brewer?"

"The word I got is that when the fight started, the marine knocked the boy he was fighting—name's Harley Shaker out of Cocke County— knocked him down and spat on him. Now I don't know Harley Shaker personally, but I know some of the Shaker family, and I would think that if you spit on one of them, even during a fight, you would do so at your peril. It'd be looked at the same as pissing on him."

"So Brewer spit on this Harley Shaker, and Shaker beat him to death?"

"That's what people who ain't supposed to be saying anything are saying."

"Heard anything about what happened to his body?"

Granny shook her head. "When something like that happens, everybody runs. So I haven't heard anybody say what happened to the body. My guess, though, is that Roby Penn would have had to take care of it. It happened at his place, from what I hear. He would have cleaned up the mess."

I was wearing gloves, but my fingers were beginning to tingle so I shoved my hands in my jacket pocket.

"What else do you know about Roby Penn?" I said.

"Quite a bit, but probably not as much as I should. They say you should keep your friends close and your enemies closer. Roby's an enemy and he doesn't even know it. I should know more about him. I know his family is from around here, that he had kinfolk who served in World War II, and that he enlisted and went to Vietnam. Wound up getting wounded. I know that a couple of years after he got out, the state government came in and wanted a piece of his property to build a highway. He told them to go to hell, so they took it under eminent domain. When they came out with the bulldozers to start the work, Roby started firing at them with a deer rifle. He could have killed several of them, but he didn't. Still, they gave him six years in prison for it. Then his son got killed in Iraq by his own guys. What do they call that? Friendly fire?"

"Yeah, that's it. Friendly fire."

"The army tried to cover it up. Roby stayed on them, though, and the truth finally came out. Several years ago, after he'd done the six years in prison, he quit filing income tax returns and quit paying taxes. That cost him another year, but he had to go to a federal pen. So he's had run-ins with local, state, and federal governments, and he hates them all. He's in his midsixties now, and these murders tell me he might be going off the deep end."

"So you want me to go at Roby the old-fashioned way or the newfangled way? Old-fashioned is figure out a way to get him into a confrontation and kill him. Newfangled is the cop way. Get informants in, do surveillance, and get him on tape. Find out who was with him when he killed Morris and his wife and jumped in the boat. Put all of them on trial and in prison."

Granny stopped and looked up at me. "Jumped in the boat? What are you talking about?"

"Nothing. Just a theory. I've already heard around the office that they escaped from Morris's house on the water."

She gave me a look that told me she didn't necessarily believe me, but she turned and started walking again. "I don't think you're going to get him the cop way. Do you know the tie between Roby Penn and the sheriff?"

"I think I've heard they're related, but I don't know how exactly."

"Roby is Tree Corker's mother's oldest brother, which makes him Tree's uncle."

"Nepotism at its finest," I said.

"That's how it's usually done. Now what was it you want to talk to me about?"

I took a deep breath and let it out slowly.

"Must be bad," she said.

"Granny, you've been so good to me, and I know when I agreed to do this district attorney thing I said you could do whatever you want, but I've changed my mind about part of it. I'd like to ask you to please not sell any drugs in Knox County. When I was out campaigning, I talked to so many people whose families had been devastated by drugs, people whose lives had been ruined. You can take on as many gambling rackets as you want, and if you insist on doing the drug trade, I won't go back on what I said, but would you please consider not selling the drugs in Knox County? It would be a huge favor to me."

"We could build that county into a million-dollar-a-year enterprise just with the pills," she said. "Probably more."

"You'll make twice that off the gambling."

"You know the old saying 'You must be talking out of your butt because your mouth has to know better?'"

"But the gambling is still good, right? With the other money you're already pulling in from other counties, how much do you need?"

"I hate the drugs, Darren. Always have. Eugene and Ronnie handle most of that side of the business because it turns my stomach. The kind of people you have to deal with, the class of people, is just disgusting. That's why we got out of it for a while. But it's just so lucrative it's hard to walk away, especially when you've been as poor as we were back in the days when my husband was alive and we went to church and followed the laws and acted like sheep in a herd. He had his little side hustles like the bar and a couple of trailers out back, but when he died, we barely had a pot to piss in, and I had to scratch and claw just to keep this place going and keep food in our bellies and clothes on our backs. That's when I made up my mind I was going to get rich and wasn't going to be poor ever again. There just can't ever be too much money."

"So I can't talk you out of it," I said.

She breathed deeply, stopped again, and looked me square in the eye.

"We can make a deal," she said. "You becoming the district attorney has been good, Darren. Good for you, good for us. But Roby's gone off the deep end if he killed Morris and the others. I can't say it for sure, but I'm usually right about these things. With Morris gone, Roby will dig in deeper than a tick in a dog's neck and dare you or anybody else to try and stop him. You can try using your informants, you can try making arrests, putting pressure on people. Maybe eventually you'll get enough to arrest and convict him, but it's going to take a long time, and if you take your shot and you miss, he'll come after you."

"So what are you saying, Granny?"

"Kill him, Darren," she said. "It'll be just like Clancy. We'll help you if you need us, and once it's over, we'll all be better off. And if you kill him, I promise we won't sell a single pill in your county."

PART III

CHAPTER 34

The summons from the governor of the state of Tennessee came early Sunday morning in the form of a telephone call from Senator Roger Tate, negating the need for Tom Masoner, my new best buddy at the DA's office, to get me some intros at the TBI. Senator Tate said I was to meet the governor, along with several other "heavy hitters," at the Tennessee Bureau of Investigation's headquarters in Strawberry Plains Monday at 8:00 a.m. sharp. The senator said neither he nor Claire would be attending.

I walked in the next morning wearing my best suit—the charcoal one Claire had purchased for me before the political rally. When I walked through the door, the governor looked at me in a way that made me feel small and insignificant, and I suppose I was, compared with a couple of the others in the room. The governor—a Republican, Theo Bradbury—sat at the head of the table. He was flanked by the director of the Tennessee Bureau of Investigation, the commissioner of the Tennessee Department of Safety & Homeland Security, the chief of police of Knoxville, and the high sheriff of Knox County, Tree Corker. Noticeably absent were representatives from the federal government. There wasn't a US attorney or an FBI agent in sight.

"Gentlemen," the governor said after everyone was seated, "I'm here to impress upon you the importance of solving these hideous murders that took place last Saturday. I mean, can you imagine the way the people of this district, and people all over Tennessee, are feeling at this minute? They're feeling unsafe and wondering whether the people they've elected to represent them can protect them. The fact that a person or persons would walk into the home of an elected district attorney general and kill both him and his wife is simply unfathomable to me. The fact that an assistant district attorney general was murdered on the same night—in his car at an abandoned warehouse—is also extremely disturbing. I've heard rumors, though no one has been able to confirm them, that the young Saban woman who was killed that night was also involved with General Morris. This case has to be tied off with no loose ends, it has to have palatable explanations for the public, and it has to be done right away. Sheriff Corker, your department has immediate jurisdiction over the case. What can you share with us?"

Corker looked uncomfortable. Beads of sweat were visible on his forehead, and his face was pinker than usual.

"I agree, it's horrible and it's important," Corker said. "We've put every resource we have into the case."

"What do you have? Are there any leads? Anything promising?"

Corker shook his head. "I'm sorry, Governor, but we have very little right now."

"Have you interviewed any suspects?"

The question came from Hanes Howell III, the director of the TBI, who was sitting to my left. He was in his midfifties, a balding, light-skinned black man who looked more like a superbureaucrat than a superagent. He'd been head of the agency for twelve years and had just been appointed by the governor to another six-year term. I'd heard early in my law career that the director of the TBI answered to no one and had done some research. It was true. He was appointed by the governor, but he had free rein. Nobody looked over his shoulder, which, I believed, was deemed necessary to make him an effective leader.

"Unfortunately, we don't have any suspects," Corker said.

"No suspects?" Howell said. "You have a man who is about to go up for reelection—and get badly beaten, from what I understand—who is murdered in his home along with his wife. This man is the district attorney and makes roughly a hundred and fifty thousand dollars a year, yet he lives on twenty acres on the lake in a six-thousand-square-foot home and has a garage full of luxury cars. Have you checked bank accounts, credit card receipts, safe-deposit boxes? Is his family wealthy?"

"We're checking into all of those things," Tree said.

"You're checking? It's been more than a week! What have you found?"

"I don't appreciate you talking to me in that tone of voice," Corker said. "You have no jurisdiction here."

"Unless the new district attorney general asks me for help," Howell said.

Tennessee law allowed local district attorney generals to ask the Tennessee Bureau of Investigation for help on matters or investigations in which the local resources may not have been adequate.

"We don't need your help," Corker barked. "We're on it, I'm telling you. All of my investigators are on it, all of my people. We're checking every lead, every angle."

"What about the girlfriend?" Howell said.

"What about her?"

"You've interviewed friends and family, gone through her financials, correct? Anything significant?"

"The girlfriend isn't my case. You'll have to talk to the chief about her."

Howell turned his attention to the Knoxville police chief, a man named Jim Boswell. Boswell was nearing retirement. He looked tired and didn't seem to want to be involved.

"What has your investigation revealed, Chief?" Howell said.

"Not much other than she was having an affair with Morris. No forensics to speak of. We found a couple of small things and sent them off to the lab, but I'm not too hopeful."

I thought briefly about informing Boswell that two of his vice cops knew Leslie Saban well, but I decided to keep it to myself. I'd no doubt have to work with him in the future, and I didn't think a couple of small-timers like Scott and Pence were worth burning the bridge.

"What about Jim Harrison?" Howell said, turning his attention back to the sheriff. "Any theory as to why he was murdered?"

"We're looking into it," Corker said.

I wanted to reach across the table and slap Corker. He'd calmed down some, his complexion had lightened a bit, and he was becoming smug.

"This absolutely will not stand," Governor Bradbury said. "What about you, Mr. Street? Or I suppose I should call you General Street now, correct? Do you have any theories on just what is going on in this mess of a district you've inherited?"

Not only did I have theories; I'd seen two of the murders that had been committed. However, that didn't mean I had cases I could take to court and prove to a jury. But Roby Penn and Tree Corker had ramped things up significantly when they decided to silence their victims in The Election Massacre, as the papers had begun to call the murders.

"I have some theories," I said, "but I have to rely on the sheriff here to bring me proof, and so far, I haven't seen anything. He hasn't asked us to help with subpoenas or warrants. He hasn't asked for a thing. So the only thing I can assume is that the sheriff isn't at a point where he needs those things."

"I'm not," Corker said. "Don't need subpoenas or warrants, at least not yet. When we get to that point, we'll come knocking."

"And when might that be?" the governor said.

"I just don't know," Corker said. "Cases go unsolved sometimes. Criminals are clever. There wasn't a single piece of forensic evidence at Morris's home outside of the bullets that got taken out of the victims' heads," Corker said. "The killer or killers even picked up the shell casings, unless they were using revolvers. Ballistics hasn't told us yet exactly what kind of gun the bullets came from. My forensics team didn't find a hair, a fiber, a footprint, or a fingerprint, not even a partial. It was like a ghost committed those crimes. As for Harrison, same thing."

"What about phones?" Howell said.

"What about them?"

"I assume you've gone through the call logs and contacts and all the other data on the victims' phones."

"We have. We haven't found a thing."

Corker was lying through his teeth, which was exactly what I'd expected him to do, but there was nothing I could do about it, at least not at the moment.

"And I don't suppose you ever made any progress on the marine you were looking for, Gary Brewer?" Howell said.

"The new investigation has taken priority over Mr. Brewer," the sheriff said.

The governor looked around the room. "Does anyone have anything else to say?"

There was so much I wanted to say I was practically bursting. My heart rate was up and my hands were trembling.

"Then I guess I've wasted my time," Governor Bradbury said.

He got up and stormed out the door, followed quickly by everyone else. As soon as I got to my car, I dug my throwaway cell phone out of my briefcase and called Claire.

"Can you get ahold of your grandfather on short notice?" I said.

"Usually."

"Good, because I need to talk to the director of the TBI. Have him call me at this number on a secure phone before he leaves to go back to Nashville."

I thanked Claire, hung up the phone, and drove toward my new office, hoping he would call.

CHAPTER 35

"What can I do for you, sir?" Hanes Howell's voice was cold and demanding over the phone.

I was back in my office, going through a pile of reassignments Tom Masoner had recommended. He was apparently already spreading the word, too, because my e-mail folder was full of messages from people who weren't happy. I got up, walked around the desk, and closed the door.

"Actually, there are some things I can do for you," I said.

"I certainly didn't hear anything useful in the meeting we had a little while ago."

"I know, and I'm sorry. I couldn't say much, but I need to talk to you. Alone. Someplace where nobody will see us together. And I mean nobody, including people from the TBI."

"Why would I want to talk to you, Mr. Street, unless you want to make a confession or two?"

"Because I can help you blow this whole thing out of the water."

Howell paused for a bit. "I don't believe you," he said. "If you have information pertinent to Mr. Morris's murder or any other murders, why don't you just call in my agents in Knoxville and get to work?"

"Because I have reason to believe your agents, or at least one of them, may have been compromised."

"Compromised how? Do you know what? You're really something. Your name has run across my desk more than once in the past as being a suspect in multiple murders. Now you have somehow managed to gain the ear of one of the most powerful men in the country and have gotten yourself elected to the district attorney's office in Knoxville, which means there will no longer be any investigation of you in that city for any crime you may have committed. And now you get me on the phone, tell me you can 'blow this whole thing out of the water,' yet you insult the integrity of my agents and my organization in the process. Do you really believe I want to have anything at all to do with you, despite what some washed-up old fool like Roger Tate says?"

"First off, I'd be careful about who I call a washed-up old fool if I want to keep my J. Edgar Hoover clone job. And secondly, if you could manage to put that tremendous ego of yours in your pocket for just ten minutes and give me a little time, I guarantee you won't regret it. Your agency will take down one of the most corrupt organizations in Tennessee since Ray Blanton was selling pardons out of the state capital, and you'll come out smelling like the proverbial rose."

"And you, Mr. Street? What will you get?"

"Some peace of mind. Maybe some redemption. A little more sleep."

He paused again for several seconds.

"All right. I'll talk to you at a safe house. You can't know where it is, though. I'm going to send one of my personal-security agents—the agent I trust the most—to pick you up. He'll be in a black SUV with tinted windows. You get in the van, he'll hand you a bag, you put it over your head until he takes it off."

"No cuffs," I said. "No shackles."

"You won't be a prisoner, Mr. Street, but if you want to do this in a secure fashion, then this is the best way. He can be at your apartment in twenty minutes."

"You know where my apartment is?"

"I know a lot about you, Mr. Street. Dress warmly. We'll be outside and it'll be cold."

I left the office and drove straight to my apartment. I went inside, grabbed an overcoat, some gloves, and a stocking cap, and went back outside. The SUV pulled in just a couple of minutes later, the back passenger door opened, and I climbed in.

"Put this on," a gruff voice said as a lightweight black hood landed in my lap. "Don't even look at me."

I did as the agent said, and we rolled out of the parking lot. Forty-five minutes later, the SUV stopped. From the sounds and the way the vehicle felt while I was riding, I was sure we had driven to Pigeon Forge or Sevierville or maybe even Gatlinburg. The mountains were full of chalets that people rented, and I was betting we were heading for one of them.

"Stay put," the agent said. "I'll come around and lead you in."

The door beside me opened a few seconds later, and the agent took me by the elbow. He guided me up three steps onto a porch, through a door, and we stepped into a house that had a neutral, unused smell to it. It smelled clean, like they had someone come in and dust and vacuum on a regular basis, but there weren't really any human smells outside of the agent's aftershave.

"We're going to step through some French doors, and you can take the hood off," the agent said. I did so, the agent closed the door behind me and disappeared, and there sat Hanes Howell III, wearing an overcoat, gloves, and a wide-brimmed hat. He was smoking a pipe and drinking a cup of coffee. He didn't bother to offer me one.

I was on the outdoor deck overlooking the mountains. They were beautiful, even without the colorful canopy of leaves on the trees. We were high up; I could see for miles, but I didn't recognize a single landmark. I had no idea where I was.

"Nice place," I said.

"We use it for our special snitches," Howell said.

"I think you live to annoy me. I hate the term *snitch*. Don't use it when you're referring to me."

"Because of the time you spent in prison?"

"Exactly, and I'm serious. If you call me a snitch again, I'll punch you in the mouth."

For the first time since we'd met, a smile crossed Howell's face. "You're a pugnacious little bastard, aren't you?"

"I suppose I am. I was always a little on the small side, and I've always had to fight to keep people from taking advantage of me."

"That's called a small-man complex," Howell said.

"Maybe so, but call me a snitch again and you're going to get a dose of it."

"How about we stop flexing our muscles at each other and get down to business?" Howell said.

"Fine. Where do you want to start?"

"I don't know. How about at the beginning?"

"I can't, because there are some things I can't tell you about."

"Okay, I'm wasting my time again." Howell started to get up.

"Wait," I said. "I might be pugnacious, but you're impatient and melodramatic. I have informants. I can't tell you who they are, but I'd trust some of them with my life. What my informants began telling me is that the district attorney of Knox County and the sheriff were allowing certain criminals to run their operations without fear of arrest or prosecution in return for a cut of the illegal proceeds. The operation began back when Ben Clancy was the district attorney general and Joe DuBose was the sheriff and has continued until this day."

"So we're talking ten years or more," Howell said.

"More."

"And what kind of criminals are being allowed to run their operations?"

"Cockfighters, dogfighters, bare-knuckle boxers, pimps, human traffickers, drug dealers, gamblers. Same old story. Where there's cash, there's corruption. In this case, they allow select people to run their operations without fear of arrest or prosecution or competition in exchange for a price. If a competitor comes in, the original criminal suddenly becomes an informant. It's basically an extortion scheme. The difference is that the extortion scheme isn't being run by gangsters, it's being run by the sheriff and the district attorney."

"How much money are we talking about here?"

"Millions. Check into the amount of money Stephen Morris made and compare it with the value of the assets he held at his death. If you dig deeply enough, you'll probably find some money stashed offshore, too."

"And the sheriff?"

"He's larger-than-life and he's dumber than a bag of hammers, but he knows better than to flaunt the money. From everything I know, he lives under the radar. God knows where his money is stashed."

"And what precipitated these murders, do you think?"

"I did, by coming in and beating Morris," I said. "I think once Morris realized he was going to lose his candy store, he threatened to go to law enforcement, and they killed him before he got the chance."

"Do you think the sheriff was involved in the murders?"

"I think he drove the boat that carried the murderers away from Morris's house."

"And why do you think that?"

"Because I saw it, but there's no way I could ever testify to it."

Howell pulled his pipe out of his mouth and set it on the table. "Start talking before you get yourself arrested."

I told him as much as I could, about how it started with Grace dying, about going to Morris, about how I made up my mind that I was going to run against Morris and told the TBI agents about it when they came to my door asking about Dr. Fraturra. I told him an old friend—but I wouldn't mention any names—knew Senator Tate from way back, and that he agreed to give me support and bring his granddaughter in to help me. I told him about how Senator Tate had pleaded with me to find out what had happened to the marine, Capt. Gary Brewer, and I told him what I suspected had happened. I told him about the rally and how great things were going, but that Morris just wouldn't shut up about the old, unproven allegations against me.

"I made a bad decision," I said. "I got it in my mind that if I could get him alone and talk to him, maybe even threaten him, that he'd shut up about all that old stuff."

I failed to tell him that I might very well have killed Morris myself had Roby Penn not beaten me to it. I did tell him about the surveillance I'd done and how I was sitting on the water the night two masked men murdered Morris and his wife. I told him about the boat that rolled in to pick up the men from Morris's dock and how the driver, while he was wearing a mask, was also massive and had what appeared to be two pearl-handled pistols in holsters tied to his thighs.

"I couldn't identify him positively," I said. "I couldn't identify any of them positively, but I've never seen anyone else carry pistols like those."

"So you think the sheriff was definitely one of them."

"One of them was the sheriff. He didn't pull any triggers, but he's guilty of conspiracy to commit murder and felony murder because he drove the boat. One of the others was more than likely a man named Roby Penn. He's Sheriff Corker's uncle, a fringe guy who hates the government and lives off the gambling rackets. Does really well with it, from what I've heard. Fixes a lot of bare-knuckle fights and cleans up. Bets on the roosters and the dogs and collects a gate and the juice. Operates some gambling machines, some card games, a small casino. It isn't a racket he'd want to lose. Roby is one of the sheriff's biggest producers, plus he's kin. The only other racket that would come close to the gambling they have set up is drugs, and I'm sure you know better than I do what kind of money drugs generate. The other rackets are smaller, but they all add up. Roby and the drugs are the big ones. They're the ones the sheriff would not want to lose."

"And how does the money get from all these people to Corker?"

"My informant tells me he just goes out and collects it. He isn't shy about it, either. He's like one of those small-time insurance salesmen who shows up at your house every month to collect the premium. Hell, he drives his cruiser, from what I understand."

"And what about Morris? How did he get his cut?"

"Jim Harrison was his bagman. Morris apparently had enough brains not to do business with the sheriff directly. He had Harrison collect the money. Harrison was just another loose end they tied up."

"And the girl? The Saban girl?"

"Morris was supplying her with drugs, but that isn't why they killed her. I think they killed her because they were afraid of what Morris may have told her."

"Yeah, pillow talk has gotten more than one person killed," Howell said. "And you didn't want to go to the Knoxville TBI because you figured since it's been going on for so long, somebody there must be involved?"

"I know the TBI has good informants. Hard for me to believe your guys didn't know anything about any of this, especially with all the time that has gone by."

"It's funny, you know," Howell said, suddenly taking on a semi-philosophical air. "These criminals have it made. I mean, you take these guys, for example. Probably doing a couple of million a year, maybe more, just off the gambling. Then you add the drugs and sex, and the numbers just go out the roof. But it's never enough for them, is it? They always need more. Always have to get greedy. And when they get greedy, somebody inevitably gets killed, and when somebody gets killed, they bring attention to themselves, and eventually their machine breaks down and everybody winds up either dead or in jail."

"So what do we do about it?" I said. "I've told you pretty much everything I know."

"I guess we'll have to bring folks in from all over the state and start from the beginning. We'll have to infiltrate the groups, identify the major players, start getting things on tape and on video. It's going to be a big case."

"And it's going to take a long time."

"No way around it," Howell said.

"That's what I figured."

"Is that a problem?"

"No, not a problem. I was just hoping to get some relief or some closure or whatever you want to call it for the Brewer family. I'd like to know what became of him."

"We'll find out eventually."

"Yeah, I suppose we will. So what do you want me to do? Do I just go about my business and leave them alone?"

"That would look too suspicious. Talk to the sheriff. Tell him as long as there isn't any more violence, you'll call a truce and let things stay as they are. But you don't take a dime. We're clear on that, right?"

"I don't want any of their money."

"And you might tell the sheriff he could throw you a bone by producing Gary Brewer's body, if there's a body left to produce. At least that'll look like some progress is being made. In the meantime, I'll mobilize my agents. We'll bring people in from Memphis, Nashville, Chattanooga, all over the state. You won't even know they're here, and neither will the agents in the Knoxville office. And rest assured, Mr. Street, I'll get to the bottom of what's going on in the Knoxville TBI office. I won't stand for corruption of any kind, even if it's just turning a blind eye."

"So you'll coordinate this entire thing from Nashville?"

"I will. It'll be top secret. Very, very few people will know about it, and those will only be people I can trust."

"Good," I said, and I stood up. "Now, if you don't mind, I think I'll ask your man to take me back down the mountain. I'm freezing."

Howell stepped toward me and reached out his hand. "You've done the right thing here today. Thank you for trusting us."

"Any chance I can ride back without the hood?" I said.

He shook his head. "Sorry. We have to keep you in the dark about some things."

CHAPTER 36

Claire called me at work around six to see whether I'd be home at seven. I told her I should be there by then, and an hour later, she showed up at my place holding two bottles of wine and a bag of takeout from the best Chinese place in Knoxville.

"This is a pleasant surprise," I said, reaching out to help her. She was dressed casually, but she looked as beautiful as ever.

"I'm afraid it's going to be bittersweet," she said. "I'm here to say goodbye."

I invited her in and we opened the wine. The food didn't seem appealing at the time. We sat down on the couch as I filled a couple of glasses.

"I'm surprised," I said. "I knew you'd head back eventually, but now that the time has come, I don't quite know how to feel. Do you really need to go back to the swamp? The job offer still stands."

"I appreciate it," she said, "but I'm not even licensed to practice law in the state of Tennessee. I haven't taken the bar."

"That's an easy enough fix."

"I will admit to you that I've looked through some materials," she said. "I don't think I'd have any problem passing."

I looked at her and winked. "I knew you wanted to stay," I said. "I knew you couldn't resist me."

"How did your meeting go?" she said.

"I don't know how much I should tell you, so I guess I'll just tell you everything." I recounted the day for her, including the clandestine meeting with Hanes Howell III.

"Will they arrest anybody for murder?" she said when I was finished.

"I think that depends on how strong the bond is between Sheriff Corker and his uncle, Roby Penn. If they turn them against each other, they'll have a shot."

"And what will you be doing?"

"Working my butt off. You've seen the mess at the office. It's going to take me a while just to get things running smoothly."

"I have no doubt you'll get it done," she said.

She surprised me like that sometimes. She would be difficult and stubborn, and then she would turn right around and say something kind that genuinely boosted my confidence, because I knew she wouldn't say it if she didn't think it was true.

"I couldn't have done any of this without you, Claire," I said. "Thank you. Before you came into my life, I was lost again, terribly angry, and had no real focus. I feel like I'm back on the right track now, and a lot of it is because of you. If you hadn't come along, I may very well have . . . Well, let's just leave it at I'm grateful for you."

Claire slid across the couch until her thigh was touching mine. She looked into my eyes and said, "I think we'll see each other again. I've never met anyone quite like you. You have this strength and resilience in you that anyone who gets to know you can see and comes to admire. You're like a strong tree in a hurricane, Darren, a tree that will bend and bend and bend and maybe lose some branches, but it refuses to break. I'm happy for you, and I'm glad I was able to help you achieve what you wanted to achieve here."

She kissed me gently on the cheek and lingered. I felt her warm breath on my face, smelled the faint odor of the wine mixed with her perfume. Just as I was about to reach for her, she stood.

"I'd better go," she said.

"Go? You just got here."

"I'm afraid this might get out of hand."

I stood in front of her and held her hands. "You're right. Thank you, again, Claire. Anytime you need a break from the swamp, you know where to find me."

"I hope you get what you want, Darren," she said. "I hope you find some peace."

She picked up her purse, and I watched her walk out the door. I felt the urge to run after her into the parking lot, to beg her to stay, but I resisted. Instead, I picked up the half-empty bottle of wine off the table and drained it.

CHAPTER 37

Sheriff Corker pulled his Dodge pickup into the corner of the parking-lot complex and parked next to the white Lexus. He got out and squeezed himself into the front seat of the Lexus next to the lawyer, who was beefy and wearing a tan suit and too much cologne. The lawyer pulled the shiny, expensive vehicle onto the highway and began to cruise north.

Today, the sheriff wasn't wearing his cowboy hat or his uniform or his Pythons. He wore bib overalls and a simple cap on his head. He could have been any farmer or auto-parts-store worker from any area of Tennessee. The lawyer called him "Sheriff." They'd met several years ago, when Corker had been appointed by the Knox County Commission to take over as sheriff after the previous one had fallen from a roof and died. Their early meetings had sometimes been strained, and Corker had occasionally been belligerent. But he eventually gave in, and the operation he'd become involved in had gone relatively smoothly for years. The recent developments had obviously changed some things, and the sheriff had been summoned.

Corker had done some research and learned that the lawyer was a solo practitioner by the name of Gates Turner. His website said he specialized in wills, estate planning, and trusts. Corker knew he also specialized in being a sleaze.

"Nice to see you, Sheriff," Turner said. "I hope you're doing well."

"Things are a little rough right now," Corker said. "I'm sure you know that."

"Yes, I've heard, and as much as I hate to be the bearer of bad news, they're about to get rougher."

"I don't see how they could," the sheriff said. "And what am I doing down here, anyway? It isn't time for our regular meeting. What does your client want?"

The sheriff had been instructed long ago to never refer to the lawyer's client by anything other than "your client." No name was ever uttered, nor was a title. Corker had been told to never inquire, and he never had. He hadn't really cared until he'd started—or at least thought he'd started—working with the FBI, but he hadn't been able to break through Turner's hard shell. Turner was smart and incredibly cautious. Sheriff Corker had absolutely no idea who Turner's client was, but he knew the client had to be powerful. Ben Clancy would never have agreed to give him a cut back in the beginning had the person not been in a position of great power.

"You're here because some information has come to light that has to do with you assisting the two men who murdered Stephen Morris and his wife. We have no doubt that you also had a hand in murdering Jim Harrison and Stephen Morris's girlfriend, Leslie Saban."

The sheriff nearly choked involuntarily. "Why would you think I'd get caught up in anything so stupid?"

His voice remained calm, but he was suddenly frantic. *How could they know? How could they possibly know?* He couldn't explain, though. He couldn't tell this lawyer he was a federal informant, or at least he'd *thought* he'd been a federal informant.

"I certainly agree that what you did was stupid, and so does my client," the lawyer said. "Why you did it remains a bit of a mystery, but we expect Morris was about to go to the feds and your uncle didn't take the news well."

"Why would Morris go to the feds?" the sheriff said. "He was in everything up to his eyeballs."

"We all know how it goes," Turner said. "First one to the courthouse gets the best deal."

"Nah, he was a district attorney. The judge would have put that whole violation-of-the-public-trust guilt trip on him. He would have done a bunch of time."

"Depends on how much he had to offer," Turner said. "Maybe he had a tape or two or a dozen. You didn't ever threaten him, did you, Sheriff? Because I had occasion to speak to Jim Harrison a couple of times, and Harrison intimated that the district attorney and his family may have been threatened."

"He didn't need to be threatened. He was in from day one, and he didn't want out. Darren Street is what changed things."

"What about Uncle Roby? Did he threaten Morris?"

"Roby stayed away from him. Didn't like him. And like I said, Morris was in. He was solid. He didn't need threatening."

"Then why did you kill him?" Turner said.

"I didn't kill him. I didn't have anything to do with it."

"You're lying. Why did you kill him?"

"I'm not lying. How many times do I have to tell you? I didn't kill the man. I didn't kill his wife. I didn't kill his girlfriend, and I didn't kill his bagman."

"Who did?"

"Don't know."

"If you continue to deny you were involved and don't give me the names of everyone who was, I've been instructed to tell you that we will bring down a firestorm of destruction on you that will make you wish you'd never been born. You'll find yourself in a federal penitentiary in less than a year, if you live that long. We'll kill your father, your sister, and that brother you don't give a damn about. We know you were driving the boat, Sheriff. Somebody saw you. You were wearing a mask, but you had to wear those damned Pythons strapped to your legs, didn't you?"

"Who told you that nonsense?"

"It doesn't matter. We believe him. He saw you, and now you have to answer for your stupidity. You basically have two options. You can do nothing and wait for the hammer to drop, or you can kill and get rid of the two men who helped you that night so we can get back to business as usual and not have to worry about further violence."

Tree turned his large head and stared at the lawyer.

"You realize you're asking me to kill my own kin, don't you? Roby Penn is crazy and he'd probably just as soon kill me as look at me, but he's been good to y'all. Your client and several others have made a fortune off him. I expect you've earned a little yourself."

"His decision to kill a sitting district attorney general—even one who was about to be beaten in an election—along with his decision to kill the man's wife, one of his coworkers, and his girlfriend shows us his judgment is failing."

"I'm in charge of the investigation. It isn't going to go anywhere. If y'all will just cool your jets for a while, everything will be fine."

The sheriff could feel his thighs trembling involuntarily. He knew his only hope was the FBI, but after what had transpired with that agency, he didn't have a lot of confidence in them.

"We don't believe the new district attorney general will be a problem. We have him neutralized. But we don't want more violence, especially this kind of high-profile violence."

"Neutralized? How do you have him neutralized?"

"We told him what he wanted to hear."

"You talked to him?"

"My client talked to him. He lied. Do you think Street will be a problem in the future?"

Scott Pratt

"I haven't talked to him much, but I don't think he cares about money. I'm not sure about other things. I don't know how aggressive he'll be."

"If he starts making noise," Turner said, "we'll employ other methods to settle him down."

"Why don't you just kill him?"

"If we think we need that done, we'll be in touch."

"I'm not killing him," the sheriff said.

"Of course you will if we need you to. And you'll kill Roby."

"You're out of your damned mind."

"And the other person who was with you. Who was it?"

"You don't know him."

"Answer the question."

"A guy named Harley Shaker. I'm sure you know about the marine that went missing. Harley killed him in a bare-knuckle fight. My uncle took care of the body, so he called in the marker when he decided to do something about Morris and his wife."

"Make them both go away, and do it soon," Turner said. "If we need you for Street later, I'll contact you."

The sheriff felt himself being squeezed against the passenger door as the car made a quick turnaround, and they cruised back to the apartment complex in silence.

CHAPTER 38

The trailer where Tree Corker grew up sat halfway up a hill, its base carved out of the red clay and rock beneath the surface. It was late afternoon by the time he returned from Cookeville, and the shadows were long beneath the quickly fading sun. A rusted, faded-green pickup sat in the gravel driveway, old but still operational. The place was marked by the signs of poverty, but Tree knew his daddy worked hard to keep the place looking respectable. He fixed leaks, caulked windows, painted when he could afford paint. He kept the wood-burning stove in perfect condition and spent hours cutting, splitting, and stacking firewood. Tree's daddy had always been distant, but the sheriff badly needed someone to talk to. Tree knew his daddy was honest, and he needed counsel from an honest man.

Calvin Corker greeted his son with a small wave of the hand as he was climbing down a ladder from the trailer's roof. It was a standard greeting and as much physical affection as he showed Tree. Calvin was a tall man like his son, although time and gravity had reduced his height from six feet five inches to just over six feet three. Unlike his son, he was lean and quiet. He'd spent his life as a laborer at a sawmill three miles from his home, eventually becoming the supervisor before the sawmill shut down and forced his retirement at the age of sixty.

"You're moving around pretty good for an old man," Tree said as his daddy put the ladder in a lean-to shed behind the trailer.

"You can call me old when I get to seventy," Calvin said. "Got two years of youth left in me. What brings you up this way? Got no criminals to catch?"

"I got a pretty serious problem, Daddy," Tree said. "You got a few minutes to talk?"

The sheriff saw an unfamiliar look come over his father's face. This was new ground for both of them.

"I was about to go in and fix me some supper," Calvin said. "You hungry?"

"Am I breathing?"

The two men went inside, and Calvin headed for the kitchen. Tree went to the wall near the television where there was a photo of his mother when she was eighteen years old. To Tree, she was the most beautiful thing he'd ever seen. She'd been a smoker all her life, though, and had died of complications due to emphysema and pneumonia five years earlier. Tree had yet to get over it, and he didn't believe Calvin had, either.

"Looking at the picture of your momma again?" Calvin said from the kitchen.

"Yep. Pretty as ever."

"Hard to believe she could produce something as ugly as you."

"Hard to believe she'd marry something as ugly as you."

"You know what they say: 'Love is blind.'"

"It's damned well true in this case."

Tree knew the banter was his daddy's way of showing affection, and he took no offense. They sniped whenever they were around each other and had since Tree could remember. Tree's older brother, Charles, wasn't close to the family. Charles had joined the air force right out of high school and was now living in Arlington, Texas. He'd come home once every four or five years prior to his mother's death. They hadn't heard from him since she'd died, though. Tree's sister, Charlotte, two years younger, was a music teacher in the Campbell County school system. She and her family didn't visit often, either, and Tree didn't see much need in visiting people who didn't seem to want to visit him. He believed his daddy felt pretty much the same way he did.

Tree could smell the food in the kitchen and walked in. His daddy was warming up a staple: leftover soup beans and corn bread.

"Smells good, Daddy," Tree said.

"There just ain't nothing better," Calvin said. "I don't care who you are or what you say, there ain't nothing better than a pot of soup beans and a skillet of corn bread. I believe man was made to exist on those two things."

"I don't mind a steak every now and then," Tree said.

"You can have your steak. I'll eat my beans."

Calvin plated the beans and buttered the corn bread. He put a pitcher of sweet tea on the table and sat down.

"Me or you?" he said.

"Your table," Tree said.

"You always say that," Calvin said, and he began to pray. When he was finished, he looked across the table and said, "So what do you want to chew on?"

"Big trouble brewing," Tree said. "You hear about the election and the district attorney and his wife and a couple of other people getting shot?"

"I hear things," Calvin said. "Don't take the paper, but I watch the news, and Trisha comes by now and then. You know how she likes to gossip. Roby mixed up in all this?"

"Why would you ask that?"

"Cause I know Roby. Known him all my life. He was in Vietnam when your momma and I got married. I was kinda glad, to tell you the truth. I figured he'd get liquored up at the reception and hurt some-body. You notice he didn't ever come around here when you were a boy, didn't you? He just ain't right in the head, never was after Vietnam. Your momma knew it and I knew it, and we made him stay away. Does he have you in trouble?"

"Daddy, there's a lot of things I haven't told you over the years. When I took over for Joe DuBose, it was a huge surprise to me. I mean, who was I? Country bumpkin, raised out here in the hills. You wasn't ever active in politics and neither was momma, as far as I could tell, so when they appointed me, I near fell over. Had no idea what I was doing. I'd only been on patrol for a couple of years after I finished working at the jail. Turned out Roby was the one who got me the job because he told this district attorney at the time, this man named Ben Clancy, that if he got me into the sheriff's office I'd do whatever Roby told me to do. And that's what I did for a while. I was a coward."

"So they been using you," Calvin said. "Roby and whoever he's in with. Who is it? Politicians?"

"Mostly, but more than that. There's a huge flow of money going. Roby and some other people do what they do, and we look the other way. And when I say 'we,' I mean the sheriff's department, the district attorney's office, maybe even the Tennessee Bureau of Investigation and the FBI."

"And he pays you? Roby pays you and them others?"

"He does. He pays, but he ain't the only one that pays, by any means. There's a pretty good crowd of them that digs in their pocket every month. But Roby is one of the biggest. He makes so much money it boggles the mind. And then there's the drug dealers and the pimps and the—"

"Drug dealers? You mean to tell me you let people sell drugs and then you take part of the money?"

"I've been working with the FBI for years hoping to put a stop to it, but they never would arrest anybody. Turns out their agent was a crook. He took all the money I'd been bringing him and left the country after I told him Roby was gonna kill those people. Nobody knows where he is. And now somebody powerful in Nashville wants me to kill Roby and another man. I ain't ever killed anybody, Daddy. I just got in way over my head. I can't do it. I can't kill Roby."

"He'd kill you in a heartbeat," Calvin said.

"I know that. I know what he's capable of. Hell, he's threatened to kill me several times over the years. He threatened to come here and kill you if I ever crossed him. And I've seen what he can do with my own two eyes. But I ain't like him. I can't kill him."

"Then arrest him."

"I might as well put a gun to my head and pull the trigger."

"Get this new district attorney to kill him for you."

"Beg your pardon?"

"There's been all kinds of talk about him killing folks. Go talk to him. Tell him what you've told me. Tell him somebody has to either arrest Roby or kill him, and you doubt anybody's gonna be arresting him anytime soon. If he really has killed people before, and if he wants to clean things up around here, maybe he'll do it."

"He'd have to kill me, too. I'd be a witness."

"So? Just because you're a witness doesn't mean you have to say anything."

"Roby's kin, Daddy. He's my uncle. The district attorney would think I'd tell."

"Will you stop going on about Roby being kin? Roby Penn doesn't give a tinker's damn about anything or anybody but Roby. He got drunk and killed his girlfriend and left her in a dumpster. He fights animals, Clifford. What kind of person fights animals and gambles on it? You say he threatened you, threatened me. You've heard the stories, just like I have. You know he's killed men, probably women and children, too. Who knows how many? Everyone he kills from this point forward is on you. You have the power to stop him. I don't know who the person in Nashville was that told you to kill Roby, but seems to me he was giving you some pretty good advice."

Scott Pratt

Tree wiped his mouth, rose, and put his bowl and bread plate in the sink.

"Thank you for the advice," he said. "I don't know how much of it I can use, but thanks just the same."

"Go talk to the district attorney," Calvin said. "What can it hurt? Just be honest. It might feel good."

Tree stopped at the door and looked back at his daddy.

"It might at that," he said. "I've never really known what it felt like to be a real sheriff. Hell, I might just like it. You be safe now. Keep an eye out."

226

CHAPTER 39

Roby Penn liked to stay close to home, but on this day, he was a little more than fifty miles from his trailer outside Knoxville. He was standing on a tree-covered hillside five hundred yards away from a house that was being built just outside of Newport, the county seat of Cocke County. The town was known for its lawlessness in East Tennessee. Its rugged mountains were home to folks who raised fighting roosters and pit bulls, operated chop shops, and grew large patches of marijuana.

Roby had made three trips to Newport before he picked out his spot. The shot wouldn't be that difficult, and the report would echo off the surrounding mountains so that nobody would know where it came from until the investigators figured out the angles many hours or even a day after Roby was long gone. He had borrowed a truck from a man who owed him a gambling debt and placed a tag he'd stolen off a car on the truck. It was parked half a mile away off an old logging road. Anyone who may have happened by would think the driver was either deer hunting or looking for deer signs since the gun-hunting season had started four days earlier.

Roby was looking through a Leupold 3-9x40mm scope that sat atop the barrel of a Remington 700 rifle. The shot would be about five hundred yards, give or take ten yards. It was a shot Roby had made hundreds of times in his life. With the combination of the Remington 700, the scope, and the 300 Winchester Magnum ammunition he was using, Roby had no doubt his target would be dead within seconds of him pulling the trigger.

The target would not be a deer, but a human. Roby had decided that Harley Shaker needed to die. Roby couldn't exactly articulate a reason why Harley had to die; it was just a feeling. Roby knew Harley haunted the honky-tonks around Newport on the weekends, and he was afraid that one night he'd get too much beer or liquor or combination of both in him and feel the need to brag. Roby shook his head a little and smiled slightly. It was funny. He'd taken Harley along the night they'd killed Morris and his wife and the lawyer and the girlfriend because he felt like Harley owed him because of the marine he'd killed. And Harley had done a damned fine job. The hit on the district attorney's wife was clean, Harley had shot the bagman lawyer without blinking, and he'd stood lookout with Tree while Roby had gone into the girl's apartment and taken care of her.

Tree, Roby thought as he pictured the sheriff staying in the kitchen while Roby went into the bedroom to finish off the girl. *He might have to be next. He's afraid of his shadow, and he's just too damned dumb to live.*

Roby's eye twitched slightly as he saw his prey walk up to a scaffold that was against the house and begin to climb. Once Harley was atop the scaffold, Roby put the crosshairs on the middle of his back, took a breath, held it, and squeezed the trigger. The Remington cracked and bucked, and Roby watched through the scope as the round found its target. Harley's arms flew up at his sides, his knees buckled, and he fell over straight onto his face.

Roby turned away and slung the rifle over his shoulder.

Another one down, he thought. *Maybe one, maybe two more, to go.*

CHAPTER 40

The second time I walked into my apartment and Sheriff Tree Corker was there, I was armed. District attorneys general in Tennessee are issued badges and are allowed to carry guns. My Walther was in a holster at the small of my back, hidden by my sport coat and my overcoat, and I almost drew it. I'd spent another day listening to people bitch because Tom Masoner had reassigned them. They still had good jobs, but you'd think from listening to them whine that their lives were about to end. I was as irritable as a snake that had just shed its skin. I'd faked smiles for so long that day my cheeks were sore. Late in the day, however, two men became so belligerent that I told them they could either accept their new assignment, resign, or step outside with me and take an ass whipping. Finally, at the end of the day, I'd called Wynken, Blynken, and Nod into my office and unceremoniously fired all three of them at the same time. The administrative side of the job was beyond distasteful to me, and to be honest, I wasn't very good at it.

The sheriff looked totally different this time. He wasn't wearing his uniform. He wasn't wearing his cowboy hat. The pistols were nowhere in sight. He was sitting at the counter in my kitchen.

"Again, Sheriff?" I said in a tired voice. "I swear to God I'd be within my rights to put a bullet in you."

"I'm not armed," he said.

"I can see that. It's like you're walking around without pants."

"We need to talk. It's serious."

Something about his tone told me he was genuine, and I walked in and took two beers out of the refrigerator.

"I had a long talk with my daddy today," he said. "You ever do that?"

"Can't say that I do. My father died a long time ago."

"Sorry to hear it. My daddy made me realize there are some things you and I need to straighten out. Some things we need to talk over. You're not going to like some of what I have to say, and I'm not going to like having to say it."

"Sounds like you're either getting ready to threaten me or confess to me," I said.

"I ain't going to threaten you."

"Okay, I'm listening."

"Do you know how I got my job?" he said. "I mean, back at the beginning? Do you know how I became sheriff?"

"I assume the county commission appointed you when Joe DuBose fell off his roof and broke his neck."

"That's right, but do you know where I'd been working up to that point? Had you ever heard of me?"

I shook my head. "Can't say that I'd ever heard of Tree Corker," I said, "but to be honest, I didn't pay that much attention."

"Nobody did, but it was Ben Clancy who got me in. Roby Penn suggested it. Clancy had a lot of political power in those days, back before you got hold of him, and he got some of his friends on the county commission to nominate me, and they ramrodded me right through. I went from applying for a job at the department at thirty-five to working in the jail for two years to being a patrol deputy for two years to being sheriff. I had no clue what I was doing. Still don't, really."

"Why are you telling me this, Sheriff?"

"Clancy already had all the hustles and rackets—all those things you mentioned to me the last time we talked—set up. Joe DuBose did what I do—kept his eyes and ears open, collected the money, distributed the money. Clancy's big earner was my uncle Roby Penn. Clancy was a terrible man, but he hated drugs, wouldn't have nothing to do with them, wouldn't let the dealers get a foothold. So Roby was his big earner. I'm scared of Roby Penn and always have been. He's a crazy, murderous man who doesn't give a damn about anybody but himself and is filled with hatred and bitterness."

"Think it was him that killed Harley Shaker?"

"What?"

"Harley Shaker was murdered this morning over in Newport. Killed by a sniper."

The news visibly shook the sheriff. "I didn't know. I've had a busy day."

"Harley have it coming?"

"I don't think so. Probably not."

"Him and Roby have any problems?"

"Not that I know of."

"You look worried."

"That's because I might be next."

"Well, we'll just have to see how it shakes out," I said. "It happened in another jurisdiction, so it isn't really my problem. So what were you saying? Oh, Roby and Clancy knew they could depend on you to keep your mouth shut and help with their scams and Clancy hated drugs. Did you bring Morris in? I doubt Clancy had much to say to him after Morris beat him in the election."

"I brought him in. It wasn't hard. He was a greedy man, Morris. He was the one who suggested we let the drug dealers start operating and skim off them, too. It's big money."

"Okay, so you brought Morris in, and he let the drugs in. That's the only thing you've told me that I didn't already know, Sheriff. I'm still not sure why you're here."

"After you got out of prison and they put Clancy in there in your place, I went to the feds. I'd had enough."

The sheriff then told me a long tale of how he'd provided an FBI agent named Wilcox with several years' worth of solid evidence and millions of dollars, only to have Wilcox disappear when the sheriff told him Roby Penn was about to murder Morris and the others. My prior experience with the FBI hadn't been good, so I wasn't all that surprised that a rogue agent had popped up, especially with all that money at stake.

"And what is the FBI doing now?" I said. "Any idea on what their plan is?"

"Honestly? I don't think they're going to do a damned thing. I think they're embarrassed."

I shook my head. "Hell of a system we have, isn't it, Sheriff?"

"There's another person involved in all of this," Corker said. "I don't know a name or a title, but I met with a lawyer this morning in Cookeville who represents him or her. I go down there once a month and take the lawyer money, same share as everybody else. But today was a special meeting. The lawyer told me that somebody saw me driving a boat the night Morris and his wife were killed. Well, they didn't see me, but they saw my pistols, and nobody else around here wears those pistols. Because this person saw those pistols, they put two and two together and knew it must have been Roby who killed Morris."

My heart nearly stopped. Only one person knew I had seen those pistols, and he was the head of the state's most powerful law enforcement agency. I wanted to scream. I wanted to kill someone immediately, and that someone was Hanes Howell III.

"You look like I just hit you in the head with a hammer," the sheriff said.

"I feel like you did," I said.

"I'm going to share something else this lawyer told me. He told me his client had neutralized you. That's the word he used. He told me his client lied to you and you shouldn't be a problem in the future. If it turns out you become a problem, though, they'll want me to kill you. They also want me to kill Roby."

"Unless he kills you first," I said. "When are you supposed to do it?"

"As soon as possible."

I drained the last of my beer, which certainly wouldn't be the only beer I'd drink that night, and stared at the sheriff. There was fear in his eyes.

"What are you going to do?" I said.

"I ain't no killer," he said. "All that stuff I do, them Pythons, it's all for show. And there's something else I want you to know. I turned over every dime of the money I took to the FBI, even the money I took in the beginning. I didn't keep a cent. As far as Roby, I don't think there's much I can do. He'd put me down in a heartbeat if I went after him."

"But then he'd have me to contend with, because the county commission isn't going to put another one of Roby Penn's relatives in the sheriff's seat. They'll appoint someone a lot different than you."

I got up and walked to the refrigerator, pulled out two more beers, and handed one to the sheriff. He was looking at me strangely, almost longingly.

"What?" I said.

"You. You should be the one."

"To do what? Kill Roby Penn? I'm the district attorney now. I can't go around playing vigilante."

"You could if you wanted to," the sheriff said. "One last time. I'll help you any way I can."

"Let me give it some thought," I said.

We sat there in silence, both lost in thought. After several minutes, the sheriff drained his beer and stood to go.

"I want you to know I'm ashamed of the things I've done," he said. "Well, some of them, anyway."

"It doesn't help much to be ashamed," I said. "I've heard some good might come from personal failings or character flaws if a person can change, but I've never been able to do it."

The sheriff handed me a card with his cell number on it. "Call me anytime. I hope we can figure something out."

He said goodbye and walked out the door. After the sheriff left, I drank three more beers. I had to just keep my hands from shaking because I was so livid. Scandal and corruption were certainly nothing new to Tennessee politics and law enforcement. I'd been reading about scandals all my life and had experienced more than my share of corruption firsthand, but to think that Hanes Howell, who acted so smug and respectable, was involved with Ben Clancy and Joe DuBose and Roby Penn and Stephen Morris, not to mention all the pimps and drug dealers and human traffickers, made my stomach turn. I remembered what he'd said about Roger Tate, and a smile crossed my face. He'd called him a "washed-up old fool." We'd just see about that.

Maybe it was the beer, and maybe, once again, I'd just reached my limit, but I began to reflect. I'd tried to do the right thing after Grace died, but Morris swatted me away like an annoying insect. Because of that, I killed Fraturra, believing I had no choice. If I hadn't killed him, who knew how many others he might have hurt?

Once that was over, I'd tried to find some solace in Grace's memory, but she rejected me. My mother had faded into nothingness.

And then the game changed completely. At Granny's suggestion, and with the help of Roger Tate and Claire, I'd thrown myself into the race for district attorney general and had largely managed to put Grace and the past out of my mind. The irony of it still slapped me in the face a couple of times a day. I wasn't running the office the way many would have liked it to be run, but with the exception of helping Granny with her gambling aspirations, I had no plans to take part in any kind of corruption.

And then Roby Penn started killing people left and right and wasn't answering for anything. The conversation with the sheriff had been insightful, if what he was saying was true. He seemed sincere, though, and I'd become a pretty good judge of who was lying and who wasn't.

With the embarrassing exception of Hanes Howell III.

I'd had it. I'd had it up to my eyeballs with worrying about what was right and what was wrong and what was just and unjust. Not many months before, I hadn't cared about any of that. Now, I found myself no longer wanting to care. I only wanted to kill. Grace had abandoned me. My mother wasn't around anymore. I had been left to my own devices, and I knew that could turn out badly and bloody.

There wasn't a single person I could trust outside of Claire and the Tiptons. There really wasn't anything Claire could do, at least not yet. Granny and her grandsons might be able to help me with Roby, but I wasn't the type to bushwhack somebody. If I was going to confront Roby, I would confront him face-to-face. To me, he was like Big Pappy. He hadn't really done anything to me personally, but I figured he was just biding his time.

I looked at my phone. It was almost ten o'clock at night. I called Claire, who had returned to the swamp.

"Am I bothering you?" I said.

"You sound like you've had a little to drink."

"I have. Not too much, but a little."

"It's good to hear your voice," she said.

"Yours, too. Listen, I'm going to do something in the morning, and it may not work out for me."

"What, Darren? What are you going to do?"

"I'm going to put an end to at least part of what's been going on here, one way or another. I'm going to put an end to it, or I'm going to die trying."

"Darren, don't make rash decisions when you've been drinking. What's happened?"

"Nothing's happened, that's why I have to do something. The man who killed Stephen Morris and all those other people is probably planning his next murder. The hustles haven't stopped, the money is still flowing. There's corruption everywhere, even at the highest level of state law enforcement."

"What are you talking about?"

"Hanes Howell is what I'm talking about. He's right in the middle of it. And the FBI has apparently committed a catastrophic clusterfuck. I'll tell you about that later. But Howell . . . I'm sure about him. He called your grandfather a washed-up old fool. Can you believe that? I should have kicked his ass for that, Claire. I'm sorry, but at the time he said it, I didn't know what he was into."

"My grandfather has been called far worse, Darren. You're overreacting. What are you going to do?"

"When I get off the phone with you, I'm going to call the sheriff. Tomorrow morning, he and I are going to drive out to Roby Penn's together, and I'm going to arrest him."

"Do you have a warrant?"

"Nope."

"So you're not going to arrest him."

"It doesn't matter. He wouldn't allow himself to be arrested, anyway."

"So you're going to a gunfight?"

"Probably."

"You said he's the sheriff's uncle. You'll wind up in a cross fire."

"Some things have come up about the sheriff I didn't know before. I think I can trust him to at least get me close to this guy. I don't know what he'll do if bullets start flying, but at least he can get me in there."

"And then what?"

"I don't know, Claire. I honestly don't know what's going to happen."

"Darren, this sounds like a bad idea. A bad plan all the way around. If you go in there, don't go without a SWAT team."

"I don't want to get a bunch of people hurt, Claire. An ATF SWAT team went into Waco. Remember that? They got shot to pieces."

"But you'll get yourself killed!"

"I hope not. Believe it or not, I've done this kind of thing before. But if it goes bad, I just wanted to hear your voice one more time. Take care, Claire. I'll call you tomorrow."

She said, "You better, Darren Street. You better call me," and I hung up.

CHAPTER 41

It was dark when I awoke. I'd managed to doze off for only a couple of hours. A chill ran through me as I rolled out of bed at 3:30 a.m. and went in to take a shower. As soon as I'd hung up with Claire, I'd called the sheriff and told him to pick me up at five in the morning.

"Why?" he'd said. "Where we going?"

"Just pick me up."

I didn't know where Roby Penn lived. Hell, I didn't even know what the man looked like. I'd heard he was a skinhead and had a white handlebar mustache. I knew him only secondhand, by his legend, the same way thousands of people knew the mobsters and Bonnie and Clyde back in their heyday. I had no idea what Tree Corker would do when I told him what I had in mind, whether the blood of family would overcome the seemingly sincere turnaround of his moral compass. And speaking of moral compasses, I had no idea where mine was pointing. I didn't know whether I was going after Roby Penn because I thought it was the right thing to do for the safety and betterment of the community or whether I just wanted to kill the man I had come to regard as a plague that needed to be eradicated.

I was the district attorney general, but I had no illusions about whether I was acting under color of law. I wasn't. There had been no meaningful investigation into Roby Penn. There was no evidence in the files of a law enforcement agency that could be brought forward in a court of law. He would receive no due process. Had I taken the time—and it would have been a long time—I could have eventually gathered enough evidence to get a judge to sign a warrant charging Roby with illegal gambling. Maybe. But in the course of gathering that evidence, I would have had to develop witnesses and informants, and every one of their lives would have been at risk. If Roby so much as suspected someone of helping the police make a case on him, I had no doubt he would have killed them, just as he'd killed Morris and the others.

I dressed, drank two cups of coffee, and cleaned the Walther pistol I'd become so proficient with. I could put a .22-caliber round into a thimble at fifteen yards with that pistol, and I could rapid-fire ten rounds into a circle the size of a teacup. When I was finished, I secured the pistol in its holster at the small of my back and thought again about whether this was something I wanted to do. I decided it was.

Maybe it was akin to a death wish. Maybe I'd lost all hope that I would ever find anything good and decent in the world that wouldn't be taken away from me. And thinking about what had been going on in and around Knoxville, the hustles and the scams and the corruption that reached all the way to Nashville, made me nauseous. I also realized the corruption was going on all over the world, all day, every day. What difference did it make if Roby Penn blew my brains out and I was no longer a part of this world? Besides, my original intent had been to gain some kind of revenge on Morris and to find an opening for Granny to get into gambling and drugs. Who was I kidding? There was nothing honorable about any of it.

I heard a soft knock on the door at precisely five o'clock and picked up my coat, a stocking cap, and a pair of gloves. A cold front had settled in, and it was chilly and blustery outside.

"Morning," the sheriff said when I opened the door. He was wearing his uniform, including the Pythons.

"Morning," I said. "I see you put your guns back on."

"Felt kind of naked without them."

"Ready to go?"

"I reckon so. Whose vehicle we taking?"

"Let's take yours," I said. "I've never ridden in a car that looks like a tank and has the words *High Sheriff* printed on it."

"Mind telling me where we're going?"

"I'm going to arrest your uncle Roby. You need to take me to where he lives."

"You got a warrant for his arrest?"

"No. I'm going to make a citizen's arrest."

We walked to his cruiser, and I was surprised to hear the sheriff chuckle as we strapped ourselves in.

"Citizen's arrest," he said as he started the car and pulled out of my complex. "That's a good one. You think you're going to just walk up to the door and knock and tell Roby Penn you're there to arrest him, and he'll just come along quietly?"

"I don't think it'll go that way, no."

"It ain't gonna go that way, I promise."

"I don't expect you to get in the middle of it. Just drop me off near his house."

"He lives in a trailer."

"Then drop me near the trailer."

"You ain't gonna be able to sneak up on him. I swear he has the senses of a wild animal. What kind of weapon you carrying?"

"It's a Walther pistol. Twenty-two-caliber, long-rifle ammo. Hollow point. It doesn't have a lot of bang, but I'm accurate. If he starts shooting, I'll shoot back, and chances are I'll hit him. If I hit him, he'll be in trouble."

"Damn, son, do you have any idea what Roby's got inside that trailer of his?" the sheriff said. "He's got military-grade weapons, fully automatic M16s. He's even got an M60 machine gun in there. I've heard he's got a grenade launcher on one of his assault rifles, but I ain't ever seen it. You might want to think this through some more. No sense in going out there and getting your head blown off."

"Made up my mind, Sheriff. A woman I know called me pigheaded not too long ago. She was right. Nothing is going to change around here unless Roby goes to jail or off to that big cockfighting ring in the sky. He's going to one of those places this morning."

"You can forget jail," the sheriff said.

"Yeah, I get it."

We rode for almost twenty minutes in silence. I concentrated on taking deep breaths, trying to calm my nerves, telling myself to just let whatever happens happen. *Stay calm, stay alert. If you get shot, keep fighting until your last breath.*

"You ready?" the sheriff said. "About a half mile on the right, I'm going to turn off onto a gravel driveway. It runs a couple of hundred yards back through the woods. Roby's trailer is at the end of the driveway. I'm gonna hit my blue lights when I get close to the trailer. He'll be up. Don't think the man ever sleeps. When he sees the lights, he'll come out, but he'll be suspicious and he'll be armed. He carries a Colt .45 everywhere he goes."

"Have you ever done this before? Come up his driveway this early in the morning with your lights on?"

The sheriff shook his head. "He'll think something is wrong. As soon as I stop, I'm going to get out and start walking toward his trailer. I'll say something like, 'Roby, we got a problem,' and then you get out. I don't know if he'll recognize you, but you've been in the papers and on television and on those buses and billboards all over town, so he probably will. You take it from there. If you want to just open up on him, go ahead."

"I'm not going to ambush him," I said. "It'll be a fair fight. What will you do when the shooting starts?"

"Probably wet my pants," the sheriff said. "Here it is."

He turned off the road onto a gravel driveway. "Ready?"

"Let's do it."

I felt a sudden sense of calm, something similar to when I stepped into the morning air to duel with Big Pappy Donovan. My senses were heightened, but my hands were perfectly still, my heart rate slow and steady. If I were to die this morning, I would do so without panic. I'd accepted my fate, whatever it might be.

The sheriff turned on his emergency lights and gunned the cruiser's powerful engine. At the end of the driveway he turned the wheel hard and did a power-slide stop that put us about thirty feet from the trailer. A porch light came on almost immediately, and the sheriff got out of the car. I pulled my pistol from the holster and held it in my lap, waiting for Roby to appear.

A skin-headed man with a wide, white handlebar mustache stepped out the door and walked down the three steps from the trailer's small front porch. He was wearing combat-fatigue pants, boots, and a white, sleeveless T-shirt. In his right hand was a nickel-plated pistol.

"What the fuck you doing out here this time of the morning, Tree?" Roby yelled.

"We've got a problem, Roby," the sheriff said.

At that moment, I opened the door and stepped out. The wind was howling, making it difficult to hear.

Roby stopped in his tracks about twenty feet away.

"The district attorney has a warrant for your arrest," the sheriff said.

I held up a piece of paper that I'd folded at my apartment and stuck in my jacket pocket. It was the rental agreement for my apartment.

Roby smiled and took two steps back. His gun started to come up, but mine came up quicker, and I squeezed a round off before he could take close aim. The bullet hit him as his gun roared. I felt the shock wave off the round he fired at me as it whizzed by my left ear, and I knelt. Roby staggered slightly, then turned and ran up the steps and back into the trailer. I fired two more shots through the door opening before he got it closed, but I wasn't sure they hit him.

I turned and looked at the sheriff, who was just standing there like a frightened child. He hadn't even pulled one of his Pythons from a holster.

"Sheriff!" I yelled. "Sheriff! Get behind the car."

I was cursing myself for not killing Roby. One shot from twenty feet should have been enough, but the combination of the wind, seeing the size of the barrel of the gun in Roby's hand, and the bullet he fired, nearly hitting me in the head, must have made me flinch a little. I moved around behind the sheriff's cruiser and waited to see what Roby's next move would be. It didn't take long to find out, and it wasn't something I was prepared for.

I'd never been in the military, so I didn't know the awesome power of a fully automatic assault rifle. The sheriff's pride and joy, his beautiful black-and-gold cruiser, was suddenly being turned into Swiss cheese as the rounds hammered into it. Roby was firing short bursts of between four and six rounds each from a window at the far left of the trailer. The windshield and all the windows exploded, and I was showered in glass.

"He's gonna kill us!" Sheriff Corker said. "I told you about what he's got in there."

The sheriff had wrapped himself into a ball on the ground.

"Shoot back, dammit!" I yelled at him. "Get off the ground and shoot back!"

I hadn't expected to get into a protracted firefight, so I only had one clip of ammunition containing ten rounds. I'd fired three shots.

"Never mind," I said to the sheriff. "Give me your gun belt."

He looked at me and shook his head. Something came over him at that moment, as though he would forever think of himself as less than a man if he gave me the Pythons. He pulled one of the pistols out and squeezed three shots off at the trailer. I was relieved to have the help. I fired two more, but we were so overmatched in firepower that I didn't think it was going to matter.

The shooting stopped for a minute, which concerned me because I didn't know what Roby was up to in there.

"We can't stay here," I said to the sheriff. "If he's got a grenade launcher, he'll blow us up. Even if he doesn't, he's eventually going to come out of the trailer and work his way around until he can pick us off from a distance."

I was wrong about the grenade launcher, but at that moment, the door to the trailer opened and a scene straight out of *Rambo* unfolded. Roby walked out with his machine gun and a long belt of ammunition wrapped around his arm.

"Oh no," I said. "We have to split up. I'm gone. Kill him if he comes after me."

I got up and started running for the tree line.

I heard Roby yell, "I'll be back for you directly!" and then the machine gun opened up.

The sound was deafening, and dirt began to fly up near my feet. The rounds tore through the trees, shredding the smaller ones. The bullets were closing in on me as I ran with everything I had through a small stand of trees and over a small hill. When I cleared the hill, the shooting stopped. I glanced to my right and saw what looked like a garbage dump just a few yards away. I ran to the dump and dove behind a berm of dirt. I pointed the pistol in the direction I thought he would be coming from and waited.

Less than ten seconds later, I saw him. He was more than thirty yards away, a little too far for a confident shot with the pistol. I needed him to get closer. He was walking slowly now, his eyes scanning the property. The front of his T-shirt was covered in blood, and his left arm appeared to be dangling. He disappeared behind a small rise, and I raised my head just a bit. When I did, he saw me, and he turned straight for me. I fired two more shots, but he opened up immediately with the machine gun, and the withering fire drove me into the dirt. If I could have, I would have started tunneling like a mole. But all I could do was duck my head and hope maybe he ran out of ammo or the gun would jam. When he was almost on top of me, I said goodbye to Claire and wondered whether I'd be seeing Grace, my little girl, and my mother soon. I wondered whether the sheriff was running away or whether Roby would kill him as soon as he was finished with me.

And then, just like that, the shooting stopped.

I looked over the berm and raised my pistol, expecting to see Roby trying to unjam his weapon, but he wasn't there. I looked around and saw nothing. The only sound now was the wind and my own heavy breathing. I raised up higher, and I saw him, lying on his face. I stood and walked slowly over to him, pointing my gun at the back of his bald head. The machine gun was on the ground by his right arm, the barrel steaming in the cold air. As I got close, I noticed a hole in the center of the back of his head. I reached down and felt for a pulse. He wasn't breathing. I tossed the machine gun to the side, rolled him over, and was confronted with a gruesome scene. Roby's forehead, along with his nose, and part of his left cheek, had been blown away.

Roby Penn, probably the most feared man in Knox County, was dead. The question was, who had killed him? Had Sheriff Corker run up behind him and put a bullet in his brain and then run away? That didn't make any sense.

I began hurrying back toward Roby's trailer, hoping I wouldn't find the sheriff shot full of holes. About halfway back, I heard an engine start. I sprinted up a hill and saw a Jeep pull slowly out of a stand of trees, drive through a field in the direction of the road, and then disappear into another stand of trees.

The Jeep looked exactly like the one owned by Eugene Tipton.

CHAPTER 42

I found Sheriff Corker walking in my direction before I got back to Roby's trailer. He was dirty from lying on the ground behind his patrol car but didn't look too much worse for the wear.

"Did you kill him?" the sheriff said.

"No, but he's dead. Somebody else killed him."

"Who?"

"I didn't see him, but I think it was an old friend."

"So somebody else knew you were going to be out here this morning?"

"I told somebody last night, and that somebody must have told somebody else."

I had no doubt that after my conversation with Claire, she had called Granny Tipton. Eugene was probably in the woods at Roby's place within hours after that phone call.

"I shot him, you know," the sheriff said. "Just so you don't think I'm a coward. When he was getting a bead on you with that machine gun, I put a round into him. I think it hit him in the left shoulder. Didn't stop him, but it bought you some time."

"Thank you, Sheriff," I said, and I reached out and shook his hand. "I thought for sure I was dead. I appreciate everything you did this morning. You showed a lot of courage."

"Me? You've got the balls of an Angus bull, son. The way you stood there toe-to-toe with him and then kept your head when he started with that M16. Hell, I peed on myself a little when he came out with that machine gun. It was a good call you made to cut and run when we did. I didn't have any idea I could move so fast."

By this time, we'd walked back to the spot where the sheriff's car lay as dead as Roby Penn. He shook his large head and removed his hat.

"Rest in peace, Felina," he said.

"Felina? You named your cruiser Felina?"

"After that Marty Robbins song 'El Paso.'"

"Yeah, yeah, I've heard that. Good song."

The car was shot to hell. All the tires were flat, all the windows shot out, and it was leaking fluids.

"I don't think she's fixable," the sheriff said.

"It doesn't look that way."

"Maybe I'll get something a little more practical."

"Sounds like a good idea. So now that Roby's dead, what do we do with him?"

"I know what we ought to do with him. We ought to bury him where he buried that marine."

"You know where Gary Brewer is?"

Corker nodded. "I hate to admit it, but I do. He's buried in a barrel underneath a garbage dump that's just over that knob."

"I was just in that garbage dump," I said. "It helped saved my life, along with you and my other friend."

I knew I was lucky to be alive. I was lucky the dump happened to be there and provided me with enough cover to keep Roby from tearing me to shreds with the machine gun, I was lucky the sheriff had grown a backbone and wounded his uncle, and I was lucky Eugene had shown up. But the thought of Brewer in a barrel so nearby dampened my spirits. Life was so fickle. I could have very easily wound up in a barrel next to him.

"So what's our story going to be?" the sheriff said.

"I think the story should be that you and I came out here to question Roby as part of the investigation into the disappearance of Gary Brewer and the murder of Stephen Morris. We don't have to say much more than that, just that an informant had told us that Brewer was buried on this property and that Roby had bragged to someone about killing Morris. When we got here, he opened fire on us with automatic weapons. We returned fire, split up, and when he went after me, you went into his house and grabbed a hunting rifle. Just as he was about to kill me, you took a shot from about two hundred yards and put a bullet in his head."

"That's what we're going to tell the TBI? They investigate officer-involved shootings."

"Not unless I tell them to. And I'm not going to tell them to. I'm the district attorney and you're the sheriff. This is our case. Screw those guys. Let's see if we can find the bullet that killed Roby. If we can come up with it, we'll get rid of it so we don't have to worry about ballistics."

"Sounds like a plan," the sheriff said.

We searched for twenty minutes in the brown grass before the sheriff found the flattened, bloody piece of metal that had torn through Roby's skull. It was about thirty feet from the body on a patch of bare dirt. I took it to the edge of a cluster of trees fifty yards to the right and buried it.

"You got a cell phone?" I said.

"It got broken during the fight."

I unzipped one of my coat pockets, pulled out my phone, and tossed it to him.

"Guess you better call in some folks. Keep it as low-key as possible. Nothing in the press. You have people you can trust, right?"

"Plenty of them."

"There's a lot of mess to clean up here, and we need to find Brewer's body," I said. "Did Roby tell you exactly where it is?"

"Pretty close. He used a front-end loader and his tractor. I don't think it'll take all that long to find him."

"His family will be grateful to you," I said.

"And to you, Counselor."

It was the first time the sheriff had ever called me "Counselor."

"Go ahead," I said. "Make the call."

CHAPTER 43

I called Claire the first chance I got, which was after one of Sheriff Corker's deputies gave me a ride to my apartment around noon. Roby Penn had been hauled off to the morgue, the sheriff's car had been hauled off to the junkyard, and Gary Brewer's body had been located and removed from a fifty-five-gallon drum that was buried very close to where the sheriff said it would be. What was left of his body was placed in a body bag and taken to the morgue.

There were other barrels in the dump, too. A deputy opened one to make sure there wasn't a body in it and found it stuffed with bundles of shrink-wrapped cash. They hadn't counted it all when I left, but there had to be more than a half million dollars, and they were just getting started.

The sheriff's deputies also hauled fifty different weapons out of Roby's trailer along with thousands of rounds of ammunition. They would be seized and eventually wind up in the sheriff department's arsenal.

"Oh my God, Darren," Claire said when she answered her phone. "I've been so worried. Are you okay?"

"I'm fine."

"What happened?"

"Roby Penn got killed this morning. The official story is that the sheriff took him out, but I think you and I both know better. Thank you for making that call."

"I didn't think you could rely on the sheriff."

"Well, thank you. You saved my life. And don't be too hard on Sheriff Corker. He's had a sudden attack of conscience. I think he and I are going to get along pretty well."

"Are you hurt?"

"A few scrapes and bruises. I came out of it far better than I should have."

"You know, I had the strangest feeling earlier," she said. "I woke up around 5:15 a.m., and I thought I very distinctly heard you say goodbye to me."

"I did say goodbye to you. At 5:30 a.m., I was lying behind a mound of dirt in a garbage pit with a crazy man walking up on me, firing an M60 machine gun. I thought I was dead, so I said goodbye. What you heard was obviously an illusion, but it's funny how those illusions can be so close to reality sometimes."

She was silent for a few seconds. Then she said, "He had a machine gun?"

"You should see the sheriff's car. It looks like it's been in a junkyard for twenty years and people have used it for target practice. No glass, no tires. It's a mess."

"That car was his pride and joy, from everything I've heard. He must be devastated."

"The car's name was Felina, but I think he's going to let her go and get something that isn't quite so loud. And I wouldn't be surprised if he quit wearing those pearl-handled pistols."

"Wow, it sounds like he's making some real strides in the right direction."

"Speaking of strides in the right direction, how would you feel about me coming up to Washington for a couple of days? I'd like to meet with your grandfather about the director of the TBI here and tell him what I know. I'd also like to see whether he can get the FBI up there to make some things happen."

"You want to come to the swamp?"

"I do. Can you recommend a good hotel?"

"I have a fantastic place near the Capitol Building. You can stay with me."

I liked that idea. I felt like it was time to see whether there was a real physical attraction between us.

"Tell your grandfather we found Captain Gary Brewer. It wasn't pretty, but we have his remains."

"Thank you, Darren. He'll be so grateful. When would you like to come to town?"

"Things have been pretty intense here for quite a while," I said. "Maybe this weekend?"

"Perfect," Claire said. "Book a flight and let me know when you're arriving. I'll pick you up at the airport."

"Sounds like a plan."

"Darren?" she said.

"Yes?"

"I don't want to deceive you. Ms. Tipton called me earlier. She said Eugene saw everything that happened. She said Eugene said you fought so bravely, that you stood in front of that maniac and didn't back down an inch."

"I backed down plenty. I ran like a scared rabbit."

"You're brave, Darren. That's the point. I'm enamored with brave men."

For the first time in a long, long time, I felt butterflies in my stomach. "I'll see you soon," I said.

"Can't wait."

CHAPTER 44

Six weeks later

I stood at the lectern in Criminal Court Division II and looked up at the judge.

"Darren Street for the prosecution," I said.

A convict with a long record of sexual offenses had been charged with raping, murdering, and burglarizing the apartment of a seventy-two-year-old woman not far from the University of Tennessee campus. It was a semi-high-profile case, but more important for me, it was the first case that I had been able to work into my schedule as a trial lawyer.

"Are you here for show, Mr. Street, or are you actually going to try this case?" Judge Richard Bell said.

"I intend to prosecute this case from arraignment to verdict to appeal, if there is one," I said.

"Well, this is certainly new. Mr. Morris, may he rest in peace, didn't try a single case in my court during his entire tenure in the district attorney's office."

"Things are being run a little differently," I said.

"They certainly are. I, for one, would like to commend you and the other prosecutors in your office for the way in which you've conducted yourselves since you took over. The dockets are already remarkably less clogged, and things seem to be running extremely efficiently."

"That has as much to do with you as it does with my office, Your Honor," I said. "You run a tight ship in here."

Why not brownnose the judge a little? What could it hurt?

"Thank you, Mr. Street," Judge Bell said. "Will the clerk call the case number?"

* * *

There had, indeed, been many changes in the past six weeks, and not just in the district attorney's office. Pimps, prostitutes, drug dealers, cockfighters, and dogfighters were no longer being extorted for money and protection. Instead, they were being arrested by the sheriff's department. Sheriff Corker had implemented a zero-tolerance policy for crime in his county, and his deputies had fanned out like a swarm of locusts into the criminal underworld. The result was a lot more work for the lawyers in my office and a steep increase in arrests in the outlying areas of the county.

The sheriff had, as I'd told Claire on the phone, stopped wearing his pistols. In fact, he didn't wear a gun at all. I'd seen him a week earlier, and he looked like he'd dropped thirty pounds. He still wore the cowboy hat, but he drove an SUV with the same decals on it that every other vehicle in his department displayed.

There remained only two discreet gambling clubs on the east and west ends of the county. They were owned and operated by the Tipton family. No alcohol was allowed, and patrons were searched with wands at the door to ensure they didn't bring weapons into the clubs. I'd talked to Granny a week after they got the clubs up and running, and she seemed genuinely pleased with how things were going.

We finished the arraignment of the defendant, and I walked up the stairs toward my office. My cell phone vibrated, and I looked at it. It was Claire's number.

"They picked him up five minutes ago," she said.

"Who?"

"Hanes Howell. You made quite an impression on my grandfather and the FBI when you came to Washington. The FBI arrested him. He's on his way to jail in Nashville. I don't think he'll be getting out for a long, long time."

"What did they charge him with?"

"You know, it seems that the FBI has some incredibly talented and imaginative investigators. I don't want to say anything else over the phone. Just keep an eye on the Nashville news this afternoon, and watch for my grandfather's call."

A couple of hours later, I found out what they'd done to him. Senator Roger Tate called me himself on a secure phone from his office in the Capitol Building and told me what happened.

"Since Hanes Howell's lawyer had apparently been incredibly proficient at hiding his money, the FBI couldn't get to him that way. So they hacked into his work computer and downloaded more than a thousand images of child pornography from various sites on the Internet and from chat rooms. They made it appear as though Howell had done it. Then they copied the images and will use them against him at trial," Tate said. "They did the same thing with a laptop Howell owns and a personal computer at Howell's house, and they did it in such a way that nobody will ever know what happened."

The news accounts made Howell look like the ultimate pervert, the worst of the worst. They said the director of the TBI had been charged with illegally downloading thousands of pornographic images of children—some of them as young as eight years old—off the Internet. He was facing thirty years in a federal penitentiary, and from experience, I knew how prisoners felt about child molesters, child abusers, and child pornography. Howell was in for a hard time.

"Thank you, Senator," I said, and I hung up.

Washed-up old fool, I thought, remembering what Howell had said about Senator Tate. *What do you think of him now, Hanes?*

CHAPTER 45

Six months later . . .

Tom Masoner, my number-two guy in the office, sat across from me. Tom had turned out to be exactly what I thought he would be—somebody I could trust. He was smart and he was tough, and he was as organized as any person I'd ever met. Number three in the office was sitting next to him. Her name was Felicia Delgado, a woman Tom had recruited from a criminal defense firm in Knoxville. She'd taken a sizable pay cut to come join the ranks of underpaid public servants, but she'd done so with a smile and a sense of purpose. Tom had transitioned from trying strictly violent felony cases to being in charge of organizing every court our office was responsible for, including the child-support division. Felicia had taken over Tom's position as the lead violent-felony prosecutor, and she was damned good at it.

"So I got a call this morning from a woman in Washington," I said to the two of them. "She wants to take me on a date on her grandfather's private jet."

"Her grandfather's private jet?" Tom said. "And who is this mystery woman?"

"Not a mystery woman. Remember my campaign manager, Claire Tate?"

"Oh yeah," Roger said. "Hottie, hottie, hottie."

"Yeah, she's cute. And absolutely filthy rich, which I don't care about, but I don't mind, either."

"Where does she want to take you on this date?" Felicia said.

"A couple of places. First, we're going to Turks and Caicos. Then we're going to check out South America."

"What part of South America? It's a big continent."

"Brazil, maybe Paraguay."

"Fantastic. Have a great time."

"So you guys are cool with this? You can get along without me?"

"We could do without you every day," Tom said. "We don't need you to run this place—do we, Felicia?"

"Ah, I don't know. He comes in handy once in a while."

"When are you leaving?" Tom said.

"It was a spur-of-the-moment thing, which is something I really like about Claire. She wants to leave Friday."

"Happy trails, my friend," Tom said. "Have a great time."

I was looking forward to the time with Claire. I'd gotten to know her better during my visit to Washington, and we'd stayed in touch regularly. I thought we might be a good fit for the long term. But I wasn't telling my coworkers the entire truth. The trip with Claire wouldn't be to South America, and it wouldn't be pleasure.

Well, maybe a little pleasure.

CHAPTER 46

As things turned out, I had one more favor to do for Senator Roger Tate. The FBI agent, Ron Wilcox, had traveled to a country that had no extradition treaty with the United States. Nothing had ever been publicized about what Wilcox had done, but the FBI and the US marshals had searched day and night for him for months. They found him in Saigon, or Ho Chi Minh City, Vietnam, living in a small apartment less than a mile from the Notre Dame Cathedral.

I was not privy to how they found him, nor was I privy to the discussions about what they wanted to do with him. Had they kidnapped him and brought him back to the United States, they apparently would have irritated the Vietnam government, and they would have had to put him on trial publicly, which meant all the sordid details about what he did to Sheriff Corker would come out. The other thing that would have come out would have been the FBI's gross negligence due to its lack of oversight of one of its own. Had they had a government agent kill him, it would have been a serious violation of diplomatic protocol. But flying a private citizen into the country who appeared to be on a weeklong vacation, and letting him handle the job aided significantly by people who were not what they appeared to be? That seemed to be the answer.

So Roger Tate requested—and I agreed after some intense negotiations—that I travel to Vietnam accompanied by his beautiful granddaughter, Claire, and take in the sights for a week. While I was there, I was discreetly contacted by only three people, one of whom was a man who provided me with what I needed to grant Senator Tate's request.

On the appointed night, our last night in town, I had a delicious dinner with Claire in the hotel restaurant and went back up to our room on the tenth floor of Saigon's luxurious Park Hyatt Hotel.

"Are you ready?" she said as I placed the gun beneath my shirt and looked in the mirror.

I nodded.

"Everything is packed. I'll have a cab waiting when you get back, and we'll head straight to the airport."

Claire knew everything, and I was comfortable with that. It brought us closer.

I took a cab to the cathedral at eleven, got out, and walked the rest of the way to Wilcox's apartment. I got there around eleven thirty. A man came out of the shadows and walked up to me. He looked Vietnamese but spoke perfect English.

"He's drunk and has already passed out," the man said. "Follow me up to the room. I have a key."

I did as he said. Before he opened the door, I removed the Smith & Wesson .38-caliber revolver I'd been given, along with a silencer, from my pocket. I attached the silencer and nodded my head. When the man opened the door, I stepped inside to a foul-smelling, filthy mess. Wilcox may have been a millionaire, but he certainly wasn't living like one. There were liquor bottles strewn all over the kitchen and den. A television was on, and the glow revealed a man slumped sideways on the couch. The voices coming from the TV were speaking Vietnamese.

I felt nothing as I stepped up to him.

"This is for the sheriff and for those miserable bastards at the FBI," I whispered, and I shot him once between the eyes.

I turned, walked out of the apartment, and handed the gun to the Vietnamese man. He locked the door while I went down the steps. I

Scott Pratt

walked back to the cathedral and hailed a cab. A short time thereafter, I was back at the hotel.

Claire was standing in the lobby, dressed casually for the long flight home.

I walked up to her and she hugged me.

"How'd it go?" she whispered in my ear.

"Perfect."

"How does it feel to have a clean slate?"

"Hard to describe," I said.

As part of my deal, Roger Tate had secured for me a pardon from the president of the United States for any crimes I may have committed up to and including the day I shot Roger Wilcox. I had a copy, a lawyer I'd chosen very carefully had a copy, the Department of Justice had a copy, and Roger Tate had a copy.

"Everything's ready to go," Claire said. "Cab's outside."

"Let's go," I said, and we walked hand in hand into the humid night.

A clean slate. What would a man with my past and in my circumstances do with a clean slate? I hoped I'd make the best of it and resist some impulses I'd given in to in the past.

But only time would tell.

ABOUT THE AUTHOR

Photo © 2015 Dwain Rowe

Scott Pratt was born in South Haven, Michigan, and grew up in Jonesborough, Tennessee. He is a veteran of the United States Air Force and earned a bachelor of arts degree in English from East Tennessee State University and a doctor of jurisprudence degree from the University of Tennessee. Pratt's first novel, *An Innocent Client*—the first book in his Joe Dillard series—was chosen as a finalist for the Mystery Readers International's Macavity Award. *Justice Lost* is the third book in his *Wall Street Journal* bestselling Darren Street series, following *Justice Redeemed* and *Justice Burning*. Pratt resides in northeast Tennessee with his wife, two dogs, and a parrot.

Printed in Great Britain
by Amazon

83721717R00154